ALSO BY ANTHONY BOURDAIN

Bone in the Throat

GONE BAMBOO

GONE
BAMBOO

ANTHONY BOURDAIN

 VILLARD • NEW YORK

Library of Congress Cataloging-in-Publication Data
Bourdain, Anthony.
     Gone bamboo / Anthony Bourdain.
        p.   cm.
     ISBN 0-679-44880-2
     I. Title.
   PS3552.O8328G6   1997
   813'.54—dc21   96-46323

Random House website address: http://www.randomhouse.com/
Printed in the United States of America on acid-free paper
98765432
First Edition
Book design by Debbie Glasserman

TO NANCY

We don't need clothes and we don't need money . . .

—from "Totally Nude,"
Talking Heads

ACKNOWLEDGMENTS

Thanks to the management and staff of the Oyster Pond Beach Hotel, Sint Maarten, the usual suspects at the Dinghy Dock, Saint Martin . . . and in New York; to my sous-chef, Steven Tempel (saucier, line cook, fixer, scrounger, and operator extraordinaire), and my night crew, Manuel Orellana and Segundo Andrango. Also, Craig Nelson, David Rosenthal, Rob and Web Stone, Brian McLendon . . . and Gordon Howard, the original true believer.

GONE BAMBOO

1

Jimmy "Pazz" Calabrese wanted room service.

"Just a san'wich or somethin' for chrissakes," he said.

"I would prefer you didn't," said the other man at the table. "Then I'd have to change motels. I don't know how you feel about it, but I'm not crazy about being seen together."

"Awright . . . awright . . . ," said Jimmy, his stomach growling, "I'll get somethin' later. Shit."

The other man at the table was tall, around six foot four, thin, and deeply tanned. He looked in his mid- to late forties, with long, dark brown hair, sun-bleached in spots and going to gray, tied back in a ponytail. He was dressed in faded blue jeans with holes in the knees and a loose-fitting long-sleeve T-shirt. He was wearing no socks or shoes, and even his feet were tan. In the dimly lit motel room, the darkness of his skin made his eyes and teeth and the gold hoop earring in his left ear flash unnaturally bright.

There were two other men in the room at the Teterboro Motor Lodge. Richie "Tic" Gianelli, a small, ferretlike man with a jail-house pallor, stood by the door, appearing nervous in a flannel-lined Burberry trench coat. The coat didn't look right on him, somehow; he looked like he'd borrowed it from an older brother. Paul "Paulie Brown" Caifano, a large man with no neck and a crew cut, sat silently on the edge of the bed in a camel hair coat, playing with the remote control for the bolted-down television, clicking from channel to channel.

"There's a reason this is comin' from me personally," said Jimmy Pazz, solemnly. "Nobody gimme permission for this piece a' work. I'm tellin' you that up front, right from the get go. It's two guys gotta go—a double. And they gotta be done this weekend 'cause you ain't gonna get another crack at 'em."

Jimmy Pazz weighed somewhere in the neighborhood of 320 pounds before lunch. He had a low, simian brow, beady, wet eyes set too close together, and a big, sloping honker of a nose. He had a dark, heavily bearded complexion, despite a recent shave and the heavy application of face powder, and he was wearing, as was often his habit among friends and business associates, a dress; on this occasion it was a blue and green tartan jumper the size of a pup tent, white kneesocks, and saddle shoes. Because he had come to discuss a matter of some gravity, he had chosen to dispense with his customary wig; it lay neglected on the dresser like a strangled chinchilla.

"What is it?" asked Jimmy, narrowing his eyes so that they almost disappeared into his face. "What?"

"I was thinking that's a good color for you," said the man with the earring. "Goes well with your eyes."

Jimmy scrutinized the other man's face for a sign of mockery. After a long, tense moment during which nothing was said by anyone in the room, he turned, satisfied, to Richie and smiled, his amethyst drop earrings wiggling.

"See?" said Richie from his place by the door. "You din't believe me. I told you green was good. Din't I say that?"

"I don't get a chance much to wear what I want around the office, the club. They takin' pitchers there. The fuckin' FBI. They'd love to get a pitcher a' me in a dress. Prolly send it to my mother. That's how they are, you know . . . they're—"

"Vindictive," interjected Richie. "They're vindictive and repressed."

On the bed, Paulie Brown rolled his eyes to the ceiling. He'd heard this before.

"You got it," said Jimmy. "Vindicative. That's what they are. They should fuckin' talk too . . . Hoover did this, you know. Friend a' mine saw him one time at Rockefeller Center, ice skatin' in a fuckin' tutu like nobody's business . . ."

The other man at the table cleared his throat.

Jimmy leaned forward in his chair, suddenly all business, his brawny, fur-covered arms coming together on the table. "Lissen, Henry," he said, "as far as anybody outside a' this room goes, this meetin' never happened—"

"Jimmy. You should get a job with the government, talking like that," said the man called Henry.

Jimmy smiled indulgently. "I get connected with this, I'm gonna have myself some serious fuckin' problems."

Henry looked around at the other men. "Hey. If you end up reading about this in the papers, it's sure as hell not coming from me," he said testily. "From what I've seen, it's you guys been opening up your books for the feds. Seems like every other member of your little fraternity's been picking up two paychecks these days. I mean, Jimmy, your admission standards are really going to hell. The old days, as I recall, membership in the FBI used to stand in the way of qualifying."

"I ain't inferrin' nothin' about you," said Jimmy.

"Implyin'," corrected Richie. "You ain't implyin' nothin'. You imply, he infers."

"Whatever," snapped Jimmy.

"So. You going to tell me what it is, Jimmy?" asked Henry.

"The thing of it is," said Jimmy, "to do this right, I gotta be there when it happens."

"Where is this taking place?" asked Henry.

"Show him that thing," said Jimmy.

Richie came over to the table with a color brochure and laid it out in front of Henry. It depicted the grounds and facilities of the Devil's Run Ski Resort in the Adirondacks. There was a map of the ski trails and surrounding slopes and some photos of the lodges, restaurants, and rooms.

"See there?" said Jimmy, placing a stubby finger at a point on the map. "This is where everybody's gonna be at. All the bosses gonna be there—Jerry Dogs, Philly, Sonny, me and Richie . . . everybody—and some other guys they gonna bring . . ."

"A convention," observed Henry, shaking his head.

Jimmy reached into his jumper pocket and unfolded two newspaper photos. One showed an old man in baggy pants and a white dress shirt standing in front of a Manhattan social club. The other showed a younger man, broad shouldered, in an expensive double-breasted jacket, shaking his fist at the camera from a loading dock somewhere.

"Donnie Wicks and Junior Lofaro," said Henry after the briefest of looks. He gave Jimmy back the pictures. "I know what they look like."

Jimmy raised half of the eyebrow that ran uninterrupted across the upper part of his face. "You know these guys?" he asked, troubled. "You done some work for these pricks?"

Henry said nothing. His expression didn't change. After a few seconds of awkward silence, Richie piped in, "Professional ethics, right? He ain't gonna tell you. It's like a doctor or a priest; you get the confidentiality. It's sacred."

Henry allowed himself a smile.

"This won't be a problem, right?" asked Jimmy, looking unsure. "I mean . . . that won't stand in the way if you know these guys . . ."

The word *problem* seemed to rouse Paulie on the bed, where he had apparently settled in on *Wheel of Fortune*. He stirred, the bed-springs squeaking as he sat up, but Henry's calm answer sent him back to his show.

"I can do it," said Henry. "It's going to cost you a whole pile of money, but I'll do it. Sure."

"Good, good," said Jimmy, relaxing visibly. "You know, we're fuckin' lucky to get a shot at the old guy. Never leaves that fuckin' club down there for nothin'. Lives at his sister's upstairs, an' if you think I got it bad with the FBI an' the cops watchin' me . . . Him, forget about. You gotta push 'em outta the fuckin' way to get in down there. Donnie's been in more movies than . . . than . . . Richie! Who's that guy?"

"Which one?" asked Richie.

"The cowboy . . ."

"John Wayne?"

"Not him. No, the other guy. Forget it. You get the point. The guy's been in a shitload a' fuckin' movies an' he never even hadda leave home. They got that place wired up like my fuckin' front yard on Christmas, so you can't do nothin' there," said Jimmy.

"But he's going to this ski thing," said Henry. "I have a hard time picturing Donnie on a snowboard. You sure he's going to be there?"

"He's gotta be there," said Jimmy. "This is a big thing. Every-body's gotta be there."

"It's compulsory," said Richie.

"Okay," said Henry. "So everybody's going to be there. So what happens, I'm supposed to pick the two of them out of the crowd? I have that right?"

"Yeah," said Jimmy. "That's pretty much it."

"This is really going to cost," said Henry.

"Just don't fuckin' shoot me by accident," said Jimmy. "Okay? I don't wanna catch no fuckin' bullet I paid for somebody else to get."

"I'll tell you what. I'll make you a special deal. I shoot you by mistake and you get your money back."

"Hey, that's not fuckin' funny," said Jimmy.

"Don't even joke," said Richie.

"So, where exactly is everybody going to be and when?" asked Henry.

"You see them five little squares there, halfway up the mountain? Them's the places they got rented for this thing. Each boss gonna get one—"

"Chalets," said Richie.

"Each boss gonna get one a' these chalets. Donnie and Junior, they gonna get the biggest one. Right here." Jimmy pointed to one of the squares.

"It's got a Jacuzzi," said Richie, turning over the brochure to show Henry an interior shot. His breath smelled of Tic-tacs. "Nice, huh?"

"So, the meeting. Where's that going to be?" asked Henry.

"Donnie's of course," said Jimmy. "We all gonna show up Saturday night late. Meeting's supposedta be aroun' lunchtime Sunday."

"You guys can't just step out for a piss, commune with nature for a few minutes? I could blow the whole place. That would be easier," suggested Henry.

"You don't get it. I gotta be there. It's gotta look like it coulda been anybody," said Jimmy.

"You could go for broke, I mean. Blow them all up."

Jimmy gave this idea a few moments of serious consideration. "Nahhh . . . some a' them guys, I wouldn't miss. I don't give a rat's ass . . . But Jerry Dogs, Sonny and them. We got business together. Nah . . . That would be wrong."

"I can't nail them on the way up?"

"I wanted that, I'd just have somebody wire up their car or somethin' an' BABOOM! I wouldn't have to pay you all the fuckin' money come up here. I can get a couple a' Irishmen do that for a case a' fuckin' beer. You the man that's so good with a rifle, right? That's what I called you for."

"Okay, okay."

"It's gotta look like it coulda been any a' us they was shootin' at. Like it was just one a' those things it's Donnie an' Junior that gets shot."

"Awfully convenient," said Henry.

"Well, nobody's gonna know for sure 'cause I'm right there. Only thing anybody's gonna know for sure is that somebody had some fuckin' balls on 'em."

Jimmy took a pack of True 100s out of his jumper. Richie came over and lit one for him. "An' by the time I make my move," said Jimmy, "nobody's gonna be in a position to do nothin' about it anyways."

"When it's time for the meeting," said Richie, "they all gonna go over to Donnie's place. He's gonna come out . . . him and Junior. Protocol. They gotta do all that huggin' an' kissin' out there."

"We'll do what we can get 'em away from the door. Outside, so's you can get a good shot at 'em," said Jimmy.

"We can get 'em in a snowball fight." Richie giggled.

"Alright," said Henry, still looking at the map. "I think I know what you want. We're talking about two targets at about five hundred yards—"

"Jeesus," said Jimmy. "You gotta be that far? That's pretty fuckin' far. You can't get any closer than that?"

"Not if I want to get away. I *had* planned on getting away."

"I want you to get away, I want you to get away," said Jimmy. "That would be fuckin' great, you get grabbed right onna fuckin' mountain there."

"I can do it," said Henry. "Wind's right I can do it up to a thousand yards. After that, you take your chances." He smiled.

"So, how much?" asked Jimmy.

"It'll be a hundred twenty-five for the old man, and a hundred for the other. In advance."

Richie whistled through his teeth.

"Okay," said Jimmy without hesitation. "Paulie. Give the man the money he wants." There was the sound of money being counted on the bed behind Henry.

Henry held up his hand and shook his head. He looked back at Paulie and Richie on the bed, both now arranging used bills into stacks.

"That's very nice," he said, turning back to Jimmy. "That's very nice. And I appreciate it—you bringing the money with you and all. But that's not how I get paid." He handed Jimmy a slip of paper with some numbers on it and a list of banks in the Netherlands Antilles and Cayman Islands. "I would prefer that you send the funds, by wire transfer, in increments not to exceed ten thousand each, to these accounts. A different bank as point of origin each time, please. Can you do that for me? It's really the only way I do business these days."

"Richie," said Jimmy. "You getting this?"

"Yeah, yeah. I got it," said Richie.

"We can do that?"

"Yeah. Pain in the ass, but we can do that."

"You don't want cash?" said Jimmy, disappointed.

Henry shook his head. "I'm not going through customs with that. No way."

Richie and Paulie began to put the money back in a gym bag.

"And of course, I'll be calling the banks Friday . . . just to see everything arrived okay," said Henry. "No offense."

"That's a lot of fuckin' money," said Jimmy.

"It's enough."

"So, you sure you got no problem doin' this without permission?" said Jimmy, trying to reassure himself. "I ain't gonna hear about you goin' cryin' to some other boss, sayin' what a terrible thing I axed you to do? I mean, I know you worked for other people . . ."

"Jimmy," said Henry. "I don't give a flying fuck about permission. Understand that about me. I'm not a member of your fraternal order. I don't know the secret handshakes, I don't want to know. I'm not looking for promotion. You get the money in those accounts there by Friday end of business and you'll get an honest day's work out of me. No money—I get on the next plane and go home. That simple. I mean, if some of your lodge brothers want to get pissed off about any bylaws getting violated, hey, that's tough shit as far as I'm concerned. You guys can work that out amongst yourselves. None of my business. Couldn't care less."

"I was thinking," said Jimmy. "When you do it. Maybe you better put a couple a' extra shots over the other fellas' heads or somethin' . . . Make it look good."

"I wanna see Jerry's face, he's lyin' inna snow, thinkin' it's him's gonna get clipped," said Richie, laughing.

"Yeah! Me too." Jimmy guffawed. "I wanna see that."

"No, no, no," said Henry. "You gentlemen want to play practical jokes on each other, buy a fuckin' whoopee cushion. I don't do that. I don't play around when I work, alright? You ever hear about me chopping anybody's hands off, jamming money up their ass, yankin' out tongues or any of that shit? No. You know why? 'Cause I don't do that. No jokes. No messages."

"Awwww," said Jimmy. "Just a couple a' extra shots to make it look good . . ."

"Nope. That's not the way it gets done. There's going to be a lot of noise. There's probably going to be a lot of people around, a weekend at a ski resort. First shot, all hell is gonna break loose. I'm not going to find myself sitting around in an orange jumpsuit because somebody thought a few extra rounds would be good for a laugh. I don't think I'd like prison. I'd lose my tan."

"Suit yourself," grumbled Jimmy. "You know your business. Least I hope you do." He stood up and walked into the bathroom to change clothes, Richie hurrying after him with a wine-colored double-breasted man's suit. Just outside the bathroom door, Jimmy caught sight of himself in the mirror over the dresser. "You sure you like this color? I think it makes me look fat. I look fat to you?"

"You look radiant," said Henry.

2

On Thursday, Henry rented a four-wheel-drive Toyota from an Avis in Paterson. He took Route 80 across the George Washington Bridge, ate lunch by himself at the Second Avenue Deli, then drove out to Brighton Beach, Brooklyn.

Sammy Avakian's stamp and coin shop was on the boardwalk, sandwiched between a coin-operated laundry and the A&B Dairy Restaurant. A bell rang when Henry opened the door to the shop, and Sammy, a shriveled little man in a dirty shirt with a face like a rhesus monkey, looked up from his Russian newspaper.

"Hey, Sammy. How's tricks?" said Henry.

Sammy scowled, exchanged his reading glasses for a pair of horn-rims, and hopped down from his stool.

"You again," he said. "I should have known you'd be around. Nice tan. Florida?"

Henry shook his head.

"Nice if you have the time," said Sammy. "So what is it? What do you need?"

Henry showed him a piece of paper, gave him a minute to read it, then put it back in his pocket. "Can you fill it?" he asked.

"Sure, sure," said Sammy. "I got just the item you want. Gimme a second." He came out from behind the counter, limping in elevator shoes, and hung a sign in the front door that said, BACK IN FIVE MINUTES. He locked the door, turned to put on an overcoat from a peg on the wall, and led Henry through the dusty stockroom to the rear parking lot.

"That your car over there?" he asked Henry.

"Yeah."

"Thought so. I haven't seen it before. We'll take mine," said Sammy. "It's not far where we gotta go."

Sammy drove a '78 LTD, his head barely able to look out over the dashboard. The backseat was filled with what seemed to be a lifetime's accumulated junk—newspapers, magazines, cartons of bric-a-brac that looked like they'd been picked up at a yard sale. It smelled of moist cardboard, cigarette smoke, and dust. Two pale orange car fresheners hung from the rearview mirror exuding papaya.

They drove to the Kwik 'N' EZ Storage Depot in a nearby industrial area, and Sammy parked in front of a lockup. It took him a while to find the right key among the scores on the chain at his hip, but he managed eventually to open the heavy padlock, and Henry helped him raise the steel shutter enough for the two of them to duck inside. They closed the shutter behind them and stood in darkness for a moment while Sammy searched for the light switch.

It was a small cinder-block room, stacked floor to ceiling with wooden crates and tarpaulin-covered objects. It smelled of Cosmoline and cat piss. Sammy scurried about the room, searching under the tarps and moving things around until he found what he was looking for. He dragged a long crate into the center of the floor and pried it open with a crowbar, making little grunts of satisfaction in the back of his throat.

"Galil 7.62 semiautomatic sniper's rifle," he announced, "got your bipod, folding stock, flash suppressor. It's got your range finder, telescopic sight . . . everything you need right inna box. Good enough for the IDF, it's good enough for you. How much ammunition you need?"

"Two clips," said Henry.

"Two?" said Sammy. "You ain't gonna test-fire the thing?"

"I'll need one clip for that, the other for the work," said Henry, holding the weapon in his arms and peering down the barrel.

"How many fuckin' Turks you gonna get with one clip?" complained Sammy. "It's not enough!"

"No Turks, Sammy. Not this time around. Sorry. Maybe one of these days I'll throw you a freebie."

"Sonofabitch! When you gonna shoot some bastard Turks? What are you waitin' for? How about I throw in the ammo for free? No, you can have the whole thing, gratis. All ya gotta do is, on the way back the City, let off a few clips. I know where the bastards live. I got plenty a' addresses. I got names—"

"Sorry, Sammy," said Henry.

Sammy spat on the floor. "You prolly gonna shoot some more fuckin' guineas," he said sadly. "Guineas, guineas, guineas, nothin' but fuckin' guineas. Where's the good? They kill each other, you leave 'em alone in a fuckin' room long enough. You . . . you really gotta give somethin' back one a' these days, Henry. Really."

"Just two clips."

"You want somethin' special? I got these fléchette rounds. When they hit the bone, they break up into splinters. Even the guy lives, they gotta do exploratory to find 'em all. They don't show up on the X ray . . ."

"Sounds like a delightful product, but no."

Sammy limped disconsolately off to a dark corner to find cartridges, returning with two boxes and an extra empty clip for the

Galil. "How about a LAWS? I got one back there. Just in. You know what that is? Light antitank weapons system. You can mess up a whole lotta people with that. Take out an armored car you want. You wanna see it? Just to look?"

"No, no really. This is all I need here," said Henry, smiling. "I *will* need a bag or something for the Galil. You have something?"

"Yeah, sure," said Sammy. He reached into a trash-filled fifty-five-gallon drum and removed a Bloomingdale's shopping bag. "Here," he said. "What sticks out, you can cover with a coat or something."

Henry packed his purchases into the bag and stood by the door.

"How about—" Sammy started to say.

"I'm fine as is," said Henry. "Really."

3

Henry, wrapped in his space blanket in his hidey-hole halfway up Curleigh Mountain, watched through his high-powered field glasses as five sets of headlights bounced through the darkness. The sodium lights that illuminated the ski trails had been switched off hours ago, as had the snow-making machinery and lifts. The mountain was black and quiet; he lay in silence under a stretched bedsheet covered with snow and twigs and dead leaves, his nose growing numb, craving coffee and cigarettes.

The vehicles came to a halt, and there was the sound of car doors slamming. The headlights were shut off, replaced by wobbling beams from handheld flashlights a few hundred yards below. Henry could hear cursing and laughter as five bosses and their attendants stumbled blindly through the snow in their dress shoes. A few moments later, the lights inside the rented chalets were turned on, one after the other. He saw dark silhouettes of large men through the curtains, watched as a few hapless lieutenants were dispatched for firewood on the icy outer decks. There was more cursing and laughter as one man slipped and fell on his ass in front of an open door. Henry heard Richie Tic's voice, complaining,

"They oughta put salt onnis fuckin' deck for fuck's sake! It's like a fuckin' skatin' rink . . . I should sue these pricks! I coulda been kilt!" There was more laughing. Dark figures holding stacks of firewood moved into the light from the open doors, came back for more, calling to each other, their voices reverberating up and down the rocky slope.

"Hey, Mags! Mags! You woulda been a good Boy Scout!"

"Ask him rub two sticks together!"

"Yeah? Rub this!"

"Where's Richie? Youse better keep an eye on Richie . . . Somethin' brush up against your ass you better hope it's only a fuckin' bear!"

"Hey, lookit Donuts! Yo, Donuts! You supposedta burn the wood, not look at it!"

"There's somethin' movin' in there! There's a rat or somethin'."

"There ain't no fuckin' rats here! It's prolly a snake!"

"A killer squirrel! You watch out. You gonna have some rabid fuckin' squirrel nibblin' on yer fuckin' nuts tonight!"

"Fuck you! Fuck alla youse! It's a chipmunk or somethin'!"

"That's cute . . . Donuts gotta new friend! Why don't you take him back the house, adopt him!"

"Fuck you! You better sleep on yer fuckin' back tonight, you prick, you gotta bunk with Richie! I'll take the fuckin' squirrel any day!"

"*Minchia al culo* . . . motherfucker."

Finally, the doors slammed shut, and in a little while there was the smell of woodsmoke.

Henry pulled the space blanket up over his head and fell asleep.

The sound of the giant compressors that drove the snow-making machinery woke him with a start. It was six-thirty in the morning under a steel gray sky. Soon the loud hiss from the spray nozzles was everywhere. Henry pulled back further from the narrow opening of his hole, wishing he could crawl out for just a minute to take a piss. The first snowmobiles began to move up the trails; maintenance workers and ski patrol checking conditions. Henry smelled bacon and home fries cooking in the kitchens at the main lodge, then the even more tantalizing scent of coffee.

He picked up his field glasses and looked down at the cluster of chalets, watched as a single mobster moved from house to house, taking breakfast orders. The man started up a gray Cutlass, tires spinning at first in the snow, finally managing to fishtail down the unpaved, icy road. A half hour later he returned, bearing parcels. When the man knocked on the door of the largest chalet, Henry was gratified to get a glimpse of Donnie Wicks and Junior Lofaro. Donnie looked older than the last time Henry had seen him. Still in his bathrobe, he took his breakfast from the man and moved quickly away from the door without comment or expression. Junior lingered for a moment, checking his bag to see that the other man had got it right.

At nine, the chairlifts ground into motion, squeaking and clanking up the mountain with the first loads of chattering skiers. Soon Henry could hear them on the nearby trails, their skis crunching on the ice under the newly made powder as they whipped past his position.

He set up the Galil on its bipod. He'd spray-painted it in a black and white camouflage pattern, and he positioned it so the flash suppressor was a few inches back from the opening of his hole. When Henry peered down through the telescopic sight, he was looking right at Donnie Wicks's front door. His fingers growing numb in the cold, he chambered a round and removed the condom stretched over the muzzle before putting his mittens back on.

At eleven o'clock, there had been no further movement in the chalets. The slopes were getting crowded. Henry could see long lines forming by the chairlifts at the base of the mountain, the whoops and shouts of skiers growing louder and more frequent around and above him. He was no longer able to look left or right for fear of giving away his position. He could only lie motionless, deep in his hunter's blind, and wait.

At least the wind was light. At the distance he'd have to shoot, it could have been a major, even prohibitive factor. He looked nervously at the sky as it grew later, aware that in a few hours the sun would pass overhead, threatening to reflect on the lenses of his field glasses or the telescopic sight. He checked his watch again, anxious that the scheduled meeting begin.

Eleven forty-five, and the doors of the chalets swung open. Henry got into firing position and removed his mittens. He looked down through the scope, breath held, ready . . . then watched in horror as instead of a delegation of bosses marching in a neat line over to Donnie's chalet, he saw an unruly cluster of hilariously dressed first-time skiers, each ludicrously attired figure indistinguishable from the next in their ski caps, goggles, ballooning down parkas, and ski boots. Flunkie, lieutenant, boss, they all looked like multicolored Michelin tire men, or overweight Smurfs, staggering anonymously about with their rented skis and poles. Henry recognized Jimmy, unmistakable in a huge, shimmering green snowsuit, a knit cap with pom-pom bobbing atop his Everest-size body. He thought he saw him look up the mountain for a second, an expression on his face that might have said, "Who knew?"

Henry could only watch Donnie's door, waiting and hoping. He saw Junior emerge, like the others, dressed to hit the slopes, but he waited in vain for Donnie. The door closed without the old man setting foot outside. It was Junior alone who led the procession of corpulent mafiosi to the bunny slope. Henry put down the rifle and watched through his field glasses as they charged down the wooded slope like drunken bison, hurling snowballs at each other and laughing loudly. He kept looking hopefully back at Donnie's door. The possibility that Donnie Wicks, a man who hadn't left his one block of Lower Manhattan in twenty years, would suddenly appear and join his subjects on the bunny slope seemed remote in the extreme. Still, Henry, his bladder nearly bursting, kept looking back and hoping.

If things had not already reached the point of cruel and absurd fuckup, it was the spectacle of thirteen mobsters clinging awkwardly to the rope tow that did the trick. Henry watched Paulie Brown lose his balance and fall onto his belly. A man who could have been Jerry Dogs stumbled over his legs, entangling his skis but refusing to let go of the rope; he was dragged the rest of the way up, his skis banging loosely behind on their safety straps. Six hundred yards away, Henry could hear them shrieking and hooting and hurling taunts at each other.

Apparently, Donnie Wicks heard them too. Henry saw a single figure step out onto the deck of the largest chalet. The old man was still in his bedroom slippers, an overcoat thrown over his pajamas. He moved slowly and carefully across the icy deck. On the bunny slope, a ski instructor was offering a few tips to a group of men who were not used to being told how to do anything. The instructor was forced to retreat by a barrage of snowballs and the shouted jeers and insults of mobsters uninterested in correct snowplowing technique. Henry saw Richie move forward clumsily and whack the man's rear with a ski pole, causing more whoops and laughter.

Henry removed his mittens and steadied the rifle. This was as good as it was going to get. He wasn't going to wait for the sun to give away his position. He wasn't going to piss in his pants and then lie in it all day waiting for a better shot. He was going to do it now,

get on a plane and go home, where it was warm, and count his
money.

Junior Lofaro was the first one down the bunny slope. He wasn't
doing too badly either, managing to stay on his feet, whereas
Jimmy and Jerry, a few yards back, stumbled and fell before they
got five feet. Junior's poles were held straight out from his hips, his
knees together, ankles apart, in a fair approximation of a snowplow.
From the corner of his eye, Henry thought he saw Donnie clap his
hands on the chalet's deck.

Henry held his breath, got Junior in the crosshairs, led him just
a little, and letting his breath out slowly, squeezed the trigger.
There was a sharp *crack* that echoed over the mountain and the valley below. A long, long second later, Junior Lofaro's head exploded
into fine pink mist. He dropped back onto his skis, feet still in his
bindings, his body continuing at a brisk clip down the slope. A
bright red trail appeared in the snow behind him. He came out of
his snowplow, kept going until he ran right off the edge of the trail
into a snow fence and lay there, dead.

There was screaming from the bunny slope. A young girl, her
canary yellow ski suit showered with Junior's brain matter, was
wailing at the top of her lungs, swatting frantically at her face to
remove bits of blood and hair. The other mobsters lay on their bellies, hugging the ground, afraid to look up. Some skiers, however,
unused to being shot at, were already pointing at various spots up
the mountain, shouting to each other.

Henry quickly swung the Galil over in Donnie's direction.
There was no time to set the range finder. Donnie was already
making for the open door across the icy wooden deck. Henry
nearly emptied the magazine, firing for the doorway, intending
Donnie to find his way into the bullets' path. A shell exploded into
the doorframe. Another disappeared into the interior of the chalet,
breaking glass somewhere. Another hit nothing. The fourth and

fifth hit Donnie in the abdomen as his feet went out from under him. A single bedroom slipper went flying as he crashed onto the deck, a wet, red stain growing large on his overcoat. He lay there without moving.

Time to go. Henry peeled off the oversize hooded white windbreaker that he'd worn over his parka all night. He left the rifle where it was, slipped out of his hole, and ran in a crouch toward the edge of the trail, where he'd hidden his skis and boots. Finding them, he tore off the rubber Totes on his feet and stepped into the frozen boots, strapped on his skis, quickly pulled on a silly-looking cap that said, SKIERS MAKE BETTER LOVERS, and charged down the trail, remembering at the last minute to put on his mirrored goggles. He joined a large group from a local ski club, skiing neither too fast nor too slow, content to look just barely in control of his skis, slightly off balance, so people would get out of his way.

The first snowmobiles of the ski patrol and mountain security began to appear, nervous young men in red jackets with radios. They drove right past him without a look. When Henry reached the bottom of the mountain, a deliberately witless-looking grin on his face, he made sure to show surprise and curiosity at the growing crowd of police and rescue workers assembling on the bunny slope. He even lingered as the first ambulances appeared, gawking with the rest of them. People were pouring out of the shops and restaurants in the main lodge for a look. Henry took off his skis and left them leaning against a ski rack by the main exit.

A high school teacher was hurrying his charges away from the carnage, and Henry moved close, following the flow of bodies into the parking lot. The rental car was where he'd left it, and Henry removed his parka, boots, cap, and goggles. When he slipped behind the wheel, he looked like any other blue-collar, work-shirted local, out for an afternoon drink. His nice, dry cowboy boots were under the dash, and he put them on, grateful for the worn, soft leather. The engine started with the first try, and he was gone.

Later, after the police and ambulances and television crews from the City had disappeared, and after the newspaper reporters had finished with their follow-up stories and their interviews with the local residents, the town of Huckapee, New York, returned to its usual grudging routine. People still talked about the shootings on Curleigh Mountain, of course. They talked about them a lot. Most people in the town were unemployed, so they had a lot of time on their hands. And the lucky few who did earn a regular paycheck worked over at Devil's Run, so most of them were right there when it happened. They were there when the Colombian Hit Man Blew Mob Bosses into Bleeding Chunks right there on the god-damn bunny slope! Few who worked at Devil's Run hadn't Seen It All.

At Mary's Luncheonette, where the maintenance crews met for breakfast, at the Wigwam Tavern, right next to the Huckapee Lodge (where the alleged Hit Man had stayed), the shootings were still the subject of much wild speculation. At the Wigwam, a framed black-and-white photo of Junior Lofaro's body hung in a place of honor behind the bar, right next to the dusty eight-by-ten of Division Champs, the Buffalo Bills. The front page of the *Huck-apee Valley Courier* was glued next to it, the headline screaming, MOB HIT AT DEVIL'S RUN! It was the biggest thing to have happened in the small mountain town since the mills closed down. Before the shootings, the headline was to have read PRINCIPAL'S SON IN CAR CRASH, describing a fender-bender between a milk truck and the notorious local drunk Billy Coombs.

Most people had come to agree with the conclusion that the Hit Man was Colombian. They'd seen *Miami Vice*. They knew what those people could do. That dark-skinned man, no question about it, had been sent all the way from the hills of Medellín to wreak bloody havoc on their mountain. Curleigh, the largest of three mountains in the valley (the other two were referred to by local wits as Moe and Larry), had taken on a whole new luster since the shootings; some folks were already talking about changing the name to something more lurid, more marketable, like Bloody Mountain. Making a buck was getting harder and harder, they said, especially in the off-season. Summer Funtime, the water slide at Devil's Run, had failed to attract. Maybe a little notoriety would be a good thing.

Definitely Colombian, most people said. The newspapers had described a dark-skinned male, possibly Hispanic, around six feet tall, who spoke with an accent. He had big feet. This much was known for sure. The rental ski boots and rubber Totes recovered near the scene were size twelves. The man had registered at the Huckapee Motor Lodge as Jaime Garcia, and Mrs. Curleigh, at the desk, remembered him as very polite, very correct. He had spoken with an accent like Ricardo Montalban, and addressed her as "Señora."

The jeep the man arrived in had been rented to someone fitting his description named Luis Chavez, resident of Puerto Rico, and the Ford Escort he'd apparently used to get away, rented in the neighboring town of Wolkill and later abandoned in the parking lot of the former Indian Burial Ground outside town, had been rented under the name Victor Lopez of Miami. To confuse matters slightly, Danny Weller, the cabdriver who took a man answering the gunman's description to a shopping mall in Quonset, remembered him as a quiet man, no accent, who said his car had broken down. "He talked kind of like an old hippie," said Danny. Most people discounted his account—Colombian Hit Man sounded so much better.

Like Elvis Presley, the Colombian Hit Man seemed to pop up everywhere for a while. He was reported seen outside Ed's Package Store, drinking Thunderbird out of the bottle. One woman claimed to have seen him at Dick's QuickStop with a cart full of groceries, calmly reading about himself in *Newsweek*. When a lift attendant at Devil's Run spotted a dark-skinned man on the lift line a few weeks later, he threw the switch, marooning a hapless Brazilian ski enthusiast until the police arrived.

The Huckapee police chief, Daryl Remick, took all of this with good humor. He refrained from pointing out that, as far as he knew, there weren't too many Colombian hit men who stood over six feet tall and wore size twelve shoes. The man was long gone in any case, the way he saw it, probably out of the country. In his comments to *Hard Copy*, Remick was positively admiring in his appraisal of the gunman's marksmanship. The chief had served in Vietnam, he explained, with a rifle company, and a head shot from six hundred yards, like the one that had sprayed Junior Lofaro's brains (a moving target no less) all over Curleigh Mountain, hell, that was "outstanding shooting."

Chief Remick was not concerned that the killer of Mr. Lofaro had yet to be captured or even identified. He knew enough about what the deceased had done for a living that his unsolved murder seemed to be something less than a tragedy.

The wounded man, however, D'Andrea "Donnie Wicks" Balistieri, was another thing. Nobody likes to see a thing like that. Mr. Balistieri had been hit by two bullets. The first entered his hip, shattering the bone and requiring its replacement with a pin. The second bullet had entered his right buttock, traveled upward at an angle, and after deflecting off the pelvis, exited slightly to the right of his navel. An emergency colostomy was performed, and Donnie Wicks would be compelled to crap in a bag for the rest of his life.

4

Henry read about it later, on the beach. He'd had to drive the scooter all the way across the island for a copy of the day's *Times,* and Frances, his wife, was still out snorkeling on the reef when he returned. Henry sat down on the empty blanket and pressed a cold Heineken bottle to his forehead, the headline on the lower right front page playing hell with an afternoon agenda that previously had concerned only where to eat dinner and whether to order the stuffed crab backs or the curried goat.

A few sunburned tourists gathered up their things a couple of yards down the beach, retreating with their Styrofoam coolers and folding beach chairs to some air-conditioned bunker in town. Soon the beach was empty. Henry looked out over the water, searching for Frances, but saw nothing. He lay back and closed his eyes, putting the thought of Donnie Wicks in his hospital bed out of his mind.

"So that's who it was," said Frances, waking him. She was reading the paper between mouthfuls of chicken leg from the barbecue shack down the beach, still dripping wet from her swim. She gave the unfinished chicken to a scraggly, feral-looking stray who'd followed her to the blanket, and peeled down her maillot to her waist. She lay down on her back next to Henry, inscrutable in her sunglasses.

"Should have gone for the head shot."

"I fucked up," said Henry, getting up on one elbow.

Frances drained the rest of Henry's beer and lit a joint, her long, well-toned body relaxing in the sun. "This going to be a problem?"

"Could be," said Henry. "Jimmy's going to be pissed for one thing . . ."

"What about Donnie?"

Henry just shrugged, all sorts of things to worry about coming to mind.

"I always liked him," said Frances, removing a seed from her lip and passing the joint to Henry. The stray dog stood up and sauntered off to the mangroves to finish the chicken bone in the shade. Frances's hand brushed Henry's arm for a second, reassuringly.

"Me too," said Henry.

5

ONE YEAR LATER

Monsieur Ribiere, in a dark blue suit, dress shirt buttoned up all the way, and striped regimental tie, poked disinterestedly at his spring rolls in the deserted dining room of the Jardin Indochine Restaurant in Marigot. He was a small man, in his late sixties, and he looked pink and scrubbed as if he'd just stepped out of a hot bath. There were angry red marks on the papery skin of his neck where the collar had dug into his flesh. His glasses, thick lensed, with military-style wire-rimmed frames, had slipped down to the end of his nose, and he peered over them with pale, watery blue eyes at his Vietnamese bodyguard, Trung, who stood by the kitchen door gossiping with the restaurant's owner, a relative.

Monsieur Ribiere was not happy with the events of the last week. Had it been in his power, he would have spiked the whole deal, answered the first Americans' approach with a resolute *non* and let them make problems for some other island. But it wasn't up to him. By the time the matter had reached his tiny outpost, it was a foregone conclusion. The decision had been made in Paris, and he was to see that the Americans got what they wanted.

A direct, written order would have been too easy, and too embarrassing if something went wrong. It had been left for him to arrange, running back and forth between his nominal office at the gendarmerie and his real offices in the Government House, the Americans insisting on the use of a secure phone for every conversation, regardless of substance.

In the event, Monsieur "Pastou" had arrived on Saint Martin with all the usual American play at top secrecy. A huge C-5 Galaxy Transport, painted ostentatiously black (just in case anybody had missed how Top Secret it all was), had touched down at one-thirty in the morning at the tiny French-side airport of L'Espérance, waking the entire village of Grand Case a few yards beyond the runway. The Galaxy's rear cargo hatch had dropped open and four, count them, four, identical new Jeep Wagoneers had come rolling out onto the tarmac. Monsieur Pastou was in the third Jeep, sandwiched between two marshals, neither of whom looked to be older than Ribiere's grandson, and Pastou himself looked decidedly un-French—even his passport photo looked like a mug shot.

If the whole operation hadn't been spectacular enough, there was the large delegation that had come out to greet the plane. Some fools from the State Department, an FBI man, more marshals (early arrivals who Ribiere's people had picked out as soon as they'd got off their flight in tourist mufti). There was even a callow youth with an impressive overbite from the always unimpressive CIA. They were all there, come to see the arrival of America's latest and greatest pet gangster. They babbled into their radios and satellite communicators, whispering code names from the four corners of the tarmac: Big Tuna, Marlin One, Swordfish—apparently it was seafood this week in the codebook. The landings at Normandy had been less noticeable, and probably less expensive.

Over his spring rolls, Monsieur Ribiere perused a rather more complete biography of the mysterious Monsieur Pastou than the Americans had seen fit to provide. That he had been previously known as D'Andrea "Donnie Wicks" Balistieri could be no secret to anyone who read *The New York Times* and then gazed upon his wizened face. His career, spanning four decades in which he had been at one time or another implicated in dozens of murders, was the subject of countless quickie paperbacks, television documentaries, and made-for-TV movies. The usual suspicions of involvement in the disappearance of witnesses fleshed out a résumé dotted with the kinds of allegations you would expect of any self-respecting capo: jury tampering, extortion, racketeering, bribery, receiving, usury, hijacking, counterfeiting, auto theft, and filing a false instrument. Following M. Wicks/Balistieri/Pastou's long life of toil in the vineyards of organized crime, Monsieur Ribiere felt a grudging respect for the wounded old murderer. They were, after all, about the same age.

Apparently M. Balistieri's brush with death a year previous (coupled with the certainty of an imminent indictment under federal RICO statutes) had convinced him to cooperate with his former tormentors. Nothing in Balistieri's file disturbed Ribiere as much as the thought of all those corn-fed, overmuscled marshals traipsing around Saint Martin with Swedish K's under their arms. In his experience, for sheer destruction and chaos, America's criminals couldn't hold a candle to the bungling, well-intentioned efforts of its official organs. Ultimately, however, it wasn't the thought of the incontinent old gangster growing tan under Saint Martin's sun that disturbed Monsieur Ribiere's enjoyment of his meal. It was something else.

The suspicion had grown in increments from one anecdotal fact in the Balistieri file. The hapless M. Balistieri, it appeared, had been shot with a Galil 7.62 sniper rifle. Though the attempt on Balistieri had failed, Monsieur Ribiere had read with interest that a Mr. Dominic "Junior" Lofaro had been effectively dispatched with a single shot to the head from over six hundred yards.

Monsieur Ribiere, over his cold, uneaten spring rolls, was uncomfortable with coincidence, especially this one. He knew somebody who liked a Galil, even insisted on one. Who did things like shoot gangsters for a living. That they had known each other well for over twenty years was cold comfort.

Monsieur Ribiere put his napkin down on the table and stood up. Across the room, Trung abruptly cut off his conversation with the owner and went ahead, out into the steamy afternoon heat. Ribiere paid his check and made his way slowly back to his office in the Government House, lost in thought. Trung walked a few dozen yards in front of him, scanning the faces of passersby, in search of enemies.

His office was no cooler than the street. The ceiling fan that droned and squeaked overhead only served to push the hot, humid air from place to place, offering no relief. Monsieur Ribiere sat rigidly behind his desk, tapping a pencil against his front teeth and thinking about Henry. Shortly, he stood up, clipped a plastic laminate to his jacket pocket, and walked down to the basement registry. A sweating security officer buzzed him through a heavy steel door into a long, narrow room lined with file cabinets. It was air-conditioned here to prevent all the valuable paper from moldering, and Ribiere got down on one knee to work the combination lock on a corner safe.

Henry's file weighed over five kilos. Monsieur Ribiere took the unwieldy pile of cables, photographs, after-action reports, and page after page of his own creative and potentially damning accounts to a reading desk against a far wall. He spread his bony fingers across the cover sheet, where Henry's cryptonym appeared in red lettering, and took a deep breath before opening the file to the first page.

6

There were pelicans circling overhead. They came down past Henry and Frances's balcony at eye level, riding the air currents; then, one by one, they plummeted out of the sky, diving straight into the water with a heavy splash. Every third or fourth attempt would yield a fish.

The sun was getting low, and the silhouettes of returning sailboats began to appear on the horizon, heading for port. Henry, still wet from the shower, a hotel towel wrapped around his waist, reclined lazily on a chaise, feet up on the balcony railing, sipping tequila.

"Look," said Frances, her white terry-cloth robe hanging carelessly open, "there's Captain Toby and Meathead."

A red Zodiac dinghy slipped out through the narrow channel from the lagoon behind the hotel into the sea. Toby was impossible to confuse, at any distance, with the other charter captains. He stood erect next to the motor, one hand on the throttle as he bounced the tiny inflatable craft over the swells to meet an incoming sailboat. Meathead, his dog, stood in the bow, ears back, face leaning proudly into the wind. Frances put two fingers in her mouth and let loose with a piercing whistle. Toby turned and waved.

The hotel rested on a spit of coral separating the Oyster Pond, a lagoon, on one side and the choppy, dark blue sea on the other. From their balcony, Henry and Frances could watch the sun rise over Saint Barts, and from the bedroom–living quarters of their suite, they could watch it set behind the mountains ringing the pond.

The Oyster Pond Yacht Club was a small Moorish structure, Spanish tile roof and white stucco walls, with twenty rooms built around a center courtyard and six suites further out on the coral peninsula. Henry and Frances lived in the one farthest out: two rooms, balcony, bathroom, and kitchenette. The furniture was white wicker, the floors glazed terra-cotta—cool on bare feet. As Henry enjoyed saying, it was like staying with a very rich friend—only the friend is away. They'd lived there for twelve years.

"Let's *not* go back to Orient tomorrow," said Frances, her green eyes catching light off the water. "I know the food is good. But if I have to look at one more fat fucking German, capering around the damn beach, naked, wagging his shriveled, uncircumcised, sunburned little dick around, I'm gonna start World War Two all over again. I mean, really. Put it *away.*"

"I think it's a status thing. You make over six million deutsche marks a year or whatever, you get to go without pants," said Henry, still groggy from the sun.

"I just don't think it's fair. I mean, *he* doesn't have to look at it—he *can't* with that belly—why do we?"

"So. You wanna go to Rouge tomorrow?"

"Don't you?" said Frances, lighting a joint and straddling Henry on the chaise. "It's much nicer. No tourists."

"You can't go naked anymore. Last time, I mean . . . remember?

French fucking cops almost hauled my ass away in leg irons," said Henry, taking the joint.

"They just asked you politely to put something on."

"So how come they didn't say anything to you? *You* were naked!"

"Maybe you were frightening the other beachgoers."

"Yeah. As much as I'd like to think that a glimpse of my mammoth dong caused panic and envy amongst the populace, I don't think that was it. I mean, I don't get it. People run around buck naked on that beach all the time. Why pick on me?"

"You were feeling me up," said Frances.

"I was *on* my stomach!"

"Oh, that's different," said Frances, taking a long hit on the joint and passing it back, the smoke making her blink. "So what does this mean? No more Rouge?"

"No, no, no . . . I just didn't like seeing cops in their pillbox hats and their dress shoes, coming down the beach, making a beeline for *my* blanket. You notice that? They came right for me. I hate that. Dress shoes on sand. Reminds me of that show, you know— 'Book 'em Dan-O.' That guy wore dress shoes on the beach too. It was embarrassing."

"Yeah, right," said Frances, fixing him with the hard look for a millisecond before breaking into a smile. Henry liked how she could do that.

"Hey. I got a reputation to consider. I don't want to read about myself as some notorious nudist in the *Chronicle,* thank you very much. 'The known nudist H. was apprehended yesterday by French-side police. After a stern warning, he was released into the custody of his wife, F.' "

"Listen," said Frances, slightly annoyed, "you're taking this entirely too seriously. They got a specific complaint, probably from that lady in the red one-piece—the one with the kids. That's who dropped the dime."

"The one with the husband with the nose shield? He was looking at *your* naked ass all day without any apparent ill effects."

"Whatever," said Frances, bored with the conversation. She stood up and wrapped the white terry cloth tightly around herself, staring out to sea.

"Okay, okay. Rouge tomorrow. I'll bring a suit. Just in case."

They both said nothing for a while, listening to the waves chopping into the coral below the balcony. Henry began to drift off to sleep as Frances headed for the shower.

Henry was still sleeping in the chair when there was a knock at the door. He woke with a start and looked around for Frances. He heard the shower running, so he threw on a robe, went to the door, and opened it.

It was a short Vietnamese man of about fifty. He wore cheap polyester slacks, leather sandals, and a white guayabera. His fingers were short and stubby, the hands and forearms muscular to excess. There was a big grin on his face as he stood there on the porch, while an ancient blue Citroën van, motor running, sat in the parking lot behind him emitting exhaust.

"Hey, Trung," said Henry. "Snapping any necks lately?"

"You come please," said Trung, still smiling.

"Come where?"

"You come see you friend now. He want to see you now. You come now please."

Still half asleep and rubbing his face, Henry struggled into a pair of jeans and a T-shirt. He stepped into some flip-flops, then stuck his head in the bathroom and told Frances he was going out.

Frances's head appeared from inside the shower curtain, shampoo running down her face. She squinted at Henry. "Is everything okay? Where you going?"

"I have to go see my French friend," said Henry. "Don't sweat. I should be back in a while."

"Tell that awful man not to keep you. Happy hour at the Dock in an hour."

Trung drove like a madman, a burning Kent in the corner of his mouth blowing ashes around the inside of the van as he bounced over potholes and fishtailed through gravel patches. Henry winced and put his hands against the dash every time they went around a turn, expecting a head-on collision with a dump truck or cement mixer at any second. When Trung took the wide turn past the Coralita Hotel, Henry had to reach out the window and grab hold of the roof to keep himself from falling onto Trung's lap. When they sped through the residential area of Orléans, heedlessly splashing pedestrians every time they went through a puddle, Henry slunk down in his seat, not wanting to be recognized as a perpetrator of such rudeness.

Trung had a country music station on the radio. Henry had always been puzzled by the popularity of country among the islanders, but it seemed even more incongruous that this Vietnamese thug next to him should be tapping his foot along with Willie Nelson and caterwauling out the window in what Henry could only guess was an approximation of singing.

"Willie Nelson Number One," said Trung. "You like?" He cranked the volume up another notch, the speakers distorting.

"Rock and roll," said Henry, not taking his eyes off the road.

Trung shook his head vigorously. "Rock and roll no good. Rock and roll make American peoples lose war. Cominiss music. No good. No good."

Willie Nelson sang about lost love and too much booze. Henry's thoughts were on the axles of the aged van, and whether they'd break before they reached their destination. They drove past the rolling pastures of La Savanne. The roadsides had been planted with evenly spaced shade trees, reminding him of the French countryside. In the fields beyond, the wind made ripples in the tall grass. Trung stomped on the gas pedal to pass a slow-moving tour bus and a flatbed truck full of construction workers. Henry held his breath as Trung jerked the van out of the way of oncoming traffic just in time to avoid crashing into a water truck. They hurtled past Pic Paradis, the highest peak on Saint Martin, bouncing over a row of crumbling sleeping policemen, and plummeted down a steep, twisting hill to Cripple Gate.

At the mouth of the verdant green valley of Colombier, they turned right and roared down a narrow dirt road, the old Citroën shaking and clattering and banging up and down on its barely functional suspension as if it was going to fall apart any second. They passed some private homes, some of them still under construction, the wheels of the van sinking almost up to the axles in the brown runoff from the nearby lagoon. Trung sped across a pitted cement bridge and pulled to a noisy stop at Friar's Beach.

It was nearly high tide on the flat, pebble-strewn stretch of beach. The sea on one side had merged in spots with the lagoon on the other, swamping most of the area. The Rastafarian bar a few hundred yards down was closed. Water lapped at the wooden supports. The beach, what was left of it, was deserted.

Trung hopped down out of the van, opened Henry's door for him, and led him over to an abandoned barbecue shack. Picnickers had torn much of the roof and walls off for firewood. The concrete foundation was breaking apart like an overcooked brownie. From behind a plywood wall covered with curling posters, Monsieur Ribiere stepped out into the failing light.

"Bonjour, Henri," he said, before switching to his British-accented English. "Perhaps we can walk a bit?"

"You don't mind getting your feet wet?" said Henry, noticing Monsieur Ribiere's dress shoes.

"I don't mind."

Henry fell in beside the old man, and they walked slowly down the swampy beach. The standing water and the mangroves in the lagoon had made the area a breeding ground for mosquitoes and no-see-ums, which were out in force. The hours between four and six were always bad in the best of circumstances, and Henry cursed himself for having neglected to apply repellent before leaving the hotel. The beach was teeming with the little bloodsuckers. He swatted at the tiny bugs that hovered around his mouth and ears, noticing with displeasure how Monsieur Ribiere ignored them entirely. Perhaps, after all the years skulking around in the bush in Africa and Asia, he had become used to them.

Henry looked back at the blue van, saw Trung squatting under a sea grape tree, his face illuminated by the glowing end of a Kent.

"Henri," said Monsieur Ribiere. "There is at the present time someone on the island . . . a man. A man who I believe you know."

"Oh?"

"Someone you maybe have had some . . . business with in the past."

"Really. You going to tell me who?"

"He arrived here a few days ago. He calls himself Pastou, but that is not his name and he is not a Frenchman. He is an American named Balistieri. You *are* familiar with this man, I think?"

Henry took a long time to consider his answer. It generally did not do to mislead the old man. He was well informed, frighteningly so at times, and he rarely asked a question to which he did not already know the answer.

Henry was not anxious to insult him with a lie or a half-truth. He was still pondering his answer when Ribiere spoke again.

"Of course you know the man," he said. "You shot him, didn't you?"

"Yes. I did," said Henry. What else could he say?

Monsieur Ribiere looked relieved. "Thank you for being so frank with me. It wouldn't have done, lying . . ."

Sneaky bastard, thought Henry.

"What's he doing here?" he asked.

"He is a guest of your Federal Witness Protection Program," said Monsieur Ribiere, a note of disapproval in his tone. "And, for now, he is also a guest of the French government." .

"No shit."

"I am informed that Monsieur Balistieri has made a very favorable arrangement with your Justice Department. He is to testify against some of his old friends and associates. In return he will be permitted to live here in safety, free from legal difficulties. He owns a home here, it appears. For some time, even I did not know."

"Me neither," said Henry, sourly. "*Quelle* fucking *surprise.*"

Monsieur Ribiere shrugged noncommittally. "It seems his recent brush with death contributed to his decision." He turned to look directly at Henry for a second. "You know, he was injured. Very gravely. Were you aware of that?"

"Yes," said Henry.

"*Dommage,*" said Monsieur Ribiere. "My interest, my concern is this: that there be no problems, no difficulties between you and Monsieur Donnie Wicks, Monsieur Balistieri, Monsieur Pastou, whatever he calls himself. You are practically neighbors, you know. He is not aware, yet, I do not think, of your presence here. I don't see that he could be or he never would have come. Perhaps, also, he is not aware that it was you who caused his injury. Still. We must assume that it is possible he will find out. Someday, perhaps, he will see you, someone will say something, in the trial, from an old friend, we do not know . . . He might see you at the beach, on the road, and perhaps he will think about things. Perhaps one of his former associates will also be anxious to stay out of prison. This is possible, you agree?"

"Yeah."

"He knows you by sight?"

"Yes. I'm afraid so. We had some . . . some business ventures together at one time."

"Mmmm . . . So."

Henry sighed, a lump forming in his throat. "Donnie's not stupid. I'd be surprised if he hadn't figured out already it was me. Like I said, we've . . . you know . . . I've done a few things for him over the years. Most guys he knows about would have done him in the street. Handguns or shotguns. The usual Sicilian surprise."

"I see. Do you think he bears you ill will? Certainly he is angry with the man who paid. I assume that it was this Monsieur Calabrese who paid? He will testify against him."

Henry thought about this for a while, plodding silently along by Ribiere's side, his feet in brown water up to the ankles now. "I don't know," he said hopefully. "Like I said, I know Donnie pretty well. At least, I think I know him pretty well. A nice guy as they go. Smart. *You'd* like him. I'd say he generally does a thing because it's the smart thing to do, because it's in his interest, not because it's something he feels like doing. He didn't get where he was knocking off every guy who got him mad. If you're asking me does he want me dead, I don't know. If you're asking me would he do something to try and make that happen, or would he tell the feds about me, I'd have to say not unless he felt it was to protect his interest. If he sees me and the wife someday, on the beach, maybe, grilling up some snapper, is he going to grab a gun and take a shot at me? No. Will he call New York, have somebody still loyal get on a plane? I doubt it. That would blow his whole deal with the feds. I don't even think he'd rat me out to the feds if he could avoid it.

Jimmy Pazz is another thing. I don't think he could avoid it there. I don't know. I don't *think* so."

"I am less concerned about what *he* will do," said Monsieur Ribiere. "He is an old man. Very sick. And surrounded at all times by marshals. I am more concerned what *you* might do. This man Calabrese is, understandably, very anxious that this man not live to testify. I imagine he'd pay a lot of money . . ."

"You can forget about that. I don't work on the island. You know that."

"So. If this man Calabrese were to contact you, offer you a great deal of money, you would not consider his request?"

"Just to make sure. What exactly is your position on this? Before I answer, I mean."

"I would prefer—in fact, I must insist—that you resist the temptation. As this man is here through the somewhat reluctant auspices of my government, we would prefer not to have any problems with the Americans. We do not want any assassinations, any shootings, any unexplained accidents at the present time, particularly if they involve this man. It is a very sensitive situation. If even my superiors in my own service were to become aware of your presence on the island, of your previous relationship with this man, they would be very, very unhappy. Should some mishap befall Monsieur Balistieri, I would of course be obliged to inform them. My career, such as it is, would be finished. And you"—Monsieur Ribiere stopped again and fixed Henry with a very unpleasant stare—"You, no doubt, I would be instructed to deal with in the harshest way possible. That is the sad fact."

"Your accent gets thicker when you're menacing," said Henry, genuinely menaced.

Monsieur Ribiere cleared his throat. They had reached the deck of the Rastafarian bar. Ribiere rolled up his pants legs, squeezing water out, and sat down on the edge of the rough wood steps. Henry sat down next to him and lit a Gitane.

"So," he said. "You going to chuck me off the island? Is that what this is all leading up to?"

Monsieur Ribiere took a deep breath, smelling the heavy salt air.

"I love it here," said Henry, sadly.

"Yes," said Monsieur Ribiere, unusually sympathetic. "I always thought that peculiar, you coming from the City. One might expect a man like you, the money you have, to live elsewhere. But maybe it is not so strange. You know, I was born in Paris. But I came to love Algérie just as you love this place. Strange, yes?"

It was completely dark now. Monsieur Ribiere looked up at the moon, took off his glasses for a moment, and rubbed his nose where the frames had pinched. "When a man thinks he has finally found a home, it's sad, very sad, to have to leave it."

Encouraged by this uncharacteristic reverie, Henry still, wisely, said nothing, waiting for the old man to finish.

"Perhaps there is another way. For me . . . for me it is always a changing situation. You say you know this man. Perhaps, as you say, he is reasonable. How well, exactly, do you know him?"

"Pretty well," said Henry. "I even like him."

"That didn't prevent you from trying to kill him."

"You know how that is." Seeing light at the end of the tunnel, Henry pressed on. "He's a funny guy. All *dese* and *dose* but smart like a whip. We got along."

"I think . . . I think you should bury the hatchet," said Monsieur Ribiere, astounding Henry. "If you were to find a way to see him, talk with him, without his guards . . . Do you think he would tell them? Myself, I don't think that a man of his experience could have much to talk about with them. They are so young. So different from him. I think, if you could talk to him, without jeopardizing your own situation, that would be for the best. Of course, if things don't work out, you will have to find someplace else to live. I would, naturally, be very sad, but . . ."

"Sure . . . I could try . . . shit." In truth, Henry had no idea if he could pull such a thing off. "Maybe if I could arrange to bump into him. Right circumstances. Got any ideas?"

"Well," said Monsieur Ribiere, enjoying himself, now. "I am informed about another man. A young friend of Monsieur Balistieri. An expatriate New Yorker like yourself. Maybe you have seen him. He owns the little restaurant, a bar really, on the beach by your hotel. Mickey's Tropical—Mickey, like Mickey Mouse. He's been here about eight months, with his woman friend. They live under the same roof as this Balistieri. You know who I refer to?"

Henry nodded, trying not to look surprised.

"Trung tells me they are very close. Yes. He prepares food for the man each day. They talk, they laugh. They are like father and son. Perhaps you could befriend this person. Or your wife. She is not without resources. She could befriend him, his girlfriend. The difference in age is not so very great. You will become great friends. They are, after all, new to the island. You can show them the sights. And you will find a way, together."

Monsieur Ribiere stood up and began to walk back to the van. "And, at all times, I expect, you will keep me informed."

"Whatever you say."

7

Mickey? You mean Rachel's Mickey?" said Frances. She was applying insect repellent, standing naked in front of the double sinks, one leg up on the counter.

"Mickey," said Henry. "As in Mickey's Tropical. The beach bar." He watched Frances from the bedroom. She had her hair up in a white bath towel; she was still stunning at thirty-six. Henry's eyes wandered over the reflection of her nut-brown body in the mirror.

"Stop gawking and tell me what the fuck's going on, please," said Frances.

"Rachel. That's the girlfriend?" asked Henry, perfectly aware that it was.

"The cute one behind the bar," said Frances, meeting his eyes in the mirror momentarily. "I have a hard time believing you haven't noticed her." She slipped into a Hawaiian shirt.

"I've been too enthralled by your own considerable charms," said Henry. "I guess I didn't notice."

"Too stuttering drunk is more likely," said Frances, searching a shelf for some pants to wear.

"So you know her? You're friends? When did this happen?"

"We've hung out a couple a' times. When you're out sailing. The place does no business. I've hung at the bar with her. She's nice."

Henry shook his head. "The guy's right down on the beach. I have to tell you, I almost shit when he told me. Right there the whole time, a friend of Donnie's. Can't believe I missed it. I mean, the one, two times I've had a beer there, I should have figured something. The guy opens his mouth and you know exactly where he's from."

"No, no," said Frances with assurance. "He's not like that. I really don't think so. Mickey's not one a' those—"

"Really?" asked Henry skeptically. "Then how come he's such good buddies with Donnie fucking Wicks?"

"They house-sit. They live up there at the house, Mickey and Rachel. I'm telling you. The kid is sweet."

"He's sweet now. Jesus. What's going on? You put Albert Anastasia on a beach with a panama hat on and you're going to say he's sweet."

"I'm not kidding," said Frances, brushing her long, dark brown hair. "He was a chef before he came down here. He worked the same restaurant as Rachel—that's how they met."

"So, how come he shows up here?"

"His place went belly-up or something. He had a few bucks, so they came down here. Can you blame him? I mean, that's what we did."

"What makes him such good pals with Donnie is what I want to know," said Henry, pacing now. "I need a drink. You ready?"

"Almost," said Frances, sorting through a salt-stained and wrinkled pile of khakis. "Don't worry. The Dinghy Dock's open for hours more."

"But happy hour—"

"We have time. Listen. You want me to ask Rachel a few things? I can do that."

"Maybe."

"You want to know if Mickey knows Donnie from before, right?"

"He must have. He must have. I want to know if he's straight. Is he a wise guy, half a wise guy, a snitch, you know."

"You want my opinion, he's straight. Just a nice Italian boy in love. He's crazy about Rachel. She's gonzo over him. They're absolutely the cutest—"

"According to you, everything about them is adorable."

"What can I say? I'm a romantic."

Henry stepped behind Frances and tried to hug her as she shimmied into a pair of cutoffs.

"Stop pawing me, I'm getting dressed."

"You're being so sentimental. I'm moved," he said.

"Yeah. I can feel what's moving. Forget it. I'm dressed."

"They live in that big stone house up on the hill," said Henry, stepping back into the bedroom while Frances braided her hair.

"I know."

"With Donnie . . . and a team of marshals."

"They look after the house."

"They hang out. That's what my friend says. Like father and son."

"He's a good cook. Maybe Donnie likes his cooking. The kid is picking up a few extra bucks. That doesn't make him a bad guy. Next you're gonna be saying he was in Dealey Plaza. Maybe we should run the Zapruder film again . . . Mickey's face might pop up in the grassy knoll."

"Hysterical," said Henry. "Listen. All I'm saying is they *hang*. It's not like an employer-employee relationship. My friend has his little Vietnamese dude watching the place, and they *hang*."

"Okay, okay. So what do you want me to do?"

"Well, I want to talk with Donnie. It's a tricky situation. There's marshals all around him. I don't want him to take it the wrong way. That would be bad."

"Uh-huh."

"I have to be careful."

"Explain, please, why you don't just kill the guy. Finish the job . . . so we can have a little peace of mind."

"No can do. My friend was . . . very specific on that point. He wants me to have a nice talk with Donnie. Let bygones be bygones and all that."

"Is that wise? I mean, you're supposed to just walk up to Donnie and say, 'Hi, Donnie, sorry I shot you in the ass. Let's be friends'?"

Henry sighed loudly. "Pretty much."

"Nice plan."

"Well. He assumes, he expects me to get an idea of the man's intentions first. If possible. You know, get an idea of his state of mind, feel things out, see what's possible, what isn't." Henry paused to lie back on the bed and stare at the ceiling. "I was thinking Mickey . . . if he's straight like you think he's straight . . ."

"What if Donnie's real pissed? Then what?"

"Then we get tossed off the island, I guess. If we're lucky. If we're not so lucky, if Donnie blabs to the marshals, then we have a serious problem."

"Bummer," said Frances. "*That* sucks. All I can say is, we better get the guy a real nice housewarming gift. Somebody shot me in the ass, I'd be kinda angry."

8

Henry lay on his back in the gin-clear water, his mask and snorkel held loosely in one hand, and gave a few desultory kicks with his flippers. A single puff of white cloud drifted slowly across the sun. Around him, the sea was flat and calm, only slightly cooler than the balmy afternoon air and his warm, sunburned skin. He raised his head and looked back toward the beach, around a hundred twenty yards away. He could see Frances, in her black thong bathing suit, the one he'd bought her on his last trip to New York, sitting on a barstool at Mickey's Tropical. She was drinking Heineken from the bottle and talking to a young woman who stood in the shadows under the bar's thatched roof.

He paddled around, repositioning himself so he had a view of his hotel, beyond the reef. Through the open French doors of the second-story balcony, he could just make out a green and black figure moving around inside, probably Esmé, the chambermaid, making up the rooms. He put his head back in the water and closed his eyes. He'd give Frances a little more time with Rachel before heading in.

He was startled by the sound of a pelican crashing into the water around twenty yards off. Henry turned and watched the big bird come up empty, water dripping from its bill. The pelican lifted itself with a few powerful strokes of its wings and quickly resumed its lazy, circular flight pattern overhead, gliding motionless over the reef, scanning the water below for fish.

Henry looked back at the beach again, at Frances. He righted himself, pushed the hair off his forehead, and fitted the dive mask over his face. He put the mouthpiece of the snorkel between his teeth and plunged deep beneath the surface. A few inches above the coral heads, he lay motionless, arms extended, and allowed the current to buffet him gently while schools of brightly colored fish darted around him, shooting in and out of the crevices and drop-offs of the reef. Blue tang, mullet, parrot fish, and grouper moved in and out of the dark areas between projections of brain and elkhorn coral, or hung in space, like Henry, avoiding the bristling black spines of sea urchins. Henry waved his hand over an electric yellow sea anemone and watched as the translucent, hollow tendrils shrank from his touch. The air in his lungs exhausted, he swam to the surface and began to kick slowly toward shore.

He swam straight in, trying not to break the surface. Even close enough to stand, he kept swimming, right up to the water's edge, the large-grained, pillowy sand finally rubbing against his chest. Only then did he remove the flippers and mask and stand up.

Frances and Rachel, both topless, lay on Henry's beach blanket, each up on one elbow, lost in conversation. Rachel wore the same black thong bathing suit as Frances, Henry noticed, making her look very much like a younger sister. She was slightly shorter, with dark, somewhat wavier brown hair cut to her shoulders, and a swimmer's body, darkly tanned like Frances's. She wore an ankle bracelet, a thin gold chain that Henry imagined was a gift from Mickey, and a pair of tortoiseshell Ray Bans. There was a tiny tattoo, a seashell, on her right shoulder, and her breasts, though small-nippled and therefore ordinarily not to Henry's taste, were in every other respect remarkably proportioned. Feeling dehydrated, Henry moved his attention to his wife, watched admiringly as the older, taller woman moved in closer to share a confidence with her new friend, was reminded yet again how beautiful she was, noticed for the millionth time her hard shoulders, long legs, strong, graceful calves, and narrow ankles. She half-whispered to Rachel, her expression impenetrable behind pitch black aviators.

All of a sudden, Frances looked up, and though Henry was certain she'd been aware of him, she put her hand to her mouth in a gesture of embarrassment. "I was just telling Rachel about you," she said, giggling uncharacteristically.

"Only about my finer qualities, I hope," said Henry, approaching the blanket. He threw his snorkel equipment on the sand and extended a hand to Rachel. "Hi. I'm Henry."

"Hi," she answered, giving him an unusually firm handshake. "I've seen you around. You bought a couple a' beers at the bar a few times I think." She sat up and drew in her knees, making room for Henry on the blanket. "We didn't have any customers, so I'm kinda playing hooky," she said. Henry glanced over at the empty bar, nodded, and began to rummage in his canvas beach bag for a cigarette.

"Mickey's in Philipsburg," said Frances. "That's Rachel's boyfriend slash business partner."

"He's trying to find us a generator for the bar," said Rachel. "We need electricity. A refrigerator if we're gonna do all the things we want to do. Mick's got a lot of food planned—"

"Mickey was a chef in New York," added Frances, as if telling Henry for the first time. "Rachel and he used to work in the same restaurant together." She took off her glasses. "You know, that's kind of how Henry and I met." Henry saw her give him a sly look out of the corner of her eye. "We were kind of working in a kind of club, a bar, really. I guess it's not the same thing."

"He's a really good chef," said Rachel, proudly. "Really good."

"I feel guilty now," said Henry. "You guys have been open, what, six months. We haven't been by to eat. I mean, we live right up there."

"We're lazy," said Frances. "*Really* lazy."

"Forget about it," said Rachel, cheerfully. "We're still kinda getting our act together. Most people don't even know we're here yet. We spent most of the time since we got here getting set up. You know, finding a truck, where to buy the food, stuff like that. We don't know too many people yet and all. Mickey's still on his Robinson Crusoe thing, a hermit."

"I'm getting kinda hungry now, actually," said Henry, giving Rachel his most winning smile. "When's the chef get back? I could eat."

"Great!" said Rachel. "I'll get you a menu!" She flashed an enormous smile, bounded to her feet, and ran for the bar. Henry, unable to avoid noticing the way the muscles moved on her taut, brown ass, followed her progress across the sand.

"Keep looking," said Frances. "Keep looking . . . see what it gets you."

"Just gathering a little intelligence, dear," said Henry. "For the cause." He pushed her back onto the blanket and cupped a hand around an oiled breast, pinching the nipple between his fingers. Frances drew a breath loudly through her teeth, hooked a leg around him, and worked a heel provocatively up his ass, pushing his crotch forward into her hip, then shoved him roughly away.

"Now behave," she said, smiling and straightening her glasses on her nose.

"We don't have everything on the menu yet," said Rachel, returning to the blanket with a hand-lettered piece of illustration board. "You know, until we get electric." She handed Henry the menu. "You should wait for Mickey to get back. I mean, I know how to make everything, but he's like a lot better at it. He'll be back soon."

"Yo—this is great," said Henry. "Shrimp fajitas. Seafood gumbo. Cool."

"We don't have that yet," confessed Rachel.

"Grilled lobster, chicken saté, blackened hamburger, ribs—gotta have that—grilled red snapper with tequila sauce—that sounds good. I hope he gets back soon. Boudin noir?"

"He makes that himself, up at the house," said Rachel.

"Grilled plantains, fried sweet potato . . . This is too good to believe."

"And there's gonna be a special every night. When we open for dinner, I mean. Once we get a light fixture and shit, we can stay open for dinner. Now it's just lunch, you know. You think people would come over for dinner from the marina, we were open for dinner?"

"I'm sure they would," said Henry, knowing full well that they wouldn't. The yachties and boat bums at the marina were creatures of habit and convenience. The wealthy among them ate just up the hill at Frogs, or they went into town. The charter crews and boat bums who made up most of Henry and Frances's friends would hardly forsake the cheap drinks and easy access of the Dinghy Dock and its shepherd's pies and ribs for a trip to the other side of the pond followed by a ten-minute walk across to Dawn Beach. Even the guests at Dawn Beach Hotel, a couple of thousand yards down from Mickey's Tropical, were unlikely to come at night. They would eat in the relative comfort of their refrigerated dining halls, untroubled by insects or scary natives, regardless of how loathsome or generic the food might be.

Still, Henry used the opening, even feeling a little bad about the lie. "I mean, maybe if you guys hung out more, got to know people around here, it would help. If you did a dollar night once a week—they like that around here. Once you get lights, people will see you're open down there at Dawn Beach, maybe come over. The food there is ridiculous. Who wants escargot fucking bourguignonne and beef Wellington in the tropics?"

"That's what Mickey says," said Rachel, entirely too happy.

"You guys should join us later at the Dinghy Dock," suggested Frances, timing the pitch perfectly. "Get to know everybody, check out the competition."

"Oh . . . I'd love to," said Rachel, smiling wickedly but clearly troubled by something. "You . . . you'd have . . . you guys have to help me talk Mickey into it. He's become such a stick in the mud. We almost never go out."

"I think this is the man now," said Henry, watching as a battered white pickup truck skidded to a stop beneath the coconut trees behind the bar. "He doesn't look too happy."

"Shit," said Rachel. "I guess no generator." She took off to meet her boyfriend, kicking sand.

Henry watched. Mickey stood next to the pickup, shaking his head, his hands balled into fists. When Rachel reached him, she put her arms around him, hugged him like a child. Fifty yards away, words were exchanged, and Henry saw Mickey turn and look over at him and Frances on the beach. Rachel tugged at Mickey's arm, playfully pulling him in their direction, then broke away and trotted back to the blanket. Mickey waited a moment, then followed slowly, looking reluctant.

"This is Mickey," said Rachel, when finally he reached them. "Mick, this is Henry and Frances. They live up at the yacht club there." She plopped down on the blanket next to Frances while Mickey shook hands, leaving him still standing, clearly wondering whether to stay and sit or simply make an excuse and walk back to the bar.

"I understand you're looking for a generator," said Henry, trying to help Mickey with his decision. He saw a look of interest come over the younger man, who then dropped to one knee and fumbled in the pocket of his cutoffs for a pack of cigarettes.

"Yeah," he said, lighting a bent Marlboro. "Those . . . miserable . . . pricks in Philipsburg have been jacking me around for weeks. Today . . . today they were absolutely, positively gonna have it for me today. I show up, and they don't have shit. 'Next week, mon. No problem.' " He sucked hard on his cigarette, still fuming. "I got hot and told them to go fuck themselves. Probably not the smartest thing I coulda done. I mean, I still need one."

"I might know somebody on the French side," said Henry. "They might be able to help."

Mickey looked skeptical. The same height as Rachel, he was darker complected, though he seemed to have spent less time in the sun. His hair was chopped short on the sides, long on top, and looked like it hadn't seen a comb or a brush in months. He had shaved, however, and Henry figured him for twenty-six, twenty-seven years old. He wore expensive Photogray prescription sunglasses, had a sensitive mouth, and Henry noticed his hands, which were heavily callused and scarred. Whereas Henry had long, graceful-looking fingers, Mickey's were shorter and wider; but the way Mickey gestured, used them to illustrate his frustration with the appliance people in Philipsburg, or reach out and stroke Rachel as if reassuring himself, made his hands look less utilitarian and more like a conductor's. Henry could easily imagine those hands dipping a fingertip into a bubbling sauce, releasing herbs into a gumbo in measured amounts, fluting a mushroom. Watching Mickey, he suspected that he was not unlike his hands; deceptively rough but capable of—even inclined toward—gentler things. He wore a sleeveless T-shirt with Yankee insignia, and Henry noticed a seashell tattoo on his right shoulder that matched Rachel's.

"I was over on the French side," Mickey was saying. "Went there first. When I started looking, I got treated like a buncha rat droppings over there by some candy-ass frog who runs the hardware store." He sat back and watched the waves lapping up on the beach, sucking on his cigarette.

"The guy I'm thinking about is different. First of all, he's local. A Saint Martiner. Black guy, bit of an entrepreneur, and he takes a lot of pride in his work. He runs . . . I guess you'd call it a sort of movable chop shop over in Sandy Ground. You should really give him a shot. One time, me and Frances, our scooter broke down on a national holiday, and nothing, I mean nothing, was open. Here we were, stuck out at Rouge Beach with a dead scooter. Anyway, the guy who runs the beach bar over there helped us out. He just chucked the scooter in the back of his truck and took us over to see Doc. Him and his little buddies, bunch of kids on bicycles, they had that thing opened up in around two seconds. The Doc looks inside, says it'll be like forty bucks, and tells the kids what parts he needs. Half hour later they have the parts we need, they put the thing together, and we're back on the road. Next day . . . next day, Frances and I bump into the guy in Marigot, and he does like a follow-up on his work. Listens to the engine, checks it out. I'm telling you, the guy's great. He'll find you a generator. And cheap. A jack-of-all-trades. He doesn't have what you want, those kids'll find one for you, know what I mean?"

"I guess you guys have lived down here a long time," Mickey said cautiously.

"Almost thirteen years, give or take," said Henry.

"Where you from? New York?"

"New Jersey . . . Frances is from New York. Upstate."

"Yeah," said Mickey, resolving something in his mind. "I think I seen you at the bar . . ."

"You're from the City, right?" said Frances, though Mickey's accent was unmistakable.

"The City." Mickey chortled. "Yeah. I still do that. People ask where I'm from, I say 'the City.' I'm so used to it. Like, what other city could there be?"

"Henry, they live up in that big stone house on the hill, the really nice one," said Frances.

"Really?" said Henry. "Nice . . . I didn't know anybody was living there. We've admired that place for years. It's always seemed to be empty."

"We're sort of house-sitting," piped in Rachel.

"The owner never comes down?" asked Frances.

"He's there now." Rachel pouted.

"Rich guy and his bodyguards," said Mickey, cutting her off, clearly uncomfortable with the subject.

"Henry was thinking of getting something to eat," said Frances, backing off.

"Yeah, Mickey. What should he have?" said Rachel.

"Oh," said Mickey, brightening. "Great . . . great . . . sure. I gotta start up the grill . . . but, yeah, great."

"We're starved," purred Frances, stretching her shoulders back and yawning. "And I could use a drink . . ."

"Rachel was just showing us the menu," said Henry.

"What do you feel like having?" asked Mickey, getting to his feet.

"I think we'll leave that to you," said Henry.

"Well, lemme buy you guys a beer or a drink or something while you wait," offered Mickey. "It'll take a little while."

"Couple a' Heinekens would be great," said Henry.

As they walked over to the empty bar together, Rachel mentioned Henry and Frances's invitation. "They asked us out to the Dinghy Dock later for a drink. Can we go? Please, please, please?"

Henry watched Mickey's expression as he scrambled for an excuse.

Frances gave him no room. "You should know now, you've got no choice in the matter. We're kidnapping Rachel whether you like it or not. So you're just going to have to say yes." She hooked an arm around Rachel's.

"It'll be funnn," said Rachel, plaintively.

"I don't know if I have the clothes," said Mickey, lamely.

"Sorry," said Frances. "Won't work. You can show up at the Dinghy Dock in a gunnysack. Nobody'll notice. As is will be fine."

"Drinks are only a buck till seven, and we're buying anyway, so money's no excuse either," said Henry.

Mickey looked around the bar like he wished he could crawl back into the dark and hide.

"We close at five anyway, Mick," said Rachel. "And it's been dead all day . . . Please?"

"You're roped in, man," said Henry. "No fighting it. You got two very determined women here."

Henry watched as Mickey's last bit of resistance faded away. "What the fuck," he said, finally. "Sure. Why not? C'mon. I'll cook us something'll knock you on your ass."

Frances and Rachel got their beers and ran into the water. Henry sat on one of the tall barstools. He could hear the women behind him, splashing around in the water as he watched Mickey behind the bar, adding some wood chips to the charcoal in the small barbecue grill and lighting it.

The day was coming to an end. The sun was getting red and heavy over the mountains, sinking slowly into pink and purple clouds. The shadows of the coconut palms played out over the white sand beach, growing longer and longer, the light growing more precise, moving with the gentle, rustling sound of the fronds in the gathering breeze.

"Snapper good for you?" said Mickey, poking at the fire with a stick.

"Excellent," said Henry, sipping his beer and trying not to press.

Mickey removed two large fillets from an aluminum foil pan filled with marinade in an ice-filled cooler. When the coals were right, he lay them down on the grill. On the side, he lit a flame under a Coleman stove and began to heat a saucepan filled with oil. Producing a gleaming mandoline, he made paper-thin waffle slices of sweet potato on a cutting board, spirits visibly lifting with each slice.

"So you're from Jersey," he said, casually. "Whereabouts?"

"Englewood," said Henry, lying.

"You know the City, then."

"Yeah, fairly well," said Henry, choosing his words carefully. "I've had business there over the years. Been some time since I was there last. I imagine it's changed."

"Nahh . . . It stays the same," said Mickey, testing the oil with a fingertip. "What exactly is it you do? You don't mind my askin'."

"I don't mind," said Henry, innocently. "I'm in real estate. I own some property here, on a few other islands. Got a tiny office on Anguilla. Go over there now and again." This was true as far as it went.

"But you live in a hotel," said Mickey, proving he wasn't a moron. "I mean, if you own places, why live in a hotel? Ain't that kinda expensive?" He glanced over at the Oyster Pond's white walls, just peeking over the palm tops in the distance. "Must cost some bucks."

"Yeah." Henry smiled, flashing a lot of teeth. "It's where Frances and I came for our honeymoon. We didn't want to leave. Sentimental thing."

"Still . . ."

"We get a good rate 'cause we stay year-round. We *like* living in a hotel. You get used to the room service—having somebody turn your bed down, change the sheets every day. Plus, we like know everybody who works the hotel, the whole staff. We're growin' old with them. At this point, it's like staying with family."

"I guess," said Mickey. He picked up the fillets with a pair of tongs, moving them forty-five degrees on the grill to burn a checkerboard pattern into the white flesh.

"You really know what you're doing," observed Henry.

"Sometimes I wonder."

The air under the thatched roof began to fill with the smell from the grilling fish. Garlic, lime, cilantro in equal parts enticing Henry's empty stomach. He turned to watch Frances and Rachel emerge from the water with their empty beer bottles. They looked like a Gauguin study—dark-skinned topless Polynesians. The two women stopped off at the blanket on the way back to the bar, Frances offering a corner of her kaffiyeh to Rachel so she could dry her face.

Moments later the two of them, dripping wet and shivering, their skin rising in goose bumps, hopped grinning onto two barstools next to Henry, Frances's nipples standing up hard and angry, Rachel's teeth chattering through laughter.

"Mickey," said Rachel. "Can we have some of the tequila? We want tequila. We're cold."

Mickey dropped a handful of the sweet potato slices into the hot oil, turned the snapper fillets over on the grill, then reached under the bar, coming up with an unopened bottle of Herradura and four shot glasses.

"Now I *know* I like this place," said Henry, while Mickey filled the glasses to their rims. He raised his, careful not to spill, and invited the others to join him. "To new friends," he said. He tilted his head back and drained his shot. When he put the glass down, Rachel was already holding the bottle, enthusiastically refilling. Things were working out.

9

Henry, fresh from the shower and wearing a ripped white dress shirt, sleeves rolled, faded blue jeans, and reef sandals, walked down the red terra-cotta steps from his rooms. Unlocking the scooter in the small parking lot, he could hear the whistling French chanteur at his microphone from the dining room of Captain Oliver's Restaurant across the pond.

The upstairs door slammed shut as he started up the engine, and a few seconds later he felt Frances slide onto the seat behind him, her left arm coming around to grasp him firmly by the midsection.

"Let's go," she said.

He turned the scooter around, and they whipped past the front desk of the hotel, giving a wave and a short beep to the security guard and the night manager, playing checkers in the lobby.

The dirt road from the hotel to the main road that circled the pond was dotted with muddy, water-filled pools from a brief thundershower a half hour earlier.

"Get your feet up," said Henry, shouting through the wind as they splashed past the deserted tennis courts.

"Just watch out for animals," replied Frances, bringing her knees up and squeezing him tighter around the waist. "Chickens, cats, *les chiens, les mangoustes . . .*"

"Yeah, yeah, yeah."

They drove up the steep, pitted incline and turned onto the paved road. Henry opened the throttle and charged full tilt toward a row of scabbed and patched sleeping policemen, braking only at the very last second to walk the scooter over the damaged humps, the metal bottom scraping cement. He drove completely around the last hump, taking the scooter momentarily off the road into a front yard, the branches of pencil trees whipping his face and Frances digging her fingernails into his ribs to get him to slow down.

The big stone house lay atop a manmade outcropping, halfway up the steep slope of the mountain overlooking the pond from the French side. The imposing stone foundation of its swimming pool and the high surrounding walls gave it a fortresslike appearance. Further up the mountain, beyond carefully landscaped and maintained rows of palmetto, avocado, banana, and flamboyant trees, the main house was just visible from the road. A gabled roof with green wood shingles was supported by heavy mahogany beams and decorated with the gingerbread curlicues and whimsical shapes popular in the islands. The enormous bay windows with heavy shutters could have been made by a master shipbuilder; they had that look of expert craftsmanship.

There was a small, Victorian-style gazebo set off to the left, near a stone archway that led to a private path down to the road. On the other side of the road, another stone archway with a swinging gate indicated the way to the water's edge, where, Henry knew from looking through his field glasses, there was a small wooden dock and a ramshackle, neglected boathouse.

Behind the main house was a smaller, lower structure, which Henry took to be a guesthouse. He imagined that this was where the marshals lived. He stopped the scooter in front of a wrought-iron gate at the foot of a steep, curving driveway and beeped the horn.

Two well-fed weimaraners pushed their snouts through the heavy bars, barking and snarling.

"Nice doggies," said Frances, meaning it.

"Can I help you?" asked an overpumped young behemoth in a J. Crew shirt and perfectly pressed khaki trousers, emerging from the darkness behind the gate. The dogs stopped barking and sat down, looking like bookends. Henry took quick stock of the man's brand-new basketball sneakers, the thick, stainless-steel chronometer around his wide wrist, the tiny earpiece in his right ear, and the concealed clip-on microphone under his collar. Mostly he noticed the gleaming Swedish K the man had slung behind his back.

"Mickey and Rachel live here?" inquired Frances. "We're supposed to go out for drinks."

Henry observed the man's square-shaped head, his blond brush cut, the thick Marine Corps neck, as he peered out at them through the bars. You could watch the man think. Jarhead, thought Henry. *Semper fi* mothafucker . . .

"Who may I say is calling?" the man asked, the words not coming naturally.

"Henry and Frances," said Henry, cheerfully, trying to look as witless and unthreatening as possible.

"One minute, please," said the man with distaste. He stepped back into the shadows, and Henry could hear him on the radio to the house.

"Marlin One at Station One. Yeah, the gate, pencil-dick . . . I got two people out here on a scooter for the kids. A Henry and a Frances."

"I wouldn't have pegged him for a Marlon," whispered Frances. "Looks more like a Buzz or a Neil. An astronaut name."

"I think he's more of a Dolph," said Henry, "Thor, maybe. You see the neck on the guy? He's lucky those dogs don't lift a leg every time they see him."

"Jealous, skinny?" joked Frances.

"Yeah. I want floppy clown shoes for tits when I get old. Just like him."

Marlin One returned and unlocked the front gate.

"Stay there," he said. "They'll be right down."

Henry heard an engine start at the head of the drive, and a moment later Mickey's white pickup appeared, Rachel smiling in the passenger seat behind the bug-encrusted windshield. Henry motioned for them to follow, and Mickey tapped the horn in acknowledgment. Rachel waved at Frances through the truck's open window.

Down a steep, sharply curving hill, past some unfinished efficiency apartments where stray cattle grazed undisturbed on newly sodded lawns, was the entrance to Captain Oliver's Marina. A uniformed security guard lifted the wood barrier blocking access to the parking lot. Henry pointed out an empty space to Mickey in the truck and slipped the scooter into a narrow space between a wall and a fragrant garbage stockade.

Rachel, in a clingy white dress, low-cut in front, appeared happy to be out and on the loose, whereas Mickey, in his sneakers and athletic socks, looked skittish and defensive. His whole posture had changed from the beach bar. Frances immediately tried to put him at ease; she hooked an arm around his and affectionately led them all down the splintering gangway onto the marina.

A big black dog came bounding out of nowhere, tail wagging.

"This is Meathead," explained Frances. "He's the Dinghy Dock dog. Aren't you, Meathead?" She bent over for a second to scratch the dog behind the ears. When she stood up and resumed walking, the dog ran alongside, panting excitedly.

She took them all the way out the crisscross of narrow planking, nearly to the dark center of the Oyster Pond. On both sides sailboats strained quietly at their lines, creaking rhythmically, masts tilting back and forth, back and forth.

Henry produced a thick, evenly rolled joint and lit it with his battered Zippo. He passed it to Rachel first; she took a big hit and immediately began coughing. Tears coming from the corners of her eyes but still smiling, she passed the joint to Mickey.

"Mick, watch out." She coughed. "It's good. Really good."

Mickey took a hit. "Yow!" he said, exhaling. "That *is* fucking good. Where . . . where do you get stuff like that? Down here . . . we've been smoking dirtweed."

"We have a friend from the States who brings it now and again," said Frances.

"What *is* this? Hawaiian?" asked Mickey, eagerly taking another hit.

"They grow it hydroponically somewhere, I think," said Henry, happy with the way things were going.

Frances sat down on an electrical junction box for the moored sailboats, and Rachel joined her, sitting cross-legged on the weathered boards. Henry lay flat on the dock looking up at the stars, Meathead next to him.

"Meteor shower," said Henry.

"And the moon," added Frances. "Look at that moon."

"We've passed out here a few times," said Henry. "After a couple of cocktails or ten."

"It's beautiful," said Rachel. "Mickey, isn't it beautiful?"

"It *is* nice," said Mickey. "Where's the music coming from?"

"That's the Dinghy Dock," said Frances. "We should go. It's only half price for another hour."

The two couples walked slowly back, Rachel thrilled to be out,

Mickey getting friendlier from the pot and the music, which was getting louder and louder as they got closer to the Dinghy Dock.

"Is that the Stooges playing? I don't believe it!" said Mickey.

"We left all our records in New York," said Rachel sadly.

"That's Henry's tape, I think," said Frances, pleased.

"Awesome," said Mickey. "Unbelievable."

The Dinghy Dock was packed with charter crews, coke smugglers, mechanics, a drunken mob of Aussies, French soldiers, American bareboaters, and the usual yachties, all clustered around three picnic tables or spilling out from under the Dock's striped canopy to sit on the rails, the chest freezers, or the milk crates. Meathead ran ahead, nails clicking against the wood, to pursue a plate of discarded ribs.

Henry found them a spot by the edge of the dock where people tied up their dinghies, and they sat down, legs dangling over the edge.

A goofy-looking Brit in an overlarge T-shirt came over from behind the bar with a bottle of iced Absolut, a bottle of cranberry juice, and some plastic cups. He put them down next to Henry.

"Henry! How you doin'? Frances. Good to see you. Cheers." Henry gave him four dollars.

"That how they serve everybody?" asked Rachel. "Or just you?"

"It's usually self-service. You know, pour your own. James is just being nice bringing it over," answered Henry, mixing drinks. Finished with his ribs, Meathead came over and dropped his head on Frances's lap. She petted him with one hand and drank with the other.

"A lot of people here think Henry's some big drug dealer 'cause they never see him work," said Frances, shaking her head and smiling.

"Doesn't that cause problems?" asked Mickey.

"Nah . . . Smuggling is an honorable profession down here. They've been doing it for centuries. An ex–dope smuggler is much more acceptable than somebody in *real estate,* so let them think what they want. If I deny it, they all smile and wink anyway, so what the fuck."

Henry saw Mickey happily moving his foot to "I Wanna Be Your Dog" and smiled covertly at Frances, who just stuck her tongue out at him. The kids were coming along.

10

With one hand, Mickey expertly cracked four eggs into a copper mixing bowl. It was seven-thirty in the morning, and bright sunlight was already streaming through the overhead skylight into the well-appointed kitchen. Rick and Burt, coming off their guard shifts, waved to Mickey as they passed through on the way to the back bedroom. They would sleep much of the day, rising around three in the afternoon for some free time before resuming duty at nine. Woody and Robbie, fresh from their morning jog, fifty laps in the pool, and an outdoor shower, moved about in the breakfast area to the rear of the kitchen, interspersing hurried mouthfuls of bran flakes with the serious business of cleaning and loading their automatic weapons.

The kitchen smelled of cloves and gun oil. Mickey sprinkled ground nutmeg into the copper bowl, added some cinnamon, a shot of Cointreau, and a few ounces of heavy cream, then whipped the mixture together with a balloon whisk. He unwrapped a loaf of panettone from the bread box and with a sharp, carbon steel knife sliced off three thick hunks from one end. Rick, the youngest of the six marshals living on the grounds, wandered into the room, doing neck rolls, a boogie board under one arm.

"Whatchya makin', man?" he inquired good-naturedly, watching as Mickey heated up a sauté pan on the eight-burner Garland range.

"French toast," said Mickey. "You goin' to the beach?"

"Roger that," said Rick. "Got the whole day for R and R. Gonna go check out that Guana Bay. They say in the guidebook they got surf there."

"You stand up on that thing like a surfboard or what?"

"Negative," said Rick. "You lay on it. Ride it like you're body-surfing."

"Yeah?" said Mickey. "Well, have fun." He dropped the slices of batter-soaked panettone into the hot pan. "You get something to eat? I got some bacon, eggs around . . . I can scramble some, you want."

"Nah," said Rick. "I had some cereal. Thanks anyway, man."

"Disgusting," muttered Mickey.

Donnie Wicks sat at a small, round table near the pool. There was a tall glass pitcher of fresh squeezed orange juice and a silver espresso pot already there. When Donnie heard the screen door slam shut, he put down his demitasse and looked up from his newspaper. "Mickey, sweetheart. Whaddya got for me today?" he said.

"French toast," said Mickey, resting a corner of the tray on the table and starting to transfer the plate and condiments to Donnie's place setting.

"I got it, I got it," said Donnie, grabbing the plate from him. "Jeez, I'm not helpless. Gimme that. You ain't a fuckin' waiter. Sid-down an' watch me eat. Have some yourself, for chrissakes."

Mickey leaned the empty tray against a table leg, pulled a deck chair over, and sat down across from Donnie.

Donnie had lost a lot of weight since his last operation. The skin on his face hung loosely, giving him the appearance of a starving basset hound. He wore chunky, black horn-rimmed sunglasses, white sun hat, pink dress shirt cuffed at the wrists, and a pair of long, baggy Bermuda shorts, waist pulled up high over his stomach. Below his knobby knees and blue-veined, hairless legs, he wore brown socks and sandals. An as yet unlit morning cigar sat at the ready in a heavy ashtray in the center of the table. The ashtray had a small figure of a woman's ass in the center, and the caption PARK YOUR BUTT HERE; a souvenir of Florida.

"So?" said Donnie, through bites of French toast. "You sleep okay?"

Mickey nodded.

"Feds bother you at all? Make any noise? They did, I can say somethin' . . ."

"No, they creep around like mice. No problem. You?"

Donnie shrugged and took a gulp of espresso. "I'm old. Old people don't sleep. I hear every fuckin' word. They can whisper all they fuckin' want, I'm gonna hear it. They can tippy-toe aroun' in their fuckin' socks . . . don't make no fuckin' difference. I know they there." He sighed dramatically. "Whaddya gonna do, right?"

"Rache's still sleeping," said Mickey. "She could sleep through anything."

"That broad sleeps too much. Whaddya doin' that girl, Mickey? Too much workin' or too much bangin'. I don't know what it is."

Mickey just smiled indulgently at the old man.

"She's nice," said Donnie. "A nice lady you got there. Don't fuck it up. That's my advice." He paused to consider something, then admitted, "You know the other night we was playin' gin? She beat the fuckin' pants offa me. Twice."

"I know. She was braggin' about it."

"Oh yeah? She was, was she?" Donnie started wheezing and had to catch his breath, his face turning red momentarily. "You gonna have to arrange a rematch."

"You can arrange it yourself," said Mickey as the screen door banged shut. "Here she is now."

"It's Sleeping Beauty!" howled Donnie, startling Don, the marshal watching them in the gazebo. Rachel came over and groggily planted a kiss on Donnie's cheek. She was wearing a short bed jacket and a pair of white panties.

"Marrone!" exclaimed Donnie. "What are you doin' to me, walkin' aroun' like that? What's with you? They din't shoot my pecker off for love a'—"

"All talk, no action, Donnie," said Rachel, dragging a chair over to the table and sitting down. She reached for one of Mickey's cigarettes, and Donnie put a spotted white hand over hers and gave it an affectionate pat.

"I was just tellin' yer boyfrien' here how beautyful you are. Look at her! First thing inna morning and she looks like an actress. Like whatsername." He fumbled for the name of a forties film star, faltered, and gave up. "Look at her! No makeup, no nothing. She just rolls outta bed and she looks like that. Mosta the broads I known in my life . . . takes 'em two hours inna bathroom and six pounds a' fuckin' makeup before they let you even look at 'em. And still, they look like shit."

"Thank you, kind sir," said Rachel.

"I tell ya, I tell ya, Mickey. I was forty years younger . . . I was forty years younger, they'd fuckin' find you inna trunk of a car somewhere out there by Idlewild. Just so's I could have a shot at yer old lady. That's how I feel about her. No shit."

"Thanks. I think," said Mickey.

"He's just buttering me up for a rematch," said Rachel. "He's a sneaky, perverted old man. And I'm gonna whip his wrinkled ass so bad next time we play he's gonna want to switch to shuffleboard or Parcheesi. Maybe you should play a game you stand a remote chance of winning, Donnie, sweetheart. 'Cause cards, you can forget about."

Donnie exploded in laughter, his face growing red again before he trailed off into a rasping cough. He took a sip of orange juice and held up a hand in a gesture of surrender. "Okay, okay," he managed to say. "I know I been whipped."

"Anything for me to eat, or did Don Corleone over here wipe us out again?" asked Rachel.

"There's plenty . . . plenty. I din't eat nothin'. A little fuckin' French toast!" protested Donnie.

"I got some fresh croissants, some brioches, eggs if you want. I can make you somethin'," said Mickey.

"No. I . . . I've got a hangover . . . That's good. Some croissant's good." She padded off to the kitchen.

"You make anything for the feds?" asked Donnie. "I don't want them eatin' all the food. An' I don't want you waitin' on them. Let 'em get their own."

"Nah. All they eat for breakfast is like bran flakes and skim milk. They bring it in themselves."

"For big boys, they eat like fuckin' squirrels those guys." Donnie sneered. "You should just throw that shit inna crapper, throw it right inna fuckin' toilet. Save everybody a step. A person that size should eat somethin' . . . Bacon. A nice steak, that ain't illegal."

"Not yet," said Mickey.

"I don't like that guys supposedta be lookin' out for my life eatin' nuts an' berries. I mean, that's no good for the strength. What if they gotta do somethin'?"

Rachel returned, nibbling the end of a chocolate croissant and carrying an empty water glass, which she promptly filled with espresso from the pot on the table.

"Nice day," she said, peering out over the patio at the view of the Oyster Pond and the reef and the sea beyond. "You know," she said to Donnie, "you should come down to the beach one of these days. See the place. Stop being such a shut-in. We could make you a nice lunch . . . I mean, what's the problem? You could have a couple a' your gladiators escort you."

"Youse two are workin' again today? Every day with you," said Donnie, scornfully. "Every day. I din't get you that place so youse could fuckin' work yourselves to death. Relax. Have some fuckin' fun."

"Sailing!" yelled Rachel, and, remembering, suddenly slammed her hand down. "We're going sailing today!"

"I forgot," said Mickey, not happy.

"We made some friends," said Rachel. "They're taking us sailing." To Mickey, she warned, "You promised."

"That's good," said Donnie. "You makin' friends."

"They're Americans. A couple," said Rachel. "They're like a little older than us, but they're pretty cool. They live over there at the yacht club. You see it? That's where they live. And they're going to get us a generator!"

"We'll see," said Mickey. "I'll see it when I believe it."

"That's good you makin' friends," said Donnie, happy with himself. "You should have people yer own age youse can go bouncin' around with. It's no good workin' alla time. Have fun. Fun. That's when you go to parties, get drunk, act stupid." He paused for a cautionary note. "As long you stay away from the drugs. That's poison. Doobies is one thing. You smokin' doobies, who am I gonna talk? But the other shit. Poison."

"You gonna be okay without us? I'll leave some sandwiches in the fridge," said Mickey.

"Get the fuck outta here. I ain't fuckin' helpless, you know," said Donnie. "I'll take a nice swim inna pool . . . maybe play some cards with the Osmond brothers over there." He winked at Rachel. "At least with them I gotta chance a' winning, right?" He sat back in his chair looking pleased with himself. "That broad, Lucy? The housekeeper? I think she's got hot pants for me. She's been lookin' at me funny. Maybe I'll give her a bang."

"She was probably just checking to see if you were still breathing," said Rachel, getting up to go dress.

11

Jimmy Pazz explained what he needed.

"I want fuckin' Godzilla," he said. "I want the meanest, murdering fucking donkey sonofabitch you got. I need somebody to go straight in, do the fuckin' job, and keep his mouth shut after. You know somebody like that?"

Brian Meehan, a sixtyish man in a pin-striped politician's suit, with snowy white hair and a genial expression, was happy to help. "I know what you're wantin', Jimma," he said, examining his fingernails. "And I have a tough old boy who's just right for you." He looked up and straight at Jimmy, his eyes electric blue, bottomless pools of bonhomie and friendly concern. "You know me, always willin' to help a friend."

Jimmy, in his caftanlike dress shirt and voluminous gray slacks, looked like Jabba the Hut next to the smaller, elegantly dressed Meehan. "You probably got a pretty good idea who it is, you been readin' the papers."

"Ahhhh," said Meehan, pressing his palms together, his fingertips touching his chin. "Yesss . . . That's a big job. The biggest."

"You got a guy?" asked Jimmy Pazz. " 'Cause it can't wait. I gotta pack this character on a fuckin' plane like immediately."

For the briefest moment, Brian Meehan's face took on an expression of uncertainty. "Jeez . . . I don't know . . . This fella, I was gonna have him do a favor for some other friends . . . but . . ." Meehan's face cleared up as a solution presented itself. "But that's alright . . . I'll work something out."

"I'd appreciate it. I got a real fuckin' labor shortage lately, and you wouldn't believe some a' the retards you got workin' today. Crackheads. Dope fiends. Kids with fuckin' skateboards."

"Don' worry yourself, Jimma," said Meehan. "This person is strictly old school. He'll do right by you."

12

The man known as Kevin sat nursing a pint of Guinness at the end of the bar. He was pale, somewhat overweight, in his early fifties, and like the other men in the Shandon Green Tavern, dressed in jeans, heavy work boots, and a denim work shirt worn over a T-shirt. He wore a New York Mets baseball cap, and his face, as he had been sitting there drinking since nine that morning, was lit with alcohol and pink around the nose and cheeks.

It was like this between jobs; dreamland, a half-life of slurred voices, stooped old men, barely remembered good intentions. Kevin, for the ninth or tenth time that day, started a list in his head— "Things to Do Today"—and again he could think of nothing.

The Jets were going down to another defeat on the silent, overhead TV screen, attracting little interest from the patrons at the bar. The man sitting two stools down from Kevin was slumped forward, his face nearly touching a half-finished plate of mashed potatoes, cabbage, and gravy in front of him. A bleary-eyed harridan, with missing teeth and makeup on sideways, loudly bemoaned her stolen welfare check on Kevin's other side, her drinking companion, a wiry old man reading a racing form, ignoring her. The stools next to Kevin were vacant. Even drunk, the customers at the Shandon Green knew enough about him to be afraid.

People drank whiskey and beer. There wasn't a screwdriver, a sea breeze, a margarita, or a mixed drink of any kind to be seen. Shots and beer—serious drinks for serious drinkers.

Kevin let his eyes pass over the familiar row of framed portraits of Joyce, Yeats, O'Casey, and other notable Irishmen behind the bar; the dusty commemorative bottles of single malt, the obligatory shillelagh, the clovers and maps of Ireland, the placards with clever sayings like YOU DON'T HAVE TO BE AN ASSHOLE TO WORK HERE, BUT IT HELPS.

The place stank of stale beer. The wooden bar sucked up spills like a sponge, year after year. Whiskey breath, the cigarettes that burned in every ashtray and dangled from the lips of the other customers, the pungent odors of pastrami, cabbage, turkey, and roast beef wafting from the long steam table near the front door—it all mixed into the particular hell-broth you found only on the West Side of Manhattan.

Kevin signaled for another pint, and in a moment his glass was refilled, the bartender fishing two wet singles and a quarter out of the pile next to Kevin's ashtray without comment. One didn't make conversation with Kevin when he was drinking. The baby-faced psychopaths who came by once a week to collect the envelope, even they were respectful of the big man. That told you all you needed to know.

Somebody in the rear dining area dropped some quarters into the jukebox—a large group of stagehands were doing some midafternoon drinking—and Van Morrison came over the speakers, drowning out the ambient sound of street noise and disappointment.

The pay phone rang by the front door, and Tom, the bowlegged sandwich man, picked it up. He listened for a second, left the receiver hanging, and walked down to Kevin's stool, where he leaned in close. "It's a parson wantin' ta speak with you, Kev'," he whispered.

Kevin slid carefully off his stool and picked his way, one foot after the other, down to the phone. He put the receiver to his ear and said, "Yeah."

"This Kevin?" asked the voice on the other end.

"Himself."

"A man wants to talk wit' you," said the voice.

"What man would that be?" asked Kevin. It wasn't Brian Meehan on the phone—the accent was all Brooklyn, and Kevin was feeling bilious and ill humored.

"You know the one," said the voice. "The man from the place . . . the place across the river there. The fat one. You know who I'm talkin' about?"

"Yeah. I think so."

"He wants to talk to you."

"Okay. Okay. So he wants to talk to me. I got that," said Kevin, the Guinness fogging his brain and a growing pressure on his bladder making it difficult to think.

"You know that place Rudy's over there? The one on Ninth?" said the voice.

"The place with the free hot dogs?"

"That's the place. That one. Okay? Be out front there at ten-thirty tonight. Somebody gonna come by in a car and pick you up."

"Yeah? And just where am I goin' in this car?"

"Lissen," said the voice, "you want the work or not? The man talked to some people said you was available to work. You want it or not? There's other people he can call."

"He talk with my friend?"

"He talked with your friend."

"Alright then."

"Ten-thirty. In front a' Rudy's."

"Right."

Kevin had a good piss in the men's room, retrieved his CPO jacket, his change, and his cigarettes, and lurched unsteadily out onto Ninth Avenue, leaving his latest Guinness untouched at the bar.

In his single room at the Globe Hotel on Eighth Avenue, Kevin took a long, cold shower and emerged from the mildewy stall looking for a towel. Unable to find one, he dried himself off with a T-shirt. He brushed his teeth and shaved, using the disposable razor the hooker he'd brought home the night before had used on her legs. He made a mess of his face, stanching the bleeding with bits of toilet paper, so many of them that the little red and white dots swam around in front of his rheumy eyes like stars when he tried to count them in the mirror.

He had something for his Things to Do list now, and he combed his thinning, straw-colored hair, scrutinizing his reflection with new purpose. It was not a terribly impressive sight, he knew. His swollen gut billowed out over his waist, pale and fish-belly white. The skin under his bloodshot eyes was pouchy and sallow. A yellowish bruise on his right temple marked where he'd stumbled into a door the week previous. But the arms—the arms still looked good. Big, veiny forearms, wide shoulders, hands with swollen knuckles and heavy calluses that resembled the claws of some giant crustacean. There were teethmarks around the second and third knuckles of the right hand, and Kevin vaguely recalled a confrontation at a bar and trying to push some mouthy nigger's teeth out the back of his head, and he wondered, momentarily, if he'd killed him.

Feeling ill now from lack of food and too much drink, Kevin opened a can of split-pea soup and placed it on the hot plate next to his unmade bed, stirring the contents with the handle of the can opener. He found a relatively clean pair of boxer shorts under an overflowing ashtray, shook them vigorously to rid them of any butts or cockroaches that might be hanging out inside. When he slipped them on, he almost lost his balance. He sat down on the edge of the bed and ate his soup, using a plastic spoon he found in a carton of calcifying Chinese takeout in the tiny refrigerator.

When he was feeling better, he pried up the floorboards behind the toilet and got out his .38 detective special and five hundred dollars of emergency money. Then he lay on the bed for a while, running his fingers over the revolver's stubby barrel, the contact with the weapon like a battery charge.

All business now, in his one suit, clean shirt, and a pair of cracked brogans, the .38 tucked snug and comfortable in his waistband, Kevin took a cab to the Tenth Street Baths.

He sat on the highest bench in the steam room, where it was hottest. Below him, shriveled old Ukrainian men, retired Jewish gangsters, a few spiky-haired punks on the nod sweated silently, occasionally pouring buckets of icy water over their heads, which they refilled from a rusty spigot. Kevin lay there on the worn, wooden bench a long time, his white skin turning pink in the atrocious heat, oozing out months of accumulated poisons. After an hour, he could take no more. He heaved himself out the door, trotted gingerly the few steps to the black and uninviting pool, and flopped into the water with a loud splash. The temperature punched the air right out of his lungs. It was cold; so cold he didn't know whether he could make it the few feet to the ladder before he went into shock and sank like a stone. He just made it, clambering up the metal rungs, his skin burning.

A wizened Uzbek with a broom of soapy oak leaves rubbed him down with mentholated lather, Kevin thinking about the job the whole time. He wouldn't take any shit this time, he resolved. If he had to go out to Jersey for this one, or up to Providence again, they were gonna pay expenses.

He had a half-hour massage from a bored-looking blond woman with a Mohawk and a nose ring. She asked him his astrological sign, and he had to say he didn't know, irritated with her for disturbing his thoughts. He was worried about his hands. They shook a little from lack of alcohol. It had been four hours since his last drink. He'd have a short one just before the meeting. Just in case he had to use the gun. Just in case they gave him any shit. He felt no loyalty to these greaseballs. This was a money job, no more. He'd ask for ten, no, twelve thousand dollars this time. Not a nickel less. He wasn't some street punk looking to make a reputation for himself. He had experience. He'd killed twenty-four men. He'd have one drink, no more. Then it was strictly maintenance until the job was over, and how long could that be?

When he went into the ancient, white-tiled shower room, only one other person was there, a tall, Nordic-looking man with one of those pumped-up bodies you got working out eight hours a day. Kevin had seen a lot of that in prison, guys who lifted weights until their bodies were so inflated they could barely touch their sides. Useless muscleheads, in love with the mirror.

"You should try the new machines," said the man.

"What?" said Kevin, annoyed that a stranger, especially a naked stranger, would talk to him.

"The machines . . . the weight machines," the man said, making lifting motions with both arms to demonstrate what he meant, and to show off an upper body he was clearly proud of. "They put in a weight room. They got everything. StairMaster, Exercycle, everything. Good for that stomach."

Kevin stepped out an inch from under the showerhead and stared stone faced at the chiseled giant.

"You should lose that belly," the man said, oblivious to Kevin's increasing irritation. He looked up and down at the older man, appraising his physique. "The rest of you is good, for your age, very good. The arms, legs . . . excellent. Pecs are good. Wasn't for that gut, you'd be in tremendous shape."

The man smiled at him, so filled with self-love he didn't see the loathing in Kevin's eyes, missed the rage and resentment that Kevin felt rushing up into his head like an electric charge. The giant Teuton moved closer, smiling idiotically, a hand extended, as if expecting to be asked for an autograph. It occurred to Kevin that maybe he should know this steroid-juiced moron, maybe he'd seen his picture somewhere, modeling underwear on a billboard, on television, wrestling maybe. He didn't know. Didn't care either. The man had pissed him off, as good as challenged him with his witless babble.

Kevin extended his hand now too. Without changing his expression, he reached down, grabbed the man's testicles, and twisted, hard. The man made a funny, sucking noise through his teeth, and Kevin brought his head forward and crashed his temple into the bridge of the muscle man's nose. As he doubled over in pain, Kevin brought his knee up to catch his head on the way down. There was a loud crack, like a bat knocking fungoes into an outfield. Then there was a wet thud as the man collapsed in a heap on the tile floor, blood running freely across his face from a flattened nose. He lay there, naked and wheezing, while Kevin looked around to see if anybody was watching. Then he looked down over his belly at the man and pissed on his head.

13

I don't see why we gotta hire a fuckin' mick," said Paulie Brown. "It don't seem right." He brought the big, gray Seville to a halt to avoid a taxi that had pulled over to pick up a fare.

"Go around him," said Richie Tic from the passenger seat. "Fuckin' rag head!" he yelled through the closed window.

"It don't seem right," repeated Paulie as he pulled back out into Second Avenue traffic, "lettin' a fuckin' mick whack a boss. It don't seem respectful. Even if the guy's a rat, it don't seem right. It sets a bad . . . a bad . . . whaddyacallit, a president. I mean, you let that happen once, and everybody's gonna feel free to take liberties . . . you gonna have every fuckin' eggplant, every porta ricken the fuckin' city thinkin' it's fine they take a shot atta boss every time they got a beef."

"Precedent? That the word you want?" said Richie. "Lemme tell you about precedent. You worried about settin' a precedent? That's what's worryin' you? Listen, somebody doesn't shut this guy's mouth an' we're all goin' . . . the whole fuckin' borghata's goin' away. Howzat for fuckin' precedent? Lemme tell you what's bad precedent: Jimmy gettin' locked down twenny-three outta twenny-four hours a day, no phone calls, nothin'—*that's* bad precedent. I don't care we gotta hire fuckin' Martians do the job, so long it gets done."

Paulie sat silently for a while, thinking things over. "An' this guy Rico?" he wondered out loud, chewing at his lower lip. "All I hear lately is this guy Rico says this, Rico says that . . . What is this Rico guy sayin' that's so bad?"

"RICO's a fuckin' statute, a law, numb-nuts. It's the law they gonna use put you, me, an' Jimmy an' just about everybody you ever talked to inna can. *Marrone!* Maybe you noticed a lotta fellas from the other families been goin' away lately? Maybe you noticed they ain't maybe never comin' back? That's what RICO is. It means like you got pinched doin' only one little thing, and the prosecutor, he puts your case in with a buncha things maybe you didn't do, some other things that maybe some other guys done, then both you and the other guys and everybody else gets to go away for it. You understand that? That penetrate in there, Paulie? You see what I'm sayin' to you?"

"I got it. I'm not fuckin' stupid, Richie." Paulie fumed silently for a few more blocks. "I still don't like usin' that mick. You see that guy last night? He looks like a fuckin' lush."

"You wanna do it, Paulie? You wanna go down there the islands? They got a whole buncha federal marshals down there just waitin' for some big guinea get off the plane from New York. You wanna like walk right over Donnie's crib an' put a couple in his head just like that? Yeah . . . why not? That'll be great. That'll look real good. Jimmy, Jimmy gets to explain to the nice prosecutor on the stand what his former close personal associate Mr. Brown, that's *former,* notice, 'cause you'll be dead by then, he gets to tell the man what his good friend Paulie is doin' down there the Caribbean tryin' to clip a protected fuckin' witness in his case. You still wanna go?"

"I don't wanna go," said Paulie. "My wife would kill me I come back with a tan. I tell her I been gone on business all I want, she ain't gonna believe it."

"He's sendin' Petey down there anyways," said Richie.

"Petey? Which Petey you talkin' about? Big or Little?"

"Little. He's sendin' Little Petey."

"He's wit' Jerry Dogs."

"Yeah . . . that's the beauty part. Jerry's like sympathetic, and he's got a casino hotel down there, he's wired up pretty good. It was his people that heard about Donnie first, so he's like sendin' Little Petey down to supervise."

"So . . . so at least it's a friend of ours who's going down with him, right?"

"Right. So shut the fuck up about the Irishman," said Richie. "He's gonna do fine, this guy. He's a real fuckin' hoodlum, don't worry. This guy, this guy, you can cut his fuckin' arm off an' he'll pick it right up an' beat you to death with it. This guy is good. This ain't the first time out for him by a fuckin' long shot, okay? Don't worry. This guy likes his work—" Richie slammed his palm into his forehead. "Fuck!"

"What is it?" said Paulie, alarmed.

"Turn it around. I forgot something."

"What?"

"Turn it around. Go up Madison. We gotta go back uptown. I forgot somethin' we gotta get for Jimmy."

"Where we goin'? What do we gotta get?" asked Paulie, swinging the Caddy across two lanes of traffic to take a right on Thirty-fourth.

"Gotta go to Lane Bryant," said Richie. "He saw somethin' he wants inna catalog."

"Jeez," said Paulie. "I hate this. Why don't he just order from the catalog?"

" 'Cause the FBI reads his fuckin' mail. He don't want people to know . . . I mean, fuck if I know. He's the skipper, okay? He wants something, I do it."

"I ain't the one goin' in this time," said Paulie.

"Why the fuck not?" said Richie. "Pretend like you're gettin' somethin' for the wife. Nobody's gonna think it's for you . . . what, you think somebody's gonna think it's for you?"

"I don't want nobody thinkin' my wife's that heavy," said Paulie. "It's embarrassin'."

14

The car arrived to take him to the airport at nine, just like Brian said, and, just like Brian said, Bobby Flannigan was at the wheel.

"You can do me a wee favor on your way to the airport," Brian had said. "As you're goin' out there anyway . . ."

It was a gray, drizzly morning, and Kevin, dressed for the tropics, was feeling shaky and cold in the front passenger seat. Bobby, a gravelly-voiced geezer, was making bitter observations on the state of the world as they crossed 125th Street to pick up the Long Island Expressway. Bobby had been around forever, and Kevin had to wonder if he sounded like that—bitter, old, his brain shriveled by alcohol.

"Look at these animals," said Bobby, moving his chin to indicate a group of young black men hanging out in front of a grocery store. "Monkeys . . . they look like fuckin' monkeys. Breed like them too . . . dirty little bastards. They're gonna be runnin' everything one a' these days, you watch. Mark my words, Kev . . . you come back—you might be workin' fer niggers."

Kevin wasn't listening. He was running over his Things to Do list in his mind.

When they got to the American Airlines terminal, Kevin directed Bobby to a parking space in the last row, explaining he had to meet somebody before he got on the plane. Bobby pulled the clapped-out Oldsmobile into the space, next to a lemon yellow Camaro.

"We gotta wait here? What time's your flight?" asked Bobby.

"Quarter of," replied Kevin, reaching in his jacket pocket.

"Don't wanna miss yer plane . . . all that fun in the sun."

"Here he comes," said Kevin, indicating a moon-faced young man in a ski parka, approaching the car from the driver's side.

"That's Timmy Moon," said Bobby, smiling. "Know his dad."

Kevin put the barrel of the Colt up against Bobby's head and fired twice. Bobby fell over the wheel, his hair on fire, a momentary spume of red painting the dash. "Thanks for the ride, Bobby," said Kevin, under his breath. He got out of the car and handed the revolver to Timmy, who put it immediately under his coat. "You got everything?" said Timmy, reminding Kevin of his bag. Kevin reached in the backseat to retrieve it.

"You touch anything?" asked Timmy.

"No," said Kevin, "just the door handle."

"I'll get it," said Timmy. "Have a nice trip."

15

Henry took Mickey over to Sandy Ground and they came away with a nearly new gas-powered generator for the amazing price of seventy-five bucks. It purred happily away beneath the palmettos, a respectable distance from the bar, bringing light and refrigeration. Rachel bought some novelty Christmas lights in the shape of chili peppers in Philipsburg and strung them around the roof. The two hopeful entrepreneurs even set up a small stereo system, playing the Bob Marley and Peter Tosh that tourists expected on vacation.

A few wanderers from Dawn Beach *did* come over now and then, checking to see if there were any naked tits on Mickey and Rachel's end of the beach. They'd have a burger and maybe a beer—*if* Frances or Rachel was sunbathing nearby—before returning to their air-conditioned bunkers and their wives and kids on the other end. A few locals would stop by occasionally, for a single soda or a milk stout, but they never came in numbers.

Henry and Frances remained Mickey's Tropical's best customers—good for lunch every day, dinner at least twice a week, and about a half case of beer and a bottle of tequila a day. They insisted on paying—in cash—and dragged a few friends over from the marina, Captain Toby and his wife, a few heavy-drinking Aussies and South Africans. They even organized a few late evening lobster-diving parties, when the bar filled up and stayed filled for hours, Mickey and Rachel rushing to keep up with the furious pace of two-fisted, career alcoholics. But none of them returned on their own.

Mickey's Tropical did not become the culinary mecca that Mickey had so fervently hoped for, and he was grateful for the distractions of their sailing trips with the older couple, their bar crawls to little Dominican whorehouses, French cafés, and waterfront lolos. He came to anticipate and even expect the gooey, high-grade dope that Henry and Frances always seemed to have in abundance.

Standing at the helm of a sleek, fifty-one-foot sailboat, a good breeze going, Mickey was thinking life in the tropics was, in spite of any business disappointments, not half bad. Rachel, grinning ear to ear, the way she had been all morning, stood next to him holding a Heineken, squealing with delight every time a wave crashed over the rails, spraying them with seawater.

"How'm I doin'?" asked Mickey, apprehensively. The sea was rough today. In their previous trips it had been nothing like this—twelve-foot swells, the deck at a steep angle, pots and pans rattling around in the cabin below, spindrift from the wave tops filling Mickey's eyes with salty mist.

"You're doing fine," said Henry from his seat. "Just keep the bow in line with that rock over there. You're doing great. Natural born sailor."

Pleased with himself, Mickey muscled the big boat up the side of another wave and surfed it down the other side into a deep trough. The next wave broke over his head, almost tearing him from the wheel and washing him overboard, thrilling him.

"Yeee-haaa!" yelled Henry.

Another wave, this one right over the bow, washed across the deck, worrying Mickey. He gave Henry an expectant look, thinking he'd want to take over, but Henry ignored him, draining his third beer since leaving port, his feet braced casually against the fold-down table in the center of the aft deck, looking dreamily over at Frances at the winches.

Isle Forchue and its surrounding rocks grew closer, and Mickey, more than a little drunk himself at ten in the morning, didn't like the way the dark sea boiled white around the projections of brown coral jutting out of the water a few hundred yards off.

"Isn't that . . . like, a reef or something?" he asked worriedly. "I don't . . . I really don't wanna rack this thing up."

"Don't worry," said Henry. "I'll take over when you get close. You're doing great. Few more times, you can sail around the world without help. Want another beer?"

Mickey shrugged, frightened and exhilarated. In a moment, Henry was pressing another cold, green bottle into his hand. This was fun. This was really fun. He was having the best goddamn time he could remember.

Rachel clambered around behind him and held on to his waist. Saint Martin was ten miles or so behind them, a faraway mountain range surrounded by dark blue. When Mickey kissed Rachel on the neck, he tasted salt.

Henry finally hopped to his feet and took the helm, swinging the boat around and through a narrow cut in the reef, using sail power the whole way. There was a towering black rock to the starboard side, and as they passed by it, into a previously unseen horseshoe-shaped lagoon, the wind died suddenly, the sails emptied and fell slack, and they drifted noiselessly over turquoise and green water, their view of Saint Martin obstructed now by Isle Forchue's outcroppings of rock and scrub-covered bluffs. Henry cranked in the main sheet, and Frances ran forward to drop anchor.

The island was deserted. Not a soul, not a house, not a boat, not a single structure of human design in sight. There was only a barren strip of white sand beach curving around the lagoon, some coconut palms, and, beyond the tree line, a hilly expanse of brown grass and low bushes. In the distance, Mickey could see sheep grazing.

"Cool," said Rachel. "I feel like a pirate."

"The British used to keep French prisoners here," said Henry, squinting into the sun. "Held them for ransom until the local governor paid up."

Without warning, Frances peeled off her wet, olive drab jump vest, kicked off her shorts, and dove stark naked into the water. Mickey caught an enticing glimpse of mahogany brown ass and a flash of pubic hair before she disappeared beneath the surface. Rachel unhesitatingly followed her example, leaving her maillot in a wet pile on the deck, leaping feet first into the lagoon. Another crash from the aft deck and Mickey saw that Henry too had dispensed with his clothes and gone cannonballing over the side.

He felt momentarily at a loss. Uncomfortable in any case with displaying himself in the nude, he was made even more uncomfortable by the fact that his quick look at Frances's rock-hard butt and that dark patch between her legs had left him with a hard-on, a noticeable semi, and the spectacle of both Frances and Rachel, frolicking like naked mermaids a few feet away, threatened to make his condition even more apparent. The two girls began chanting from the water, "Mick-ey! Miiick-ey!" and he saw he had no choice. Before his penis popped out of the top of his bathing suit like a hand puppet, he belly flopped into the water.

It almost knocked the wind out of him. Swallowing water, he could only gasp for air as Rachel came up behind him and dragged his suit down over his feet.

"That's better," she said, tossing the balled up suit onto the sailboat.

Rachel ran her hands over his chest, and he thought for a second something was going to happen right there, with Henry and Frances only a few feet away. Things were different now. Something had changed, and the liberating sensation of treading water naked was pleasantly disorienting. When Rachel slipped around and pressed her belly against his hard-on, he pushed her away, dog-paddling in a wide circle until less excited, trying to think of other things. He held his breath and dove as far down as he could, his eyes shut, and when he surfaced the two women were climbing onto the aft deck. Frances reached for the freshwater hose, and Mickey gaped appreciatively as she ran cold water over her body and Rachel's. She was so tan. Completely untroubled by her nakedness, her long, brown body unmarred by a single white line. Mickey's eyes drifted over to Rachel, noting with sadness the triangular white patch over her pubis where the sun had never reached.

"I'm hungry!" called out Henry, from behind him somewhere, churning water, and with a few even strokes he was pulling himself onto the deck. "Let's eat, man . . . you going to paddle around all day?"

Frances brought a large picnic basket from below, laying out a spread on the table. There was lobster salad, some cheese, two loaves of crusty French bread, a thick *saucisson à l'ail,* and some soppresata. There were olives and dark pommerey mustard, and the last thing to hit the table was an enormous survival knife, a military issue KayBar. Henry used it to slice the sausage.

They ate greedily, without saying much, washing down the food with chilled Beaujolais drunk out of jelly jars, the only sounds the cries of the frigate birds, gulls, and boobies overhead and the gentle slapping of water against the fiberglass hull.

Chewing happily on a hunk of French bread, Mickey watched Henry slice sausage, noticing for the first time how muscled he was for such a long, thin guy. And the scars, he'd never noticed them either. They'd become livid in the water, and they were remarkable, a chronicle of incredible, violent violations of the flesh. Two large discs of scar tissue were noticeable on Henry's left side, under the rib cage—they puckered when he leaned forward to grab the cheese. Mickey wondered for a moment if he'd been gored by a bull. When Henry turned to root around in the picnic basket for a plastic fork, Mickey saw a whole constellation of jagged trails and old suture marks running diagonally across his back. He stopped chewing, transfixed, tabulating wounds, more and more of them, everywhere he looked. Suture marks under the right knee, a sizable hunk missing from the right foot, two more shiny punctures on the left instep, and just visible now, in the noonday sun, a hairline scar extending from Henry's left ear to his right collarbone, below the Adam's apple. Jesus, thought Mickey, where did he get those scars?

"Henry, sweetheart," said Frances, startling Mickey. "Mickey's checking out your scars. Be a love and tell him how you got them. He's probably dying to know."

Mickey stammered a few protestations. "No . . . no . . . that's okay," he said, feeling guilty at having been caught staring.

"Well, I don't want you to think it was *me,*" said Frances, laughing. "Though there have been times—"

"It's alright," said Mickey. "Really."

"No, don't be embarrassed. Everybody who sees them wants to know." She smiled indulgently. "I mean, how could you not? He looks like Dr. Frankenstein put him back together, poor thing." She leaned down and ran the tip of her tongue lasciviously along the hairline scar on Henry's neck, Henry grinning agreeably the whole time.

"Veet-nam." Henry sighed without drama. Bored with the subject.

Rachel, naked still, like the rest of them, except for Henry's red-

and-white kaffiyeh draped around her neck, sat down next to Frances and gaped openly at Henry's appalling collection of wounds, clearly fascinated. She leaned forward, wobbling a little drunkenly, one arm resting on Frances's leg, Mickey not liking at all the way her eyes were traveling over Henry's body.

"Wow!" said Rachel, reaching the two punctures below Henry's rib cage. "I guess you got shot, huh?"

"Henry's been shot a gazillion times," said Frances. "A regular magnet for flying pieces of metal and sharp, nasty objects. Fortunately," she added, pausing to eyeball his crotch lewdly, "nothing vital got hit." She lifted the tip of Henry's penis with a pinkie finger before letting it drop back against his leg. The two women exchanged looks and burst out laughing.

"I was trying to be the boy hero. You know, Audie Murphy time. Too many damn movies. That was the problem," said Henry, still completely at ease with the difficult subject and Frances's casual handling of his privates.

"Did it hurt?" asked Rachel, this time, at least, looking him in the face.

"Some more than others," replied Henry, cheerfully. "This one here hurt the most." He pointed to the round scar on his instep. "Stepped on a punji stake. Went right through the boot. That hurt. That hurt like a motherfucker."

"Ewww!" said Rachel, grimacing.

"He was shot *five* times," said Frances.

"Well . . . it was on only two different occasions," Henry hastened to add, modestly. "After the first one hits you, you tend not to notice so much the ones that come after."

"Then some nasty commie threw a grenade at him," said Frances. "And this one here"—she traced the thin scar down his neck—"that's where he got stuck with a bayonet. Can you believe it? A bayonet!"

"No shit," said Mickey. "I thought they cut that shit out after like the Civil War."

"Victor Charles was sort of short on high tech," said Henry patiently. "But he was long on enthusiasm. Guy who gave me this came at me wearing nothing but swim trunks and a satchel charge. I thought, Wow! Swimsuit! . . . Wow! Bayonet! By the time I got over the surprise, he was making neck kabob outta me." He laughed and popped a heel of French bread into his mouth. Standing up, he grabbed a disposable camera and a jumble of snorkel equipment from a storage locker.

"Mickey, let's you and me climb that big rock over there. The view is sensational. We'll swim over. There's a big moray down there we can look at on the way. Check it out."

He tossed a pair of flippers and a mask at Mickey's feet and went over the side. Mickey looked wistfully at the two women, who were just stretching out for some sun, then reluctantly dove in after him.

Underwater, Mickey had to exert himself to keep up, breathing hard into his snorkel. He saw Henry stop and point over at a large, round hump of brain coral rooted in the sandy bottom of the lagoon. Seeking to impress, he dove deep for a closer look. Henry waved him off, and he immediately saw why. A snakelike thing, all eyes and angry-looking teeth, came darting out at him, mouth open. It was the moray Henry had spoken of, and it was enormous. The whole rock was teeming with them, a nest of smaller ones visible inside the hollows; yellow colored with bluish speckles, they squirmed and slithered noiselessly, their evil-looking heads extending out a few feet, all eyes on Mickey, row after row of jagged little teeth. Turning, Mickey caught a flash as Henry captured the moment on film—Mickey and the Medusa.

They swam on, the water grew shallow, and soon Mickey could

stand on the soft, swaying sea grass. A few moments later, they were sitting side by side, Henry storing the snorkel gear on a dry rock by the water's edge.

"Onwards and upwards," said Henry. "This way."

Mickey followed, able to walk upright at first, using his hands occasionally for support. Henry was up over the first pile of black rock very quickly. From there, leaping like a mountain goat, he picked out the most direct route to the top. They reached an almost vertical incline, and Henry just went straight up—there were plenty of moss-covered ledges and pits in the rock face where one could grab hold, so Mickey labored, sweating, after him. At first, each new handhold led fairly easily to another, but soon it became more difficult to keep up with the older man. When Mickey stopped and looked down, he was horrified at how high they were. Below, on the sailboat, he saw Frances and Rachel watching him through binoculars. Rachel waved, and then they were whistling and cheering, Mickey was suddenly reminded that he was still buck naked.

He'd fallen behind. Now painfully aware of how far he had to fall if he lost his grip, he began to pick his way up more carefully. He didn't know how he was ever going to get down. His knees felt trembly and uncertain, and little bits of pebble and dirt began to roll past his head as Henry hoisted himself over yet another ledge and waited for him to catch up.

When they were standing side by side under an outcropping of scrub-covered rock, the wind began to pick up. They were above the protective barrier of grassy bluff now. Mickey could see the ocean and feel the salty gusts coming off it. He wanted to go back.

"I'll help you over this part," said Henry. "It's a little tricky here." His back to the wall, legs splayed, he held his hands together to give Mickey a boost. When Mickey put his right foot in Henry's hands,

he heaved him easily up and over the scrubby projection overhead.
A mass of twigs and spongy vegetation in his face, Mickey grabbed
frantically with both hands for somewhere to hold on.

There was a terrifying, inhuman screech, and a barely apprehended flash of white—the beating of wings, Mickey thought—
as he felt himself falling backward.

He plummeted straight down. For a long, a very long second, he
was free from the earth, death an absolute certainty.

Then he felt himself grabbed out of the sky. Henry's arm was
around him, and in the next second he felt himself slapped against
the rock face like a stolen pass. He was alive. And Henry had saved
his life.

"Almost lost you there, bro'," said Henry.

"Wha . . . what *was* that?" gibbered Mickey. "That *noise?*"

"Baby boobie," said Henry, calm and smiling like it was only
laundry he'd just saved from a two-hundred-foot fall onto the
coral, the deep creases around his eyes indicating amusement.
"Must have disturbed a nest. Good thing mama boobie wasn't
around. Now she *really* would have caused a racket. Anyway . . .
No problem, mon. We can go around."

"I don't know," said Mickey, his legs Jell-O now.

"Not to worry," said Henry, moving laterally along the ledge.
"It's not bad from here. Besides," he said casually, "you really don't
want to try to go down this way. The other side is easier. We could
have come up that way, but this way is more fun."

"Fun," said Mickey.

They moved around the rock horizontally until they were over
the sea. Waves rolled over sharp coral beneath them, the wind
stronger than ever. Mickey fought to regain control of his shaking
limbs, not wanting to show fear but desperate to get back to the
safety of the boat. Finally reaching a more gradual incline, Henry
led him up to one last heap of boulders, made a few perilous

hops, and was quickly at the top. Mickey, his knuckles and knees scraped and bleeding, reached up, took hold of Henry's proffered ankle, and was pulled to the bald, black peak. Exhausted, he sat down across from Henry and took his first breathless look around.

"Nice," he said. "Nice view."

He was grateful to be alive. Leaning into the wind, the sweat drying at his hairline, he looked at the endless body of water below them. The sailboat in the lagoon looked like a bathtub toy, and on one side he could see Saint Martin on the horizon, on the other, Saint Barts.

"Hey, Mickey," joked Henry, squatting on his haunches, "I can see your house from here." He raised the camera and snapped off a few shots of cowed Mickey on the peak.

"What's that one?" asked Mickey, doing his best to show interest in something other than clinging to life. He pointed to a shadowy silhouette in the distant sea, afraid to remove his hand from the rock for more than a second.

"Oh, that's Saba," said Henry. "It's a volcano." He identified the surrounding islands of Saint Eustatius and Saint Kitts, named the barren rocks of Hen and Chicks and Molly Beday. Unexpectedly, he prodded the disposable camera into Mickey's hand and said, "Take my picture."

It sounded, unusually, like an order, and Mickey was surprised how quickly he responded, without thinking about it. He took two quick shots of Henry, squatting atop the rocky crag, high above the sea.

"Shoot the roll," said Henry. "There's only a few shots left." He rose and adopted a mock heroic pose, standing on one leg, like a running Mercury, leaning precariously over the edge. Another pose, this one Washington crossing the Delaware, eyes shielded from the sun. Mickey kept taking pictures, anxious for the film to run out so he could go back to holding the rock with both hands, but Henry kept at it. One minute an Egyptian hieroglyph, the next, Nijinsky, each pose loonier and more dangerous. Finally the film ran out, and Mickey tried to hand him back the camera, but Henry ignored it, fixing him with a stare of such sudden and unexpected gravity that Mickey thought he might be knocked off the rock by the force. Henry sat cross-legged across from him, his eyes steely gray and unblinking, a panther examining its lunch. "I want you to do something for me," said Henry, and Mickey knew, with terrible certainty, that whatever Henry was about to say was what this had all been about from the first. The boat, the rock, maybe everything—it all came down to this. Frightened and unbalanced, he cocked his head and held on, trying his best not to show fear, pretending it was the Lower East Side, not the top of a rock in the middle of the ocean.

"I want you to do me a favor. And I want it to be a secret. Between us."

Mickey couldn't imagine what favor, what outrage could possibly follow. What could Henry want from him that was worth all this? He wondered for a millisecond if Henry was gay.

"Take the camera," said Henry. "Take it to the Dock Shop when we get back. They'll develop it right quick for you, you put a rush on it, pay a couple extra dollars. I'd like you to take those pictures . . . and show them to Donnie."

There it was. There it was. Mickey felt as if the rock under him had moved. He felt cut loose, like he was holding on to the top of a teetering flagpole. Donnie. He knew about Donnie. This changed . . . everything.

Henry placed a hand on Mickey's shoulder. "It's not what you think." Mickey shook off the hand and almost lost his balance.

"Steady, steady," said Henry, withdrawing the hand. "Just listen . . . listen to me. I just want to talk to the man. Show him the pictures. See if he wants to talk to me. It's simple."

"You knew. The whole fucking time. The whole time."

"Mick, please understand . . . I've known Donnie a long time. It's been a while since I've seen him, and there's something I want to talk to him about."

Angry and betrayed, Mickey just shook his head, barely able to hear Henry over the rush of blood in his ears. "Sonofabitch" was all he could manage.

"It was a surprise for me," said Henry, "when Donnie showed up here. It presents me . . . to be honest, with some difficulties. Especially with his new friends. I imagine . . . I hope . . . it was a surprise for you too." He stopped to examine Mickey's reaction. "I mean . . . you were never involved . . . in the crew . . . nothing like that. I'm right about that, right? I'd sort of counted on you not . . . you know . . ."

He was silent for a moment, just watching Mickey. "No. I didn't think so."

Feeling like an utter and complete fool, Mickey blinked away tears. "That's what all of this is about. Isn't it? The generator, the bar, the boat trips . . . it's all about this." He looked down again at the boat, at the two brown shapes stretched out on the deck. "Your wife . . . she's in on this too."

"I tell Frances everything."

"Friends," he said, bitterly. "Big friends. So helpful . . . so nice. I guess we look pretty stupid to you."

"Look," said Henry, trying to be conciliatory. "I couldn't just walk up to the house with a potted plant and say, 'Donnie, ol' pal.' I've worked for the old man. Okay? Back in the bad old days. Like a lot of folks down here, I'm not terribly anxious for the U.S. government to take a sudden interest in my life. I am what I say I am. Just a guy with a wife he adores, a home . . . who just wants to spend the rest of his life in the sun, grab a little happiness, live simply. I didn't lie to you. I'm not a bad guy. Being an old friend of

Donnie's is not exactly an asset these days, you've gotta admit. Apparently a lot of them are going to jail."

"And you're working for them," said Mickey.

"No. I don't work for anybody. Not here."

"Who the fuck are you? How . . . how . . . how do you know him then? He hasn't left his corner in twenty years. You make it sound like you met him at a cocktail party."

"Look . . . you're pissed at me, and I don't blame you. We used you. A little bit. But the friendship part. That's for real. That's not bullshit. This is not a scam. This is my home, okay? We've lived here for over ten years, and this is who we are. I'm not here to hurt Donnie. There's no ill will. Not from me. Donnie could hurt me. Badly. I just want to talk to him. My intentions"—Henry smiled for the first time in a while—"are strictly honorable."

"Who are you to him?" asked Mickey.

"I worked for him once," said Henry. Mickey was taking indecent pleasure in his apparent discomfort. "I did some things for him . . . Look. I'm not asking you to betray the man. I know you wouldn't do that. Just give him the fucking pictures. Show him the pictures of your new friend—the silly American expatriate. Tell him what I said. Tell him any damn thing you want. There's nothing I can do about that. Just . . . let him decide, okay? I'd rather you didn't go squawking to the marshals. That's all I ask. Donnie wants to blab to them, let it be *his* move. Show us both that respect is all I ask . . . please. The old man wants to drop a dime on me, there's nothing I can do about it."

Henry sighed and looked forlornly over at Saint Martin. "See that piece of ground over there? That's *home* for us, man. That's everything to us. We've gotten to know you, you've gotten to know us. We let you in. That's who we are now. We decided to put our faith in you. We're in your hands, okay? Just pass the message. Show him the pictures. Then we'll both find out . . . what he wants to do." Henry stood up and shook off whatever else he was thinking about. He looked older. "That's it," he said. He extended the hand once more, this time to muss Mickey's hair like his father had once done. "Let's go back."

They were halfway back to Saint Martin. Mickey sat sullenly by the bow with a beer forgotten in his hand, Rachel asleep below. Frances approached Henry at the wheel and whispered in his ear. "How'd it go?" she asked.

"*Mezza mezz*," said Henry. "We'll just have to wait and see."

16

Donnie Wicks, in an apron, baggy blue jeans, espadrilles, and a T-shirt that said HEY MON! stuck a bony finger into Mickey's lobster sauce and took a taste.

"Nice flavor," he said.

Mickey, standing next to him at the range, arms crossed across his chest, explained. "It's all about reduction. You gotta reduce, reduce, reduce. And you don't let the brandy flame the shells. That's the mistake everybody makes. You burn the little hairs the lobster got on his tail there, you do that . . . you get a burnt taste. And you roast the garlic first, before you use it."

"You gonna put some butter?" Donnie wanted to know.

"At the end I put the butter," said Mickey. "Right at the end. That's called *monter au beurre* you wanta know."

"The fish . . . can I flip 'em?"

"Yeah, go for it."

Donnie turned down the flame under the copper *sautoir* next to the saucepan and drained the extra oil into a coffee can by the edge of the range, holding three grouper fillets in place with a spatula.

He confidently turned the fillets over, skin-side down now, and put the whole pan into the oven.

"What's that gotta go, like, five, six minutes?" he said, wiping his hands on his apron.

"Little more," said Mickey, "if you don't want it wet in the center."

"I don't," said Donnie. "Call me a fuckin' philistine all you want. I like fish cooked alla way through. Meat, that's another thing. I can have that rare. But fish . . . I want that cooked."

"Okay. Seven minutes." Mickey sighed. In another pan, he sweated some shallots in butter, added some mussels, some stock, and some white wine, threw in a few sprigs of fresh thyme from Donnie's garden and, as the mussels began to steam open, tossed them with a few medallions of lobster and some bay scallops.

"Again . . . you mount with the butter. Heart attack food, that's what I like." At the very end, as he removed the pan from the flame, he stirred in a heaping teaspoon of red lobster roe. "Where's the vegetables? The vegetables! Shit!"

"Awright, awright!" said Donnie. "You're a fuckin' ball-breaker . . . Here." He sprinkled some blanched, julienned vegetables in with the mussels—carrots, zucchini, yellow squash, and snow peas. "I know, I know . . . correct seasoning . . . I'm tellin' ya, I dunno how that broad puts up with you over there." He ground some fresh pepper into the mix and then sprinkled a little kosher salt.

"Okay. Now all we gotta do is eat it," said Mickey. "I wish I was hungry."

"What's eatin' you is what I wanna know," said Donnie. "You been on the rag all day."

"I gotta talk to you. After," said Mickey.

"Talk to me now, you got a problem."

"After. We'll talk after," said Mickey, turning his back and yelling down the hall. "Rachel! Where the fuck is she? Ra-chel!"

Don, the lead marshal, an older man with a barrel chest and gray hair, stuck his head into the kitchen from the patio. "I think she's still in the shower, Mick, I can hear the water running."

Mickey shook his head, pissed off.

"You smell what those jerks ate for dinner tonight?" asked Donnie, when Don disappeared. "You can *still* smell it. Smells like a buncha chinks livin' here . . . boilin' dogs or some shit."

"They burned the garlic and the ginger," said Mickey, in no mood.

"I got a nice wine picked out. Nice an' cold," said Donnie, proudly. "Pooly Foomay. That okay?"

"That's fine," said Mickey. "I'm gonna go get her. The food's fuckin' dyin' here."

"Give the girl a fuckin' break, willya?" said Donnie. "She's inna shower. You don't want her clean? What's with you?"

Mickey stalked down the hall into the bedroom he shared with Rachel, opened the bathroom door, and said, "Dinner's ready. You're holding up dinner."

"I'll be out in a second," said Rachel. "I'm just rinsing."

"Hurry," said Mickey, closing the door.

It was an uncomfortable dinner with little conversation. Rachel, still wet from the shower, ate in her bathrobe, not speaking to Mickey. Mickey, anticipating his talk with Donnie, picked at his food, lost in thought. The fish was dry and overcooked, and Donnie was defensive and a little hurt that no one was saying anything nice about the meal.

When the plates were finally stacked in the dishwasher, after the espresso was finished and Donnie had lit his after-dinner cigar,

Rachel went back to the living room to do her toenails in front of the TV.

"Can I talk to you now?" asked Mickey, worried about the marshals overhearing. "Downstairs?"

"Let's have an Amaretto," said Donnie. "Maybe we can shoot some pool." He pushed his chair back and headed for the recreation room.

He had difficulty on the stairs, a tightly wound spiral of decorative wrought iron. Mickey had to help him down. The room was done all in green. Back in the late fifties, it had been a sort of sanctum for the old man; now, with the difficulty of negotiating the steps, he seldom came down here.

Behind a broad teak bar, an enormous picture window faced into the swimming pool below water level. On the other side of the thick glass, there was a muted splash, and two pairs of legs, exercising marshals, swam silently past. There were trophy fish, marlins and sailfish, mounted on the walls. An antique pool table stood in the center of the room, green felt lit by a Tiffany chandelier, color, green. The other light fixtures, scallop-shaped wall sconces, only added to the undersea effect, and the moving ripples from the pool lights played over the green leather easy chairs, green felt card table, green and beige carpet. A few listless tropicals hung in the water in a recessed aquarium, opening and closing their mouths, and the liquor bottles behind the bar were illuminated from below by little spots, recessed into the wood, the tiny green points reflecting off Donnie's glasses.

Mickey took the photographs from his back pocket and slid them across the bar to Donnie.

"What's 'is? Dirty pictures?" said Donnie, coming around the bar with two snifters of Amaretto. He glanced up at the swimmers, not yet touching the photos.

"We went sailing with that American couple," Mickey began. "I told you about them . . . Anyways, I'm sitting on a rock out there in the middle of the ocean, and this guy—his name's Henry—he asks me to take these pictures." He paused for a sip of Amaretto, his mouth dry. "So I take the pictures, right? And this is the thing . . . He says to me, he says he wants me to give the pictures to you."

"To me?" said Donnie, startled. "He mention my name?" He lifted the photographs in one hand, lost his purchase, and they spilled onto the floor. Mickey got down on his hands and knees and collected them. This time he laid the pictures out on the bar for Donnie to look at.

"He said, 'Give these to Donnie.' He says he wants to meet with you, talk . . . without, you know, *them* knowin' about it."

"You didn't tell him nothin' . . ."

"No!"

"I mean before. I mean, how's 'is sonofa——"

"That's the whole thing. I didn't say nothin', *nothing*. He knew it all already. He knows you. He says you know him."

Donnie leaned over. His eyes moved slowly along the row of color snaps. He picked one up off the bar with hands that trembled slightly and stepped over to the pool table to examine it under the light. It was a full-length pose, Henry leaning naked over the edge of the rock, hand shielding his eyes, a silly grin on his face. Donnie went back and looked at another one, the color gone from his lips.

"And what's this guy callin' himself?" he asked.

"Henry."

"That's right, Henry. You said that. Henry what?"

"I don't know," said Mickey, feeling foolish. "Just Henry is all I know. I . . . I never asked. I could probably find out for you, you want."

Donnie looked at each photograph carefully, each pose more ridiculous than the one before.

"Where'd you meet this guy again?"

"On the beach. Rachel met them on the beach."

"She didn't say nothin'?" Donnie thought better of the notion and dispelled it. "Nah . . . she didn't say nothin'."

"She wouldn't."

"I know, I know."

Donnie shook his head, exasperated by a picture of Henry, this time posing as a nude King Tut, high atop the peak on Isle For-chue.

"The wife . . . She a good-lookin' broad, tall, dark, green eyes . . . name a' . . . Frances?"

"Yeah!" said Mickey, anxious to know what was going on. "You *know* them?"

Suddenly, Donnie exploded with laughter, his whole body shaking. "Yeah," he wheezed. "I know this guy. I know this *tes-tadura*. Henry. Sure, I know him pretty good." He kept laughing, wiping his eyes with a cocktail napkin from the bar, his face growing red. "Mickey, I'm slippin' . . . I tell you. I shoulda heard this guy comin'. This guy, this guy, you can hear his balls clankin' to-gether a mile away. An' the wife. The wife! *Minchia!* She got balls even bigger. The biggest! Sonofabitch . . . Henry an' Frances . . . She still look good? She was a good-lookin' woman. It's . . . it's been a while."

Mickey just nodded, confused and somewhat displeased at Don-nie's reaction. He'd felt betrayed at being used to get to Donnie. He'd expected, hoped for an ally, and now this reaction. It wasn't at all what he'd anticipated.

"They live here?" asked Donnie.

"In the hotel, the yacht club over there, the other side a' the pond."

"They stayin' in a hotel?"

"They *live* there, he says. They say they been in the same place for years."

"You believe him?"

"About what? About livin' here? Yeah. They know everybody, everything on the island. They're wired up down here."

"That's fuckin' rich," said Donnie, chuckling now, his color returning to normal. "Them livin' here the whole time."

"You're gonna talk to the guy?"

Donnie looked again at the photos. "He's worried, I bet, right?" He jerked a thumb at the pool, the two marshals still swimming back and forth. "About them. He knows I'm a rat now, an' he's worried."

"You ain't a rat, Donnie."

"You call it what you wanna call it. So. What else he say?"

"He said it was up to you. He said you had to decide whether to tell anybody or not, that it would mess him up bad if you did."

"I'll bet it would," said Donnie. He picked up the picture of Henry leaning over the edge. "Look at this guy . . . Look. He's got his balls hangin' right over the cliff. You know what he's sayin'?"

Mickey had not the slightest idea.

"He's sayin', 'Here I am, Donnie.' That's what he's sayin'. An' he's askin' me what I'm gonna do about it. He's bettin' I ain't gonna do nothin'. That's what he's sayin'."

"What are you gonna do?" asked Mickey. "You gonna see him like he wants?"

"Of course I'm gonna see him," said Donnie. "Are you kiddin'?" He laughed out loud again, a thin, raspy cackle. "I wouldn't miss this . . . I wouldn't miss this for the world."

17

United States Marshal Donald Reginald Burke, fifty-two years old, divorced, with two teenage kids who hated him, $820 in the bank, and a painful case of sciatica, sat on the edge of his bed in the guesthouse, considering Donnie's request to go fishing.

As senior marshal of the unit charged with protecting the peripatetic gangster, he had two divergent instructions: Keep Donnie safe, and Keep Donnie happy.

Burke was having a difficult time making a decision. He'd immediately cabled Washington, requesting information on Henry Charles Denard and wife, which was all he could do at the moment. He'd even watched Mr. and Mrs. Denard, through binoculars from across the pond as they headed off to the beach on their little Honda scooter. He'd told Donnie he could of course go fishing with his friends, if Woody and Burt could tag along with their radios and their weapons.

Donnie wouldn't play along. He wanted solitude. Just him and Mickey and this mysterious "fishing guide" who lived in a three-hundred-dollar-a-night hotel. Burke didn't like it, and he didn't want to make the call. He decided to pass the buck. Let somebody else take the blame if things went bad. He picked up the phone and called Washington.

"So?" said Donnie, padding onto the pool patio in his bare feet. He was wearing a T-shirt Rachel had bought him, depicting the continent of Africa in black, green, and orange with a large marijuana leaf superimposed over it. "Can I go, Dad? Huh? Can I? Huh? All my friends are goin'. Huh?"

Burke shook his head. "I don't know yet. I don't know. They have to call me back." He almost felt bad for the old gangster. Donnie just wanted to go fishing, and here he was, waiting for permission from some pencil-necked suit in New York, a kid, really, who was probably conceived about the time Donnie was making his bones.

"Whaddya think they gonna say?" asked Donnie, sitting down at the small table and lighting a stogie-size joint.

Burke winced at the sight and found himself reflexively looking away. Rachel had taken to providing little packets of Jamaican pot to the old man. He seemed to love the stuff, said it helped his appetite after all the operations. Burke had felt it was better to ignore it, but lately Donnie had begun taking a perverse delight in lighting up next to him. Burke had a horrifying vision of Donnie on the stand, recanting his depositions, telling the jury how the prosecutors and marshals had supplied him with mind-altering drugs.

"Get that away from me," said Burke. "Please. Okay?"

"You worry too much," said Donnie. "Look at yer little partners there. They got the right idear . . . Ain't nothin' in those heads, just rabbit chow and muscle magazines . . . not a care inna world."

"It's the other guy," confided Burke. "This Henry. I don't know anything about him."

"He knows where the fish are. He lives down here. What's to know?"

"More," said Burke. "A lot more."

18

The man lobbed a golf ball onto the green at the ninth hole, then walked slowly after it. He winked at Monsieur Ribiere, a few feet away, and carelessly tapped the ball toward the cup. It went wide.

"Do you play?" asked the man, ignoring his ball. He was a tall man, wide shouldered; he might, when he was young, have been a football player. Now his face was jowly and deeply etched with lines; the sad Doberman eyes and dark rings under them spoke of someone who had suffered many disappointments.

"No," said Monsieur Ribiere, looking very uncomfortable in checked Lycra golf pants and a striped, short-sleeved polo shirt. "Never."

"Me neither," said the man. He had a deep, boozy voice, mellifluous but tired. He reached down, picked up his ball, and began walking to the next tee. Monsieur Ribiere signaled Trung, who was acting as caddy, to follow with their clubs.

"Still got your little friend with you," observed the man.

"Yes," said Monsieur Ribiere. "He is very loyal."

"I remember," said the man, giving a short, barking laugh.

Six o'clock in the morning at the Mullet Bay golf course. The sprinkler system had just been turned off. Black, desalinated lagoon water collected in puddles on the parched sod, in the tracks the golf carts had made. On a nearby hill, an earthmover cleared ground for a new hotel; the solitary figure of a black woman, visible at the foot, was setting up a folding table with tinfoil containers of food and black and yellow bananas for the construction crews. In the distance, they could hear the sound of tennis balls hitting rackets.

"Two things," said the man, lighting a Viceroy with a tarnished Dunhill lighter. "My shop got a request for a file search yesterday from the Organized Crime Section over at Justice. I thought I better come down and talk to you before deciding whether to comply. Henri Charles Denard. Somebody over there wants to know what we have."

"I see," said Monsieur Ribiere, walking past the tee without stopping. "Thank you. It was good of you to see me first."

"Yeah . . . well . . . I remembered. He was a protégé of yours a while back, wasn't he? I thought, you know, there might be some exposure on that. Figured it wouldn't hurt to ask."

"How interested are they?" asked Monsieur Ribiere.

"The request originated with the Marshals Service. Got piped through Justice. All Agencies Request for Information, so, you know, it got around to us. How interested? You tell me. How interested should they be?"

"You know about our guest down here? This gentleman from New York, Balistieri?"

"I might have heard something about that. Something crossed my desk, I think . . . They got him stashed down here, don't they? Super Snitch. Gonna bring down the Cosa Nostra single-handed, right?"

"Yes."

"You must be thrilled."

"Delighted to assist our ally in any way we can," said Monsieur Ribiere, acidly.

"That what they're saying back at La Piscine, you don't mind my asking?"

"Well . . ."

"That's what I thought."

"I am to cooperate."

The man grunted.

"Do you have an interest?" asked Monsieur Ribiere, raising an eyebrow.

"Could care less," said the man. "Not my patch, my friend. We're happy to assist other agencies, if we can, as far as that goes. It's a matter of degrees, isn't it, sometimes. Thought I'd talk to you first, though. Our relationship is somewhat . . . more sensitive."

"Yes . . . yes," said Monsieur Ribiere, trying not to sound encouraged.

"So you tell me. What's going on? I don't want to blow an asset for you, but I don't . . . I don't want to have to take a trip up to the hill and get asked the hard questions either. The boys back home know about this Denard?"

"No. Not that he's here. The past, yes. I'm sure there's something on paper, but they would rather forget."

The man laughed that short, ugly hack again. "Okay. I got you . . . It's tough all over. So what's your friend doing, crossing paths with Donnie Wicks?"

"They have a prior business relationship," said Monsieur Ribiere, driving his ball sideways into the brush. *"Merde."* He put down another ball and kicked it onto the fairway. "I suggested that, as they are neighbors, he have a discreet word with the gentleman. Straighten out any misunderstandings."

"Oh, I don't like that."

"It was a bad surprise, this Balistieri, this Wicks coming here."

"I can imagine."

"My man will be discreet."

"I hope so. I really do. You trust him to behave? I can see considerable potential for blowback here. This Denard . . . he did some things"—the man smiled wryly—"He did some things a while back for us, didn't he? A liaison thing. I mean, I seem to remember—"

"There's nothing in the files," Monsieur Ribiere assured him. "It was our operation, always. If there was some mutual interest . . ."

"You trust the guy."

"I trust him."

"Okay. I'll rely on your take on the situation. What do you want me to do? They need some kind of an answer."

"What are my choices?"

"I can treat them like mushrooms over at Justice; that's option one: keep them in the dark and feed them shit. They generally don't like when we do that. Somebody always ends up going and crying to Congress or whispering to the press. Option two: I can jerk them around for a while, dribble out a few uninteresting tidbits a page at a time. Bore them into submission. Option three: I can give them chapter and verse and see what happens. Just throw a classified slug on the memo, tell them it will compromise Liaison Agreements with a Friendly Unnamed Power. That'll keep them quiet for a while, but . . ."

Monsieur Ribiere screwed up his face into a look of utter skepticism.

"I take it you don't like option three. Probably right."

"My friend has a long and distinguished history of service. It would be unfortunate . . . unfortunate for us both, if the past were to be dragged up and examined."

"Say no more." The man sighed. He was, apparently, not entirely unused to being blackmailed before breakfast. He took a vicious swing at his ball, missing it completely. "Fuck."

"For him, for me . . . even for you . . . it would be bad."

"Hey, buddy. I got it. You don't have to lay it on so thick. A little subtlety, please." He clapped an arm around Monsieur Ribiere's bony shoulders. "God, I love this," he said, startling Ribiere. He picked up his ball and headed back to the clubhouse, his club over his shoulder like a baseball bat. A few early-bird golfers were beginning to appear at the first tee, a jumble of brightly colored fat men disgorged from golf carts.

19

The giant underbelly of American Airlines Flight 557 from New York, landing gear down, dropped out of the clouds over Simpson Bay Beach, covering the horrified weekend tourists below with a fine mist of jet fuel. The end of the runway for Juliana Airport, to the tourists' surprise, lay only a hundred yards beyond the tree line, and the hapless beachgoers could hear the squealing tires and the roar of the air brakes as the big airbus touched down, the exhaust from three Rolls-Royce jet engines kicking up sand and curling over beach blankets.

Passenger Kevin Aloysius Coonan, in khaki SanSabelt slacks, a stiff Johnny Carson button-down dress shirt fresh from its wrapping, and a pair of Korean-made moccasins, stepped onto the hot tarmac. He carried a wilted blue blazer over one arm; in the other, he held a cracked leather carry-on containing toothbrush, disposable razors, some balled up white tube socks, a copy of *Sports Illustrated,* and a bottle of Jameson whiskey. Everything else, Kevin figured he could buy on the island.

He could hardly breathe. Sweat ran into his eyes behind the blue-framed aviator sunglasses that threatened to slide off his nose at any second. He took his place in the line of restive new arrivals waiting at passport control, wedged between two corpulent retirees in new vacation outfits. The man on his right had a skin condition, the pale white turkey wattle under his neck becoming red and blotchy as the line moved slowly forward in the sweltering hallway. Kevin tried to shrink back from the man, afraid of catching something, in near despair at the way he was scratching the skin now, little white flakes dropping onto his shirtfront. By the time Kevin reached the immigration shed, the man's face was affected, fiery welts creeping up into his cheeks, his wife, an even larger blob of flesh with a slash of fire-engine red lipstick misapplied diagonally across her lips, was saying, "Don't scratch! Don't scratch. It'll make it worse."

Kevin didn't feel too good himself. The flight down had been torment. He'd denied himself drinks since he'd be meeting his contact in the arrivals lounge, and the talkative crone in the seat next to him had smelled like the conga line at Century Village, all perfume, urine, and spite. She'd polished off six or seven gin and tonics, the tiny bottles forming a neat row on her tray, all the while railing about that damn Rooosevelt and the conversion from the gold standard. Roosevelt was a Jew, she confided, after her third gin, lowering her voice and moving in close so Kevin could smell the tartar on her teeth. He had suffered his deprivation badly, focusing on the woman's wig, the way it seemed to move independently of her head when she turned, staring at the frightening copper-colored hairpiece like it was some lurid religious icon, willing her to die right there so she'd leave him alone.

The in-flight movie had been *Harry and the Hendersons.* From what Kevin had been able to gather from the soundless movements of its characters, it was about some cute little kids and an adorable Bigfoot who moves in with them. Kevin had found himself wondering where the hairy, pantless giant's sexual organs were concealed, and where the beast went to take a dump. One of those photogenic little tykes stepped into a pile of yeti shit, he had thought, and it would have been a different movie altogether. He might have sprung for the headset to see that.

He got his passport stamped and wandered about in the arrivals lounge until Little Petey found him.

Little Petey was not little. The man who nodded at Kevin from the sliding doors by the taxi stands was of more than average height, big chested, with his black hair swept back tightly into a stylish little rattail, which hung over the collar of his silk shirt. He was thirtyish, tan, and comfortable looking in summer-weight chamois pants, sandals, two-toned orange aviators with the name of a sports car written in tiny letters on the frames. He looked like a vacationing movie producer, or a retired fireman who'd hit Lotto. Kevin hated him on sight.

"Car's over there," said Little Petey, not shaking Kevin's hand. He led Kevin across a shadeless parking lot, completely unconcerned, like he was taking him to see some time-shares, his gait lazy and carefree, the bulge of a handgun under his waistband the only indication of his true associations.

"It's a rental," said Little Petey, not so apologetically, swinging behind the wheel of a white Hyundai jeep. "You need a fuckin' tank to drive down here. The jigs, they can't drive, an' the roads . . . forget about . . . you lucky if there is one." He ground the gears for a while, lurching and stalling and starting up again until he found reverse. The roof was down, and Kevin thought that if he didn't get some air-conditioning soon, or at least a breeze, his brain was going to boil over and start bubbling out his ears. When at long last Little Petey successfully shifted into first, and then second, Kevin had sweat right through his shirt.

"Car I been drivin's back at the casino," said Little Petey, one arm outside the door, tapping out a beat to a reggae tune on the radio. "Guy who runs the place didn't think it was a good idea you stayin' there. He's got his own thing down here, and he didn't want no complications."

Kevin's imagined hotel room—air-conditioning, fresh sheets, swimming pool, tall blender drinks, and steel band—evaporated.

"How 'bout a beach where I'm stayin'? Place got a beach?"

"Well," said Little Petey, smiling good-naturedly, "the place we goin' is like a hunnert, two hunnert yards . . . maybe half a mile from the water. You can walk there no problem. It's nice."

"And where you stayin'?"

"Uh . . . I stay at the casino," said Little Petey.

Kevin sank in his seat, leaning against the window frame, grateful at least for the wind as the jeep picked up speed. They passed a Kentucky Fried Chicken, a Burger King, a Subway, then turned up a steep, winding mountain road, where they ran into traffic. A few wiry black youths whipped by them on scooters.

"Nice view, huh?" said Little Petey when they reached the top. Below them, the French lowlands, a narrow squiggle of sand and trees, snaked around a giant inner lagoon, the red tile roofs of vacation homes peeking through the green.

"A bar," said Kevin. "This place have a bar?"

"Oh, yeah. This place got a bar. Broads . . . all the broads you want. They got a string a' hooers workin' outta this place. I'm tellin' you, you'll love it. This guy runs the place, Dominican guy? Brings the hooers in in fuckin' cargo containers." He started to laugh. "This guy was tellin' me . . . last year, they sent in a load onna boat, right? So they get the container in, only nobody tells the guy it's there. Three days later somebody finally gets aroun' to callin' this guy an' says you got a cargo container down here onna docks, come an' pick it up. So he goes down the docks and cracks the thing open, and there's nothin' in there but a pile a' dead hooers. They been sittin' inside that thing for . . . for days, and they like started to cook in there. By the time he opens the thing up, they look like a pile a' boiled shrimp."

"What about the guns?" asked Kevin.

"They gonna be here in a few days. No problem there. That's all handled. Everything you need. I got that under control personally."

"The vans."

"They're up there already. I got a garage behind the place you stayin' at. They in there. And the others, the kids you gonna need, they'll be by in a few days too. Tough little bastards, perfect for what you wanna do. They'll go chargin' right in the front door that what you want. They're happy for the work, believe me."

So am I, thought Kevin. Happy for the work. He unbuttoned his shirt, feeling a little better now. "They any good?" he asked.

"How good they gotta be?" said Little Petey.

Kevin shrugged.

"They'll do fine," said Little Petey. "They don't know nothin' . . . they figger it's a drug thing. The guy owes money, we told 'em. They unnerstand that. Pisses 'em off on principle, some rich guy doesn't pay what he owes. Where these guys come from you do that, they come and saw yer fuckin' legs off. You see that movie? Al Pacino? 'I wanchoo to meet my li' frien'.' " Little Petey laughed uproariously. "I love that pitcher."

"You payin' these kids?"

"Sure. Peanuts, but we payin' 'em. That's the beauty part. These guys are right outta the fuckin' trees. Show one a' these animals a fuckin' Uzi, he'll come in his pants an' be yer best friend for life. They'd do it for the guns, I axed 'em to. This one kid, he shows me this clapped-out fuckin' Smith, musta been twenny years old, you . . . you wouldn't think the thing had ever been fired. This kid's so proud of this gun. He waves it aroun' in fronta my face an' tells me how many mean hombres he's put inna ground with this thing, what a bad dude he is. You'll see. They're gonna be fine.

They just gotta get you in there anyways, right? I mean, they don't come out again it's no skin off my ass."

As they descended the mountain road approaching Philipsburg, Kevin saw a row of beachfront hotels and casinos. Beyond them, in the Great Bay, two cruise ships, dispatched ferry loads of bargain hunters to the duty-free shops in town. Kevin found himself again yearning for a piña colada in a cavernous, air-conditioned necropolis, an anonymous, sterile room with a paper strip across the toilet bowl and crinkly waxed paper covering the water glasses.

But Little Petey took a hard left turn away from the town, past the Great Salt Pond, a charitably named stagnant lake of foul-smelling brown water, and back into the mountains. The landscaped condominiums and newer villas gave way gradually to ugly, unpainted cinder-block motels, wooden shacks that sold lottery tickets, a few smoky roadside barbecue joints, and shantylike homes, built haphazardly on the hillsides.

"You hungry?" asked Little Petey. "You want some ribs or somethin'?"

"No. Thanks same," said Kevin. "I jus' wanna lay down, maybe have a nice drink or two. I'll look around a little bit later, get the lay of things."

"You'll get the lay a' things all right where you goin'," said Little Petey. "I can promise you. This a regular pussy palace."

"I wouldn't be stayin' in a whorehouse, would I, Petey?" said Kevin. "This *is* a hotel we're goin' to?"

"What can I say?" said Little Petey, slapping Kevin on the back in a friendly way. "People stay there. It's a whorehouse, but it's a hotel. Don't worry. They gonna take real good care a' you there. They keep their mouth shut an' they take care a' our friends. It's nice. You'll see. We almost there."

"Jayzuss," muttered Kevin.

They turned onto a dirt road, more like a dry riverbed, the jeep bouncing over exposed roots and large stones broken loose from a crumbling, weed-covered wall on one side. In a cloud of choking dust, Little Petey navigated between the rocks and wall and a deep drainage ditch, past a run-down plantation house with a rusting pickup on blocks in the front yard, a few goats picking over a discarded bag of potato chips. They passed a few low wood and plaster sheds with beer signs out front and cars parked under the trees in their backyards.

"The competition," said Little Petey.

A few locals, walking single file at the edge of the road, didn't even look up as they roared past them, leaving them in a cloud of dust.

La Ronda was by no stretch of the imagination a hotel. Kevin could see that before they'd even pulled up into the trash-strewn parking lot. It was a large, ramshackle structure, three stories high with precariously sagging balconies built around the upper floors. The first floor was stone and beams and might once have been a respectable structure. But first one, then another, then many more annexes had been added on haphazardly, cheap plywood and sheet metal, cobbled together into a top-heavy junk pile of small cubicles, all connected by inner and outer walkways. A single neon sign advertised Presidente beer from behind a dirt-smeared window. Curling political posters urging the reader to Vote for Rudy papered the front on both sides of the entrance. Upstairs, sheets and pillowcases hung from a network of clotheslines. Somewhere a dog was barking to get out. Kevin saw a few empty taxis parked in the lot, back from the road, and a moldering pile of cardboard beer cases stacked against the wall, reaching to the second floor.

"Taxi drivers like this place for a little love in the afternoon." Little Petey chortled, trying to put a good face on things. Kevin didn't want to get out of the car. He'd thought this trip would be an escape from the squalor of his recent circumstances. This was even worse.

"This is crap," said Kevin.

"Don't knock it," said Little Petey. "It's safe. Nobody's gonna see you here. You can do anything you want . . . Someplace else, you got yer marshals, you got your cops, DEA, all sorts a' snitches and scumbags you don't want pokin' their nose in . . . I mean, this is business, right? Come on, man, it ain't so bad. Give it a fuckin' chance. I'll buy ya a drink, introduce you to Ruben."

Now even a drink would be a blessing, Kevin decided. He got out of the car, took his bag and jacket, and followed Little Petey into the front entrance to La Ronda, the familiar smell of spilled beer making the ugliness recede as he got closer to his first drink in over twelve hours.

The main bar was a large, wood-paneled room, decorated by beer advertisements of buxom, Spanish-looking women in skimpy bathing suits. A warped pool table occupied the center of the room, where a gold-toothed Dominican with tattooed hands was struggling to sink the eight ball while a fleshy whore jerked him off through his open fly. The Dominican was drunk. He kept swatting at a nonexistent insect on his nose, rubbing his face and eyes with one hand while the whore continued valiantly to maintain his apparently uncooperative erection. Every few seconds the man would return his attention to his cue stick, trying to focus on the ball, dangerously on the verge of falling over. When he scratched on the eight, he staggered off into a back room, the whore still alongside, half-carrying him with one arm, the other pumping determinedly away inside his pants.

"Nice, high-class joint," said Kevin, bellying up to the bar.

"Whatya havin', Kev'?" asked Little Petey.

"Beer," said Kevin, licking his dry lips.

A dark woman with a flat nose and earrings the size of door

knockers opened two Presidentes for them. "Bunny, this is my friend Mr. Smith," said Little Petey. "This here's Bunny. She's Mrs. Ruben. Where's Ruben at, sweetheart?"

"He coming now," said Bunny. "This your frien' Meester Smeet who wanna room?"

"*Sí*," said Little Petey. "The very one. This the man who gonna stay here for a while. You look after him real good. This a good friend a' mine. Anything he wants, you make sure he gets it."

Kevin drained off half his beer in one gulp and then finished it with another. He ordered a second. A short, balding man with a big grin and a heavy gold cuff on his wrist came down the stairs, counting a stack of aged singles. Seeing Little Petey, he straightened up and came immediately over, an expansive air of self-importance in his walk.

"Meester Petey. So good you are with us again. An' this is your friend? The Señor Smeet you spoke of? It is so excellent to make your acquaintance please," he said, pumping Kevin's hand vigorously. "You are most welcome to my home please. You are drinking? Yes. Anything I can do? You justa ask me. I have a room, the best. Is ready now. I take your bag, Señor Smeet? Here. Please."

Ruben gestured to a bored-looking teenager who was watching cartoons on TV from a broken couch in the corner. The young man came over, took Kevin's bag, and loped upstairs, squeezing past a trio of drunken taxi drivers coming down at the same time.

"I do what you do, you know," said Little Petey, feeling chatty after a couple of drinks. "Or, I did, anyways. I'm like semiretired now. You'll like it down here, really. It's nice."

Kevin ordered a Chivas, pleased, at least, that nobody was asking him to pay for drinks. There was music playing upstairs, merengue, and he could hear women's voices, laughing and talking in Spanish.

"So whad are ya doin' now?" he asked Little Petey, wanting to goad the gun-toting hood with the tan into admitting he wasn't up to the job himself. "You gonna be in on the thing or what?"

"Me?" said Little Petey, raising an eyebrow. "Nah . . . I'm here on somethin' else. I'm lookin' for a guy. Another guy. I been all over the Caribbean—Anguilla, Antigua, Virgin Islands, you name it, tryin' to locate this prick. It ain't easy, believe me."

"Sounds tough," said Kevin, thinking again about how Little Petey's accommodations differed from his own.

"Hey. It is tough! This guy don't wanna be found. And when I do find him, it ain't gonna be easy. This guy ain't no old man. He's a stone fuckin' killer, and I'm supposed to be retired."

"You ain't up to it, when I'm through with this—"

"Fuck you," said Little Petey, straightening up and looking directly at Kevin. "I'm no fuckin' virgin at this, asshole. Okay? I may *look* like fuckin' Island Jim over here right now, but don't make that mistake. I done plenty . . . plenty back in the City. A year ago . . . a year ago, I severed a guy's fuckin' head off."

"That's nice," said Kevin, clinking his glass against Petey's. There was no point getting his back up any further. This was the biggest job he'd had in years. As much as he'd have liked to grind a broken shot glass into Little Petey's neck, what was the use? Like they used to say back in the City, not for nothing.

There was more laughing from upstairs, and Kevin looked up, hoping to see women better looking than the one slag at the pool table. The alcohol was working now; a few more, Kevin knew, and he'd fuck a barbershop floor if there was enough hair on it.

"Relax," said Little Petey, his feelings still hurt. "Have fun. Try out the beach. Ruben'll fix ya up with a broad, take you down there, show you the lay a' the land. Life could be a hell of a lot worse, believe me."

"You leavin'?"

"Yeah. I gotta get back, check in with some people. It ain't all play down here. So enjoy it while you can. I'll be in touch." Little Petey put down his empty glass, patted the gun in his waistband.

"Good luck," said Kevin. "I guess I'll be seeing you, then."

"Yeah. I'll be by."

When he was gone, Kevin sat down on a broken couch by the single fan in the room and closed his eyes. The music sounded good . . . music and the voices of laughing women . . . creaking bedsprings. In a while, he'd check out the beach. Maybe this wasn't going to be so bad after all.

20

From the dock, Burke watched unhappily as Mickey and Henry helped Donnie Wicks aboard the fifty-foot Chris-Craft. Henry had brought the boat over from Captain Oliver's Marina an hour ago, and Burke and the other marshals spent most of that time searching the vessel for weapons, explosives, or places where someone might be hiding. It was seven-thirty on a cloudless morning. The little information Burke had received over the weekend about Henri Charles Denard, while tantalizing to an experienced reader of government documents, had been insufficiently incriminating to deny Donnie his fishing trip. This Henry fellow looked the part of the fishing guide, at least, thought Burke, trying to assuage his doubts. The deep tan, the earring, the graying ponytail—he looked like other boat bums and burnouts he'd come across, ex-dopers, juice-heads, failed Unitarian ministers, former businessmen making up for lost adolescence. Maybe it would be okay.

Introducing themselves as the notional Monsieur Pastou's security team, they'd asked Henry a few cursory questions, patted him down for weapons, a light frisk; unnecessary, but Burke had insisted on one anyway, just to see how he reacted. Sometimes you can tell when a guy has been through a frisk before. He reacted well, not going limp, the way ex-cons do, looking down at the ground, all yessirs and nosirs the way people who've spent a long stretch in prison come to respond to authority when challenged. This Henry seemed, if anything, relaxed, submitting to the pat-down with amusement. That was in his favor. As far as Burke could see, however, there weren't too many more in that column.

The bare outlines of Henri Charles Denard's life and times had arrived by fax the day before. A few sheets of paper, culled from DMV records, Selective Service, army discharge papers, a transcript from two years at Columbia University . . .

Henri Charles Denard, born April 8, 1950, in New York City to parents Jean-Pierre and Marie-Thérèse, Belgian nationals who had been naturalized during the Second World War. Son Henri (by now Henry) was educated at the prestigious McBurney School, a private boys' academy in New York, until his expulsion for cheating in 1967. He finished his last months in New Jersey, at the Englewood School for Boys, a slightly less tony establishment, and after graduating applied to join the Peace Corps. Rejected for less than stellar grades, he had, strangely enough, joined the army.

Burke, a veteran of two tours of Vietnam himself, was surprised at this. In 1968, at a time when everybody else was actively seeking to avoid the draft, young Henry had enlisted. This was *after* Tet, when even Burke's fellow soldiers in country knew it was hopeless, and here comes Henry, joining the Airborne fucking Rangers.

Specialist Denard served with the Seventy-fifth Infantry Division along the Cambodian border, receiving, in the space of three years, three Purple Hearts, the Combat Infantryman Badge, and the Bronze Star. A weapons specialist, Burke had noted with displeasure.

After receiving his third Purple Heart, Henry had been evacuated stateside, where Uncle Sam, uncharacteristically, had been generous enough to send him off to the Monterey Language School and then, even more uncharacteristically, to Columbia University. This aspect of Henri Charles Denard's particulars really ate at Burke. What did the army, or whoever, expect in return for their investment in young Denard? Burke wondered. The whole thing reeked of spookism. Burke's jaw tightened, the lack of response from subsequent inquiries of DIA and CIA burning a hole in his stomach. Whereas Woody and Robbie, both veterans of the Panama adventure, had been impressed by Henry's military records, he had been made uncomfortable. To him, young Henry Denard, in 1973 a war hero fluent in French, Spanish, and Vietnamese, had been exactly the sort of misguided young man they liked to take under their wings in the climate-controlled fool factories of Langley, Fort Meade, and certain windowless subcellars of the Pentagon. In those heady years of Nixon and Watergate, all sorts of death freaks and chest-thumping war lovers found employment informing on fellow students, doing black bag jobs, and worse.

Burke looked over at Rick, joyfully revving the twin Mercury engines of the marshals' rented speedboat, Woody sitting behind him, cradling an MX-70 rifle with scope. Henry would be familiar with that weapon, Burke thought. He remembered Woody that morning discussing the slim file on Henry, expressing regret he couldn't go along on the Chris-Craft. "I'd love to talk with this guy," he'd said. "You know, just to shoot the shit."

Burke wanted to talk to the guy, too. Where Woody saw "War Hero," Burke saw "War Lover." In his worst fears, he imagined Henry as a reader of *Soldier of Fortune,* a man with an overheated imagination, a grandiose sense of himself as a maker of history, G. Gordon Liddy with a ponytail. That was, however, hard to reconcile with the laid-back aging hippie he gazed at now, another troubling possibility.

That morning, frustrated by the lack of response from Washington, Burke had watched from the pool deck, through his field glasses, as Henry left his room at the Oyster Pond, boarded the little inflatable Zodiac, and buzzed across the pond to rent the Chris-Craft. He'd watched him load the fishing equipment, the beers and provisions, thinking all the while how he'd like to take a look inside Henry's rooms. Now, having made up his mind, he waited impatiently for the fishing trip to get under way so he could go through every square inch of Henri Charles Denard's lair with a goddamn microscope.

"I hope you jamokes are hungry," yelled Donnie from the stern of the big boat, " 'cause I'm gonna be cookin' up some serious fish I get back!" Henry, on the flying bridge, threw the burbling engine into reverse, and they pulled slowly away from the dock. Mickey, strangely silent, hovered over Donnie. For a young man going fishing, he didn't look very happy. When they swung around and headed out to the channel, only Donnie waved.

Rick hit the throttle on the speedboat and roared away from the dock. He made a wide arc, coming back in toward shore, waiting for the Chris-Craft to gain some distance, turning sharply away from the dock at the last second, showering Burke, Burt, and Robbie with his wake. The VHF radio in Burke's hand crackled to life, Rick screaming into it, "Yeeeeeee-hahhhhhh! This bad boy can move!"

Burt and Robbie went back to the house. They would maintain radio contact from there. Burke, ostensibly to watch from the beach, took his leave in one of the jeeps.

He drove immediately over to the Oyster Pond Yacht Club and parked down by the tennis courts, away from the hotel parking lot. Walking the short distance up the dirt road past the reception area, he saw that the chambermaids had just begun to clean the rooms in the main building of the hotel, their linen-filled carts parked outside on the side away from Henry's rooms.

Burke figured he had an hour. He took a thin plastic strip out of his pocket, walked casually up the steps to Henry's room, and began working on the latch. It gave him no trouble at all.

He shouldn't be doing this, he knew. But by the time he'd stepped into the room, underarms running with sweat, it was too late. He was committed. The French doors on the sea side of the room were open. Burke steered clear, not wanting to be visible from the Chris-Craft in the water. There was something hanging over the open doorway, a piece of clothing drying in the breeze. A woman's bathing suit.

Burke hadn't considered that possibility at all. Did Henry have his girlfriend living with him? Was he married? He cursed himself for not having thought this through. He froze in position in the empty room, listening.

There was no sound. Turning his head, he saw that Henry did not live here alone. The evidence of a woman's presence was abundant. Two impressions in the unmade bed, sheets torn back, an ashtray on each nightstand loaded with cigarette butts. A row of dresses hung on hangers in the open walk-in closet, and a battery of cosmetics bottles and jars, two deep, crowded the bathroom counter by the his and hers sinks.

He considered leaving immediately. There was no telling when she'd be back. She could be down at the pool, the beach, due back at any second. But he couldn't resist. A peek. Just a peek inside Henry's nightstand drawer, maybe a look in the white wicker desk in the corner. He stepped silently over to the bed and saw on the nightstand a framed photograph of a woman, an out-of-focus posed shot of a dark-skinned, attractive brunette, features blurred, standing under a palm tree, a wide smile on her face.

Someone had written in lipstick over the photo the words GONE BAMBOO!

He leaned over and, as gently as he could, slid open the drawer. Swelled by humidity, it gave him a hard time. He had to use both hands, one to brace himself and keep the nightstand from pulling away from the wall, the other to slide the drawer. It gave a slight creak, but he got it open. He was reaching for a U.S. passport when something very hard smashed against his head over the right ear. Suddenly, his cheek was resting on the cool terra-cotta floor.

"Who the fuck are *you?*" hissed the voice.

Burke tried to turn his head, but something sharp and threatening was pressing into his ear.

"Don't move," said a woman's voice. The pressure in his ear increased, the pain pinning him to the floor like a frog in biology class. "One fucking twitch out of you and I hammer this thing through your skull."

The pain from the head blow diminishing ever so slightly, his cheek flat against the ground, Burke peered cautiously out of the corner of one eye and saw a tall, slim, very tanned woman sitting astride him, holding a heavy glass ashtray over his head in one hand. He couldn't see what was in the other, but it felt like an ice pick, or a meat skewer. Whatever it was, it was sharp.

"If you think I won't hammer this thing right into your brain-pan," she said, "if you think that"—she pushed a little harder— "then you're making a bad fucking mistake."

From what he saw of her expression and the calm, even tone of her voice, Burke had no doubt at all that she'd do it.

"I don't get all wobbly, the sight of blood," she said. "You should know that."

He felt her press a knee into the small of his back where he kept his Glock.

"Uh-oh. What's this?" she said. "Alright . . . slowly, very slowly,

I want you to reach down and remove the gun and your wallet and put them on the floor. Left hand. And slowly. Any other part of your body moves an inch and you get a cut-rate lobotomy. Gun first, then wallet."

She sat back down on him with her full weight, the sharp object in his ear probing deep again, the other hand tensing with the ashtray, ready to pound it into his cortex.

To get the gun, he had to slide his hand down behind his back. He did that, removing the Glock and placing it to his left.

The wallet was farther down, in his right back pocket. He hesitated. He'd have to move his hand between her legs to get it.

"Wallet next. Come on. I want to see who you are. Breaking into a lady's rooms. It's deplorable."

He pushed his hand down behind, felt terry cloth move out of its way. Christ, she wasn't wearing anything under the towel! His wrist brushed against pubic hair, passed under her, his fingers feeling awkwardly for the wallet. And she didn't flinch. Not a muscle moved the whole time. He finally managed to get two fingers around his wallet.

"Now pull it out slow. Don't hang out to enjoy yourself down there . . . I'm not," she said, the weight on her pubic bone not diminishing in the slightest.

He pulled the wallet through and let it fall from his grasp onto the floor, relieved. Jesus, this broad was tough. He hoped she wasn't going to kill him. Sweat was running into his eyes, and he felt something warm on his neck. Probably blood from the head wound.

"Open it. Open the wallet," she said. He flipped it open, revealing his gold marshal's badge. She picked up the Glock. So quickly and efficiently did she do it that he didn't realize the thing in his ear was gone until he saw a Bic pen clatter to the floor next to his face. He heard her rack a round into the chamber.

"A fine-point," she said, talking about the pen. "Woulda worked. Now put both hands behind your back."

She removed his belt, looped it around his wrists, and tightened it, all with one hand, quickly, as if she did this for a living.

"Alright, now. Let's see what we've got." She got up off his back and stepped back toward the French doors.

When he pushed himself up onto his knees, finally managing to stand, his pants dropped around his ankles.

"Turn around, Marshal Dillon. You're sort of out of your jurisdiction here, ain't you?"

She was standing in a picture-perfect two-handed Webster firing stance, holding his own gun on him like she meant to use it. Even with the look of near-fanatical seriousness on her face, he could see she was a stunning woman. Ordinarily, he would have liked to have taken fuller account of the long expanse of brown flesh, looking even darker against the white terry-cloth towel she'd tied just over her breasts. But instead, he kept his eyes on hers, looking for a sign that he wasn't going to die.

"Why don't we step out on the veranda, have a little chat?" she said, motioning with the gun. He shuffled awkwardly onto the balcony, tiny steps, his legs constricted by the trousers around his ankles. She stepped aside and back as he passed, the gun swinging around slowly to follow him.

"Sit there," she said.

There was a pitcher of Bloody Marys, sweating in the sun next to a chaise lounge. She had been there when he came in, he saw, sunning herself, watching the Chris-Craft with the field glasses on the little table. He sat down, almost reclining, on the chaise.

"I guess you can pull your pants up now," she said, leaning against the railing across from him, the gun held waist high now but still pointing at him.

He pulled his pants up, awkward with his hands tied, feeling utterly defeated; the ramifications of what was happening beginning to sink in. He almost hoped she would shoot him. Worse could happen. If she called the cops, it was all over. There would have to be an investigation. A hearing. The IG would be down. And they'd bury him. He thought about what the younger marshals back at the house—Burt, Woody, Rick, Robbie—what they'd say. They'd laugh, of course. Compromise of a protected witness, loss of service weapon, unauthorized, illegal break-in. His head swam, and the pitcher of Bloody Marys began to look real, real good.

"Shit," he said.

"Have a drink?" she said. "You look like you could use one." The gun was still aimed at his belly.

"No, thanks . . . I . . ." he began to say, automatically.

"On duty?" she said, skeptically. "I have difficulty believing that." She threw him a towel from where it had been drying in the sun on the railing. "You might want to clean up a bit, Marshal. You're bleeding. If you promise to be good, I'll untie the belt."

"Thanks," he murmured. She untied him.

"There's ice in a bucket next to you, for the swelling."

"Thanks," he said, wrapping some ice in the towel and pressing it over his ear. There wasn't much blood. "Sorry about the towel," he said lamely.

"Now . . . maybe you can explain to me what the hell you think you're doing. Breaking and entering. Menacing a lady with firearms, indecent exposure." She laughed. "Really, I should just call the French cops . . ."

"No, please," he heard himself say.

"What the fuck are you *doing* here?" she said.

"I . . . uh . . . I was searching for a fugitive," said Burke, trying to cling to some vestige of a cover story, hoping that the name Balistieri would not have to come up.

"A fugitive," she repeated, not believing it.

"A guy . . . a guy jumped bail and came down here. I thought . . . I thought this was where he was."

"Have a drink," she said, filling a glass for him. "I'm surprised, you know. I'd think that if, as you say, you were on duty, you'd have a whole army of French police out there in the parking lot. This . . . this fugitive you're looking for . . ."

"Well, it's sort of on my own," said Burke, looking at the pitcher of Bloody Marys, then back at his gun. "Can you take that gun off me, lady? Please. That thing could go off. It's loaded."

She smiled and let the gun drop a little. The safety was still off, though, and he remembered that she had a round in the hole, ready to go. He poured himself a drink. Fuck it. New rules.

"You broke your radio," she said, referring to his VHF, its plastic housing shattered, in his chest pocket.

She had to know. She'd been sitting there watching Henry, watching Mickey, Donnie Wicks, the chase boat. The whole pretense falling to bits around him, Burke took a big gulp of Bloody Mary, blinking into the sun.

"Those your friends in the speedboat?" she asked. It was not really a question but an observation. "Hope they didn't pay over a hundred for it. If they did, they got robbed."

In fact, Burke knew, the boat had cost them two hundred for the day. He had used his own Visa card for the deposit; the boat's owner was a rummy-looking Frenchman with no love for Americans.

"Fuel line's fucked," the woman said. "They'll be lucky if they get in without a tow." She came over, poured herself a drink, and left the Glock on the table next to the pitcher.

"What happens now, lady?" asked Burke. "I'm sorry, really sorry about this. I guess I got the wrong room. That's all I can say."

"Donald Burke," she said. "That's your name?"

"Yeah."

"I'm Frances." She pulled over a chair and sat down. Together they watched the two boats for a while. The Chris-Craft was around a half mile offshore now, drifting slowly in the water, lines out, Donnie's seated figure just visible in the aft, Henry and Mickey seated nearby. The speedboat was a few hundred yards away, idling in the sun. "Nothing sinister about my husband if that's what you were looking for," said Frances, casually. "Relax. Whoever the rich guy on the boat is . . . he's got nothing to worry about. You really shouldn't have bothered."

"Sorry," said Burke, rubbing the bump on his head.

"That looks like it hurts," she observed, not terribly sympathetic.

"It's okay," said Burke. The bleeding had stopped at least. With luck, nobody at the house would notice. "You gonna call the cops?" he asked.

"I don't know. I guess not."

"I appreciate it, really."

"What the fuck, right?" she said, raising her glass. "Cheers."

He was going to survive this. No disgrace. No investigation. No younger agents snickering at him in the hallways. He'd still have a job.

She got up, and he forced himself to think about something other than what he'd felt when he'd reached for his wallet.

She went into the bathroom and was in there a long time. When she came out she was dressed.

"You still here?" she said. "I figured you'd be gone by now."

"No . . . sorry . . . I . . . ," Burke stammered.

"No, that's okay, finish your drink. I'm just going out. I have to do some shopping in town. If it'll settle your mind, you can search the room. There's nothing to see. No body parts in the fridge, no codebooks. We're both registered Democrats. Henry's a well-respected, well-liked member of the community down here. Ask around if you like. Maybe you mistook him for someone else. Actually, we're a very boring couple."

Burke doubted that very much. He got up to leave, retrieving his wallet from the floor on the way out.

He got behind the wheel of the jeep, his head aching, his shirt, drenched through with sweat, stuck to the vinyl seat. He felt a million things at once. He felt relieved. He felt humiliated. He was a little drunk. How much vodka had she put in that pitcher of Bloody Marys? He was worried and anxious, more curious than ever about Henry. There had to be something to a man with a wife like that. And more troublesome still, worse even than the glimpse he got of himself in the rearview mirror—an aging, defeated, frightened man—was the tightening in his throat, the feeling, which he hadn't had since adolescence, of having been somehow . . . jilted.

21

As soon as they'd cut the engine, Henry came back to sit on the gunwale and smoke a cigarette. Donnie's line was limp in the water, the old man looking uncomfortable in the sun.

"Does it hurt?" Henry asked Donnie, giving him a long, meaningful look.

"It hurts," said Donnie. "Every day it hurts."

"I'm sorry," said Henry, shaking his head.

"I gotta take pills," said Donnie.

"That's a bitch."

Donnie held up a hand to stop Henry from saying more and unclipped the VHF radio from his hip.

"Mickey, baby, take this thing downstairs there. Maybe those guys . . . they got a bug innit maybe. I don't want them findin' out any fishin' secrets." He looked disdainfully over at the speedboat, a few hundred yards off the port bow, drifting aimlessly, Rick and Woody, their shirts off, lying back in their seats, watching though binoculars.

When Henry and he were alone, Donnie looked at him hard and said, "It was you, wasn't it? You shot me."

"Yeah," said Henry. "It was me."

"I always thought so," said Donnie. "Soon as I come around there, I think, Henry. Henry was up there somewheres. He done this."

"I figured you'd know. If you lived . . ."

"You fucked up big time," said Donnie.

"Yeah."

"I guess Pazz is pretty pissed off at you. He prolly wants a piece a' you almost as bad as he wants me. You get paid in advance?"

"Yeah."

"Then you can count on it. Jimmy don't like to pay for nothing he can't wear. Especially things don't work the way they supposed to."

Henry shrugged and looked out at the water.

"Junior . . . Now that, that was good shootin'. I saw it happen. I seen that, I started to haul ass, I can tell you. Almost made it too." Donnie played with his reel for a second, winding it in, then letting it out again. "I shit in a bag now," he said. "They . . . the doctors there, they gave me a colostomy. You know what that is?"

"Yeah. I heard. I'm sorry, Donnie, really. I felt bad as soon as I read about it."

"They cut me a new asshole," said Donnie, a bitter chuckle escaping.

"You mad at me?" asked Henry.

Donnie only shrugged. "He hadn't got you, he woulda got somebody else."

Mickey returned and sat down, protectively near Donnie, on a cushioned seat by the helm, his jaw set in a look of enforced seriousness. Henry took Donnie's fishing pole, reeled in the hook, and baited it with a piece of turkey dog from an open can.

"They like that, the fish?" said Donnie. "That works?"

"Yeah," said Henry. "They love it. Some friends a' mine down here, they run a sea walk on the other side of the island. They take people out with like diving bells over their heads, weight belts, and they look at the fishes. They've been hand-feeding the fish turkey dogs for years. To keep them around. Give the tourists something to look at for their money."

"Pazz gonna want to feed you to some fish," said Donnie, taking back the pole. "He must figure you brought him all kindsa trouble with me testifyin' and all."

Henry looked over at Mickey, uncomfortable about talking in front of him.

"You don't gotta be shy about Mickey," said Donnie. "He knows. He knows what you do. He ain't prejudiced."

Mickey looked away, avoiding Henry's eyes.

"You gotta be livin' in the worst place inna world, my friend," said Donnie. "Right down the street from me." He laughed out loud. "That fat fuck Jimmy. He's sittin' up there right now, tryin' to find me, tryin' to figure out a way to shut my mouth for good . . . and here you are. His whole fuckin' hit parade, livin' in one place." He adjusted his sunglasses and relaxed in his chair a little. Taking one foot out of its sandal, he rested it on the gunwale and wiggled his toes. "This feels nice."

"Think he'll come looking?" asked Henry.

"Oh, yeah," said Donnie. "He'll send somebody around, eventually. You know Jimmy had his own brother whacked? D'you know that?"

"No, I didn't," said Henry.

"Well, he did. His brother made fun of him at a party. For dressin' up. Most people din't know back then. Jimmy was still just a skipper, and his brother got drunk and told a bunch a' people at a party. They found him 'bout a month later upstate. He had a size fourteen woman's shoe stuffed in his mouth. What kinda animal kills his own brother?"

"The feds treating you okay?" asked Henry.

"Far as it goes. What can you expect from cops? I'm still inna hospital when they start to pile on. Say they're gonna transfer me to Bellevue I don't cooperate, let Jimmy finish the job. I'm lyin' there, half outta my fuckin' mind on the dope they give you. I got tubes runnin' in, runnin' out, I don't know if I'm even gonna walk again, and these fucks are sittin' there, askin' this, askin' that. Every time I wake up, this one guy is sayin', 'Donnie, Donnie. You tole us this and that an' the other thing. How about you just fill in a few more little details?' Course, I go, 'What the fuck you mean? I din't say boo!' But they got me believin' it. They're tellin' me, 'Donnie, you just said . . . when you was a little woozy back there . . . Maybe, maybe you don't remember.' "

Donnie let out a deep breath, the memory clearly painful. "Course, what they was doin' was just readin' from the fuckin' files they got. They'd read up the wiretaps they had, other stuff people was tellin' 'em. And then they'd make like it was me that said it. This one guy, he's alone with me for a while, and he leans over an' says, 'Donnie, Donnie . . . we gonna tell the papers. They gonna be sayin' you fuckin' blabbed anyways. Let it go. You're a sick man . . . very sick. Even if you make it out the hospital, whaddya think it's gonna be like for you, gettin' pushed aroun' Marion like Raymond Burr? Some nigger gonna come at you with a shank, you can't even run away?' "

"Fucked up," said Henry, feeling genuinely bad for the old man.

"No shit." His thin lips trembling slightly, Donnie said, "So I did what they wanted. I fuckin' ratted on Jimmy fuckin' Pazz an' every yellow, mutt cocksucker in his crew. I didn't say nothin' about Dogs, but I told 'em all I ever knew about Junior. I figured he was dead anyways, so I put a lot a' stuff on him. They prolly dug up Junior's cellar lookin' for Jimmy fuckin' Hoffa, time I was through talkin' . . . They don't care. They don't give a shit about nothin' but makin' a case against Jimmy. I help put Jimmy away and my deal is finished. Spend the rest of my life fishin' . . . Where *are* the fuckin' fish anyways?"

"Jesus, Donnie, I don't know. This the first time I've been."

"That figures. Well, I hope I catch somethin'. I was shootin' my mouth off, tellin' everybody I was gonna land the fuckin' big one. I better get somethin'. It'll look bad. You sure about these turkey dogs?"

"The fish I saw sure seemed to like them," said Henry. "Tear the things right out of your hands."

"I hope so."

"So . . . you liking it down here? All things considered?"

"Yeah," said Donnie. "Funny thing. I am. The kids. You know . . . you met Rachel . . . it's nice bein' around. The weather . . . I bought the place back inna fifties. Before Castro. Everybody else was in Cuba. I got this. Never got down here much. It was always one thing or the other. Always somethin'. Twenny years—couldn't talk onna phone, even pay phones. I couldn't call my niece, that's Mickey's mother, wish her happy birthday without people hearin' every word. Always lookin' over my shoulder. I was spendin' more time with the fuckin' lawyers than I was with my friends . . . and half a' my friends are either talkin' with the cops or they was talkin' with Jimmy. Fuck it. I ain't sad I turned my back on it."

"You didn't have a lot of choices," said Henry.

"Yeah," said Donnie. "I always used to see you. All tan, lookin' relaxed. I'd say to myself, This guy's got it all figured out. Come into town for some work, make a little money, and poof! Gone. Off there somewhere's where they got sun and the beach."

Donnie looked up suddenly, remembering something. "How's

that wife a' yours? Frances. Howzat crazy broad? Mick here says you still together."

"She's good, thanks. She sends her love."

"Does she? Does she?" Donnie laughed. "That crazy bitch. Good! Good! I'm glad youse still together. That's great . . . Mickey, you met Frances, right?"

"Yeah," said Mickey, still looking morose, pretending to concentrate on his cigarette.

"Yeah, yeah," said Donnie. "Rachel and Frances. Two a' my favorite women. They should know each other. They should be friends."

"They are friends," said Henry.

Mickey snorted with disgust.

"Hey," said Donnie. "Don't be like that. You're actin' like some girl somebody forgot to call." To Henry, he said, "So, Henry . . . what do you want?"

"I just wanted to have a talk. Now that we're neighbors and all . . . see if we could bury the hatchet. Sensible thing . . . sensible thing as soon as I found out you were here, was to just pick up and run away. I didn't want to do that. Frances doesn't. For once, I thought, fuck sensible."

"Now you seen me, the marshals, they gonna be in your fuckin' shorts."

"I imagined they would be," said Henry.

"How hard can they look before you got a problem?" asked Donnie.

"I don't know. Pretty hard, I guess."

"So. Another thing we got in common," said Donnie, slapping Henry's knee. "We both got a lotta people interested in us."

"What's the other thing?" asked Henry.

"The other thing? The other thing is, some a' the things we done, we feel bad about now. Am I right?"

"You're right," said Henry, his smile disappearing.

The reel on Donnie's fishing pole started to spin, fast and hard, surprising the three men. Mickey jumped to his feet, startled.

"Holy shit!" cried Donnie, overjoyed. "I got one! Son of a bitch!"

22

Something less than a full moon illuminated the grassy crest of Crystal Mountain, the windy bluff that guarded the mouth of the Oyster Pond, opposite the hotel. Frances stubbed her toe on a rock and grunted with pain.

"Hurt yourself?" inquired Henry, moving past her in the dark.

"You could say that," said Frances, limping after him.

"No flashlight yet, okay?" said Henry. "Sorry."

"Yeah, yeah."

Below them, at the bottom of a steep slope, waves exploded against the rock and coral. The churning white water almost glowed in the moonlight. Gusts of wind combed the tall, silver-peaked grass, whipping it one way, then another. Here and there, little round humps of cactus poked out of the grass, and a dark pile of boulders at the very top of the hill threw long, black shadows.

Henry found the spot, just beyond the drop-off, and began to dig, using his folding field shovel. Frances, sitting on a rock, swatted a mosquito on her neck and said, "What could I do? I was thinking about shooting the guy but, *really,* right in the hotel? I didn't know who knew he was there. And the only thing he had was a Glock. The noise would have been ridiculous."

"You did exactly the right thing," said Henry, still digging.

"I just figured, what's the point?"

"We have to assume we're blown. I mean, if the one guy is so interested, others will be too. It's really just a matter of time."

"If I thought we had to split the island 'cause of him, I *would* have killed him," said Frances. "That's not going to happen, is it?"

"Not yet," said Henry. "Really. You did the right thing. Shooting federal marshals is not something we should be doing right now. Too bad he didn't die of embarrassment."

"He came close, I think. You should have seen the poor guy, trying to walk with his pants around his ankles."

Henry's shovel hit something solid.

"The flashlight," he said. "Just for a second."

Frances played the beam over the freshly dug hole. Henry plunged his fingers into the soft, sandy earth and tugged on a plastic parcel until it came free. "Okay, turn it off," he said.

He fiddled with the package for a few minutes, unwinding layers of hurricane tape and plastic trash bag from around a Tupperware container.

"Your weapon, ma'am," he announced, finally. He tossed a Walther P-5 automatic over to Frances.

He kept the Heckler and Koch VP70 for himself, then stuffed boxes of 9-millimeter shells into the pockets of his windbreaker.

"So, who are we planning on shooting?" asked Frances, kicking dirt back into the hole while Henry shoveled. She slid the Walther into her pants in front, under her sweater. Henry had his weapon in the back pocket of his jeans, sticking out. "I mean, do we have a plan here?"

"Proper prior preparation prevents piss-poor performance," said

Henry, quoting his old drill sergeant. "Be prepared," he added. "That's what the Boy Scouts say."

"Henry . . ."

"We were smart, we'd leave. Now. That would be the smart thing," said Henry sadly, the hole filled. "We could pop off to another island, move to one of the other places. The place in Belize would be perfect, for instance. We have no tenant there now . . . There's the place in Antigua that's not too shabby. We could do that."

"Who has to get shot for us to stay here?" said Frances, impatiently.

"Don't know, baby," said Henry. "Maybe nobody gets shot."

"We're not going to leave unless and until it's absolutely, *absolutely* necessary," said Frances.

Henry came over and wrapped his arms around her. She hugged him back. Hard. "I don't want to go either," he said.

"I'm not going," insisted Frances.

"I got a call from Anguilla the other day," Henry confessed. "From Angus at the real estate office."

"Yes?"

"A very suspicious-looking American was asking for the proprietor."

"Meaning you, of course."

"One would assume so."

"More cops?"

"I don't think so. Angus said he came in a car he knew. Hotel car from the Tropica. He thought he should mention it. I have a pretty good idea who owns the Tropica."

"Thanks for mentioning it to me," said Frances, bitterly. She started back down the hill.

"I was thinking about what to do," said Henry, catching up to her.

"I would've liked to have known."

"Yeah, sorry. I should have."

"So, what you're telling me is Jimmy knows where we are."

"Not yet, I don't think," said Henry, with less than complete confidence. "He's looking. We can be sure of that. And he's getting close. Like Donnie said, Jimmy's not a forgive-and-forget sort of a guy."

"So things are bad. Already. They're really bad," said Frances, stopping. "Shit!" In the moonlight, Henry saw that she was blinking away tears, something she almost never did. The last time he'd seen her cry was when their taxi had hit the goat. Or . . . no . . . there was the time that beach dog with the broken leg didn't show up as usual. She'd cried then, too. He felt like crying now himself.

"Let's face it," he said, patting the automatic wedged down the front of her jeans. "These are not the sort of beach accessories that leap immediately to mind when you live in a place like this." He kissed her lightly, on the lips, hooked his little finger around hers, and pulled her down slowly into the long grass.

"Christ, Henry. We're gonna get eaten alive up here," she said, unzipping his fly, kissing him so hard their teeth clicked.

When they were through, walking slowly down the mountain to where they'd left their scooter, Frances said, "So we're going to be shooting Italians." A gust of strong wind and the pounding of the surf made her have to almost yell. Henry didn't say anything.

"I guess it's better than cops," said Frances, almost to herself, her words disappearing over the water.

23

I notice the boys aren't speaking to each other," said Rachel, rolling over onto her stomach and lighting a cigarette.

"I think Mickey's still mad at Henry," said Frances, lifting a breast to oil the underside, then moving on to the other. The two women were stretched out on a nearly deserted Dawn Beach, a scraggly-looking mutt with floppy ears sleeping in the sun at the head of their blanket, legs twitching, dreaming of the chase.

"Mick's just sulking for a while," said Rachel. "He's a sulker."

"So, it's temporary, you think," said Frances, screwing on the top to her suntan lotion and replacing it in a plastic sandwich bag.

"Yeah," said Rachel. "He's mad 'cause of you-know-who. Henry not telling him and all. He thinks he's some sort of hit man or something. I don't know what his problem is."

"You talked about it?"

"Yeah. I said, 'What's the problem? I mean, we're living with a gangster, right? Donnie's nice. We like him. So why can't we be friends with Henry and Frances?' " She turned her face to Frances. "How's my face? Am I getting burned?"

"No. Looks okay."

"He's got hurt feelings. That Henry didn't tell him he knew. He doesn't open up to a lot of people, and, you know . . . He felt silly. And he's jealous. That they seem to be such good friends and all . . . I don't know . . . He'll get over it."

"I hope so," said Frances. "Henry's upset about it. He likes Mickey. It's just not a thing he felt he could come out and say, you know."

"I know."

"He's a careful person. He tries to be careful."

"Where is he today?" asked Rachel. "I haven't seen him."

"He took the ferry over to Anguilla. Business. He's got to talk to somebody about some property we're thinking of selling."

"Oh," said Rachel. "I've been meaning to ask, where'd you two meet? I mean, you know, how?"

Frances smiled wickedly. "Oh, that's a good story. I met him in New York—"

"How old were you?" asked Rachel, enjoying the confidence.

"I was really young. I'd been out of college for only a year. I got kicked out actually. I'd been in New York about two years. I met him at this club where I was working. He asked me out on a date. He was very sweet."

Frances was smiling. She tucked an errant strand of hair back into her French braid and then lowered her voice, needlessly, since there was no one else on the beach. "I was stripping—"

"No!" exclaimed Rachel, clearly delighted and intrigued. "What was it like? Oh God! Tell me everything." She moved her head and shoulders closer to Frances on the blanket. "I *don't* believe it."

"Yeah . . . me and a friend from college were stripping at this club. We were dancers, but, you know, you don't really dance, you just kinda roll around on stage and pretend to finger-fuck yourself through a G-string. It was pretty lame. Twenty-minute sets, five times a night. But the money was good, and I needed money."

"Henry was a customer?"

"No, no. He worked there for a while. Bouncing. You could see right away he was different. You should have seen him. The middle of all these guys with their gold chains and Sta-Prest pants—you know, big lapels, the hair just right—there's Henry. He was still wearing his green fatigue jacket from the army, dirty blue jeans. He had practically a crew cut. And this was, like, shag era. Nobody looked like that. He looked totally . . . lost . . . and kind of dangerous. But he was smart. When he talked, which wasn't often in those days, you could tell he wasn't like everybody else. He read books. He thought about things. He never had to lay a hand on anybody, any customers, he looked so weird, if he said to somebody they were eighty-sixed, they left."

Frances reached in her beach bag, pausing long enough to light a fat joint. She took a long hit and passed it to Rachel.

"So, what was it like? How'd he ask you out?"

"He just came over and asked if I wanted to have dinner with him. I said yes just to piss off my boss and all his manicured buddies. They'd been trying to get into my pants since day one. Actually, some of them had been *in* my pants already, but it pissed them off all the same."

She took the joint back, took another hit, and passed it over.

"He took me to a little French place in the theater district. Some shabby little joint. Said it reminded him of someplace he'd been. He spoke French to the waiters, and it shocked the shit outta me. We had dinner, and then . . . then he took me bowling."

"You're kidding!"

"No. I couldn't believe it. In New Jersey, no less. Drove over in this clapped-out Beetle he had. Drove past where he went to school for a while, pointed out houses where he said friends had lived, a real sentimental journey. Then we went bowling. Drank long-neck Budweisers and held hands between frames. It was the craziest thing." She laughed. "I guess it's fair to say, I was impressed."

"Too much," said Rachel. "So, did you put out on the first date?"

"Nope. The whole time, I'm thinking, end of the night, we're going over to his place or he's coming to my place and he's gonna ask for a blow job and he's probably going to get one too, 'cause I liked the guy. I thought he was interesting. But, no. He drops me off, kiss on the cheek and 'I'll see you at work tomorrow.' "

"Were you, like, weirded out by it?"

"Kind of. I thought, maybe he got his dick shot off in the war or something. Or he's like some guys who hung out in the club, all he wants to do is hang around strippers, get their laundry and shit, do them favors. You get that a lot. But, next night, Henry comes in, and he's got a big bouquet of flowers and a nice, I mean *really* nice, antique bowling shirt with my name stitched over the pocket. Walks right up to me onstage and gives it to me. My boss almost burst a blood vessel. Of course, me being the cunt that I am, I insist on wearing the damn thing all night, so my boss, he's not too happy. I left the thing unbuttoned, so they could still see my tits, but I wore that shirt all night. My boss is getting more and more pissed off, he keeps gesturing from the bar to take it off, take it off, getting all red in the face. Then he goes over and says something to Henry at the door. We had to leave in a hurry."

"What happened?" said Rachel, breathless.

"You're not going to take this the wrong way, I hope. I don't want you to get the wrong idea about Henry. He's a *very* sweet guy . . ."

"What happened?"

"Well, I don't know what he said to Henry, but it must have been pretty bad, 'cause Henry broke both his collarbones."

"Holy *shit!*"

"Yeah . . . I asked him later what was said. He wouldn't tell me. I had a pretty good idea though."

Recovered slightly, Rachel spluttered, "Well, *what?*"

"I'm sure he called me a whore," said Frances, with a matter-of-factness that Rachel found chilling. "I mean, it had to be that. Besides . . . it was true."

Rachel rolled over onto her back and collapsed, arms akimbo. "Whew! I mean . . . Ayiyi!"

Frances laughed and took a last hit on the burning roach. A pale, knobby-kneed tourist strolled by, eyeballing the two half-naked women openly. Neither woman said anything for a while.

"You should know something about Henry, though," Frances finally said. "He's a really *gentle* person."

Rachel tried not to look skeptical, but something in her expression must have given her away.

"Really," said Frances. "He's a sweetheart. I was pretty fucked up back then. For a long time after, I was fucked up. I was doing a lot of drugs. I looked like shit . . . He was always sweet to me. Always gentle. And in all the years we've been together, he's never been unfaithful."

"Come *on,*" said Rachel. "How do you know?"

"I know," said Frances, convincingly. "Worst thing you can say about Henry is he can be lazy."

"Mickey's a little scared of him, I think," confided Rachel.

"I know," said Frances. "He shouldn't be. Really. That's why I'm telling you all this. So you know what he's really like. He shouldn't be scared of Henry. Henry would never do anything to hurt Mickey or Donnie."

"I can, like, take that as an assurance?" said Rachel.

"Henry's not about that at all."

24

For the first time in his life, Kevin was getting a suntan. He was pleasantly drunk. Also, he was in love.

It had been a week since he'd moved into La Ronda. Other than work on the vans, there hadn't been much to do. The guns had yet to arrive. The planning, such as it was, had been completed.

He spent his time at the beach, or drinking at the bar, with Violetta.

Though his nose, cheeks, and shoulders were still painfully red, the rest of his body, rapidly slimming from exercise, was becoming golden brown. That morning, in the streaked mirror of the communal bathroom, he had barely recognized the grinning, healthy-looking bugger who greeted him over the sink.

He swam every day. He ate breakfast with the whores in the rear kitchen each morning, their children tugging at his sleeves to play with them, television blaring Spanish soap operas. Then he'd jog down to the beach, heave himself into the water, and swim until he could stand it no more. Then he'd visit the trash-strewn gully by the mouth of the dirt road, where the abandoned earthmover was, and drag whatever parts he needed back to the garage behind La

Ronda. Little Petey had managed to find him an oxyacetylene torch and some tools, and the work went well.

He'd usually knock off around noon. By that time it was too hot to continue. Time for drinks. Then maybe a trip upstairs with Violetta. Sex, a nap. Then back to the beach.

Kevin liked the beach best during those magic hours from three until five-thirty. The shadows grew long, and the light from the sinking sun made glimmering white peaks on the water. Not too hot, not too cold, he'd lie there with the silent Violetta, drinking beer, napping some more, maybe taking a short walk down to the little barbecue shed at Dawn Beach Hotel for a burger or some hot dogs.

Violetta seemed to like the piña coladas there, foamy and thick in the plastic cups. He always made them give her extra cherries.

Violetta, Violetta, Violet, Vi—he called her Vi. He gazed down at her now, at the foot of the blanket where she was massaging his feet, the tip of her tongue poking earnestly from the corner of her mouth. She spoke no English as far as he could tell. If the other whores were to be believed, she didn't speak much Spanish either. They had been surprised and much amused when he chose her. An Indian, they said contemptuously, barely out of the jungle. What would he want *her* for? To the others, Violetta's broad nose, large, almond-shaped eyes, straight, black hair and bangs were an affront that detracted from their somewhat more metropolitan airs. They made fun of the scars on her legs, her thick ankles and powerful forearms, her slightly stooped posture, as if she were carrying a great weight.

But to Kevin she was beautiful. An exotic, an Amazon, a girl like he'd seen in *Mutiny on the Bounty*. Watching her at the beach, splashing water over her shoulders, skin shining in the failing light, gave him the most excruciating pleasure.

"Vi . . . Vi," he said, patting the blanket next to him. She came up and sat next to him. He took her hairbrush from her little red plastic purse and began to brush her hair.

A man in a hat woven from palm fronds came by, selling jewelry from an attaché case. Kevin paid ten dollars for a necklace made of seashells and mother-of-pearl, an item he could easily have had for a dollar in town. He didn't care. Reaching around Violetta's throat to fasten the clasp, seeing the corners of her mouth turn slightly upward, her Toltec mask face softening into a smile, he was happy, happier than he'd ever been.

Late in the afternoon, the locals came down to the beach. Whole families, parents and all their children, came to swim in their underwear, black skin reflecting in the late afternoon sun. They'd lived by the beach their whole lives, Kevin thought, watching them splash each other, children doing headstands on the wet sand at the water's edge, yet each time he saw them, they appeared to be newly thrilled, as if visiting this beach for the very first time. He could live here, he thought. He really could.

Near the end of the day, the water crowded with families, the white tourists long gone, he'd swim among them, sometimes holding Violetta in his arms, drifting in the shoulder-deep water, and it was as if he was sharing a bathtub with them, the blacks looking at him with amused benevolence.

"Yo!" came a voice from the palm trees. "Yo! Kevin!"

It was Little Petey, wearing a Hawaiian shirt and khaki shorts, sweating behind mirrored sunglasses. Kevin, annoyed, got up from his blanket and walked back into the shade.

"Jeesusss," said Little Petey. "Lookit 'em all."

"What is it?" said Kevin.

"The guns are here," said Little Petey. "And some people you should meet."

"Now?"

"Yeah, now," said Little Petey. He was looking at Violetta on the blanket, fingering her necklace. "She speak any English?"

"No," said Kevin.

"We'll take my car," said Little Petey. "Leave her. She can walk back."

It was an impressive array of firepower. Laid out on a sheet-metal billboard advertising Ting orange soda were enough guns to over-throw a medium-size Caribbean country. There were Uzis, four of them. M-16's, two of those, two pump-action Remington shot-guns, an assortment of handguns, fragmentation grenades, and, drawing the most attention from the awestruck, shabbily dressed Dominicans who stood gaping and transfixed like a cargo cult around the guns, was a South African special purpose automatic shotgun, its huge drum canister and wide, ugly steel snout already the subject of heated debate.

Two of them, both in flower print shorts and sleeveless T-shirts, were arguing over who would get to wield this fearsome weapon. They were pushing and shoving like little kids, voices rising into curses and threats.

Little Petey had to step in, telling them to shut up in his high school Spanish. The Dominicans fell into sullen silence, eyes still glued to the big shotgun.

"This is Orlando," said Little Petey, throwing an arm roughly around a slightly built youth with a scorpion tattoo on his wrist. "Orlando is one bad dude, right, Orlando?"

Kevin wasn't so sure. They looked like spindly, underfed little bed wetters to him. If this was what he had to work with, it was not going to be easy.

Kevin unfastened the lock on the rotting wood garage door behind La Ronda's garbage area. The whole group followed, stepping over the empty propane tanks, beer cartons, and torn mattresses. When he pulled the doors open, a waft of damp, stifling air escaped. Everyone squeezed inside the dark garage to admire Kevin's work.

There were two Ford vans, their passenger compartments heavily reinforced by heavy steel plates, still rusted from years in the weeds. The rear cargo areas were similarly protected, top and sides, with large X-shaped gunports crudely cut through the centers of the plates on both sides. Smaller metal plates had been attached over the outer wheel wells to shield the tires, and protruding from the front of the first van, like the horn of a mutant stegosaurus, was an intimidating orange hunk of steel, a section of hydraulic arm from a front-end loader. Kevin had mounted the thing right through the dash; it rested on the floor between the two front seats and protruded at an angle, three feet beyond the bumper. He'd had to put a counterweight in the rear of the van so the back wheels didn't lift off the ground. Orlando whistled admiringly through his teeth at the fearsome-looking battering ram and stroked the flattened tip with his hand like he was petting an animal.

"Paf! Paf!" Somebody was yelling outside the garage. It was Flaco, Orlando's rail-thin brother with one drifting, milky eye, dry-firing the automatic shotgun. Jorge, a near child wearing an Orioles cap, grabbed his chest and feigned being shot. Suddenly, the whole group was joining the fun, grabbing at weapons and pointing them at each other, the scene degenerating into a children's game. Hector and Alfredo, two dwarfish cousins, wrestled on the ground, competing to get the single remaining Uzi, while Papo, the only normally proportioned member of the group, tried to fit all of the grenades into the pockets of his threadbare cotton shorts.

Little Petey was embarrassed by the scene. *"Calma!"* he yelled.

"*Tranquillo!*" He made them put the guns down, waiting until everything had been returned to the metal sign. Only Flaco still held a weapon, the automatic shotgun, which he'd managed to snatch out of Jorge's hands at the last second.

"Gimme!" commanded Little Petey, unsuited as a schoolmarm, wresting the weapon from the resentful Dominican only by exerting his superior strength.

They stood once more around the sign, looking sheepishly at their feet while Orlando, their apparent spiritual leader, hurled abuse at them in Spanish. Every once in a while, one of them would look up from his sneakers to gaze longingly at the guns.

"This a bloody fucking kinnergarten you got here. I'm supposedta work with these pitiable bastards? They're . . . they're fuckin' hopeless!" grumbled Kevin.

"Don't worry about it," said Little Petey. "Watch. Watch this." He picked up an Uzi and slapped a clip in, handing it to Flaco, the one with the walleye. With startling ease, the skinny Dominican had the safety off and was firing away on full auto, the tamarind tree a few feet over Kevin's shoulder bursting into confetti. Kevin dove for the ground and waited for the firing to stop. When the clip was exhausted, he got to his feet, walked over to the shooter, and hit him full in the face with his fist.

Flaco fell backward, knocked clean out of one of his sneakers. But, to Kevin's surprise, he didn't drop the gun. He didn't lie there, collecting his wits, or spitting out teeth, or rubbing his badly split lip. Instead, he bounced right back up, smiling, blood smeared across his large white teeth, and cheerfully held out the Uzi to Kevin. "Ees good," he said. "*Muy bueno.* You want gun?" His grin grew wider at Kevin's look of astonishment.

"See?" said Little Petey. "They make 'em tough where these kids come from. Flaco, baby," he asked. "How many, *cuanto hombres* you kill, Flaco?"

Flaco's smile stretched even wider, and he beamed with pride as he held up ten fingers, closed his hands, and then held up three more. *"Sí!"* he insisted, serious now. *"Es verdad!* Very bad people!" adding, "Paf! Paf! Paf!" to stress his point.

"See?" said Little Petey. "They're *not* bad boys. They got experience this kinda thing."

"Christ Jesus," said Kevin, wiping dead leaves and bits of tree bark off the front of his shirt. He examined the tree where the bullets had gone home, a tight little grouping, good shooting for a kid who'd probably never handled an Uzi before.

"See?" said Little Petey, again. "What I tell ya?"

Violetta was only halfway back when Kevin found her. He'd borrowed Little Petey's car, racing down the dry riverbed to meet her. She was walking impassively up the hill, picking her way barefoot over the exposed roots and rocky humps, Kevin's beach bag perched on her head. Headed back to her cramped, clapboard cubicle at La Ronda.

As Kevin pulled the car up to give her a lift, calling out to her through the open window, he noticed that she'd removed the necklace he'd bought her, and his heart sank. When she slid silently into the seat next to him, he considered saying something to her about it, but he didn't.

On the short drive back, he was surprised at the depths of pain and unhappiness this simple development had brought on him. That she no longer wore the cheap string of shells hurt him in ways he hadn't felt since childhood. He found himself blinking rapidly, trying to get rid of the sickly sweet sensation that was washing over him like an illness. As if each time he opened his eyes again, the pain would be gone.

He suspected she'd sold the thing back to the man with the attaché case. Pocketed the one or two dollars he would have given her for it. Kevin tried to put a caliber on it, the amount of pain he was feeling now. On the hierarchy of pain, how bad, really, did this hurt? Kneecaps busted? No, it wasn't *that* bad . . . Stabbed? Yes, more like that, the same icy tendril of fear and uncertainty was working its way into his chest as it had when he'd been stabbed. Kevin's chest hurt.

He looked over at Violetta, her hands crossed demurely on her lap, smiling shyly as the car bounced and jolted over the dirt road. He slowed down and, without thinking about it, leaned across the seat and pecked her on the cheek. When she turned and kissed him back, opening up her hand to show him the necklace, speaking for the first time since he'd known her, since he'd picked her out from a group of curlered, painted women on the couch at La Ronda, he felt better again.

"Gracias," she said, filling Kevin with joy. He sang all the way back, humming when he forgot the lyrics.

25

Little Petey was drinking a banana daiquiri from a plastic cup, half-listening to the steel band on the casino's pool deck, and contemplating another pass at the complimentary buffet when he hit the jackpot.

Bored with watching tourists squealing and laughing as one Farrah-cut behemoth attempted to squeeze her bulk beneath a limbo pole, Petey drifted away from the beach side of the deck, leaving a pile of gnawed spareribs on his paper plate. His drink looked and tasted like fabric softener, and, half drunk and in a pissed-off mood, he wandered over to the street side, considering dropping the cup two floors into the Tropica's gurgling fountain.

On this side of the building, he was looking down onto Philipsburg's main drag. Unlike those on the narrow strip of trucked-in sand on the bay side, the faces here were black. People stood outside their taxis, hoping for fares, played dominoes in doorways, hustled jewelry and prerecorded cassettes from makeshift stands. There was a busy take-out joint under a stand of ratty-looking palms a little way down, and more of them huddled around two picnic tables with their barefoot children, awaiting their orders.

Food was probably a damn sight better than the crap on the casino's buffet, Petey thought, regretting his meal already. These were locals, after all; they *had* to know the good places to eat. And this place was doing gangbuster business; it was a whole social scene, he saw—young men on scooters and motorcycles flirted with shy girls in brightly colored braids by the roadside. People beeped as they passed in their cars. An updraft brought the scent of grilling chicken and frying johnnycakes to his nose, and Little Petey almost shuddered with desire. He was thinking seriously about going down there and giving it a try when he saw Henry.

Hard to miss in these surroundings—Henry's was the only white face in sight. Taller than anybody around him, he stepped away from the counter with two plastic bags filled with take-out food, not a care in the world, thought Little Petey. Just look at him. Dressed in cutoffs, dirty T-shirt, and flip-flops, he sauntered over to a parked scooter, exchanged greetings with some dreadlocked young men sitting on a step (did he see Henry give *them* a joint?), and after some backslapping, hand-shaking, and laughing about who knew what (Petey couldn't hear them), Henry got on his scooter, the bags of takeout at his feet, and zipped off down Main Street.

This, thought Little Petey, should make Jimmy happy.

26

Henry and Frances had a long, boozy dinner at Orient Beach. They ate swordfish, rice, and peas, washed down with a lot of vodka and many beers. By the time they finished, it was dark, and the beach chairs and chaises had been piled up and chained, the Jet Skis returned to their sheds, the Hobie Cats and sailboards stripped and put away for the night.

They walked down the empty beach for a while, smoking a joint, collapsing on a stack of chaises to watch the shooting stars.

Feeling loose and happy, they exchanged deep, vodka-tasting kisses and ended up fumbling with each other's clothes on the wobbling stack of chaises. Soon Henry was inside her, Frances astride him, riding him like a rocking horse, the two of them giggling like truants.

When they were done, Frances wouldn't put her jeans back on until she'd wiped up. "I just got them back. They're clean," she said. They broke the lock on a closed barbecue shack so she could find a napkin. When the door was open, she crept inside, jeans in one hand, and bumped into a table. Suddenly she came bolting from the door, shrieking with laughter.

"Watchman!" she managed to say, as she ran full speed past Henry toward the parked scooter. The dark figure of a man loomed in the doorway, more stunned, most likely, by the sight of Frances's naked ass charging across the sandy parking lot in the moonlight than concerned with a possible burglary. Henry, caught flat-footed, stammered a few lame apologies.

"Pardon, monsieur . . . Ma femme . . . elle a besoin d'une serviette." He handed the man a fifty-dollar bill to cover the damage and trotted off to the scooter.

"Let's get out of here!" said Frances, hurrying him to start the engine, the two of them laughing and excited.

"I have to get the lock off."

"Hurry," she said. "I've never been so embarrassed in my life."

"I doubt that," said Henry, finally starting the engine. They sped down the dirt track to the main road.

"Do you think he was watching us the whole time?"

"Probably," said Henry.

"God," said Frances. "Get us out of here."

"Maybe you should put your pants on before we hit the main road."

When they got to the long section of loose dirt and gravel that curved around the high windward bluff over Baie Embouchure, they were still laughing about the incident. Henry was driving too fast, and he felt Frances digging her knuckles into his ribs so he'd slow down. They sped around the ungraded turn, rear wheel sliding a little, past the sign marked only with an exclamation point. Still drunk from dinner and feeling mischievous, Henry ignored the knuckles in his side and opened up the throttle even more.

They rounded the final bend, high over the crashing waves, a sudden blast of wind hitting them hard, broadside, forcing Henry to veer to the right as he struggled to keep the wheels aligned.

There was a car parked at the crest of the hill, a jeep with its headlights on, the door on the driver's side open. The driver was nowhere in sight.

Two, three muzzle flashes came from the other side of the drop-off, a few yards behind the car. As the reports from the gun were whipped away by the wind, Henry felt the impact of the slug slamming into the scooter's front fender. He only had time to yell, "We're going down!" before he lost his grip on the handlebars and they were on the ground, Henry rolling for the ditch on his right, the terrible, hollow sound of the scooter sliding on gravel in his ears, and more gunshots, distant snapping sounds coming from somewhere in the dark.

Feeling instinctively for the butt of the H & K, he called out to Frances. "You okay?"

But she was already on her feet, running straight at the shooter, her Walther blazing. Henry raised himself onto bloody knees and shot out the jeep's headlights. After the lights went out in a shatter of glass, for a moment the only sounds were the heavy thumping of the waves below and the wind.

There were two more shots, then a loud yelp from somewhere over the rise. Henry raced forward in a crouch to see Frances, walking erect, illuminated now by the light from the fallen scooter. She was walking along the edge, firing her weapon—*Pop, pop, pop*—as if she were spraying cockroaches. He caught up with her as she stepped out of the single beam of light, his hands shaking, and pointed his gun blindly in the same direction as hers. He looked over the edge.

"Oh, man," said the man in the dark summer-weight suit. He was lying on his back, shirt pulled up over his navel, both hands wrapped tightly around a large wet area on his thigh. A Colt 9-millimeter automatic pistol lay useless near the man's head.

"Why do they always pull their shirts up?" said Frances, her voice funny, eyes shining in the moonlight. "You ever notice that?"

"Checking their dicks," said Henry. He'd seen that before. A lot.

"Please," said the man, looking up at Henry, "Don't let her shoot me again."

Henry put the back of his hand against the barrel of Frances's Walther and nudged it aside. "You okay?" he asked her. When she nodded breathlessly, he leaned down, took the man's Colt, and put it in his waistband.

"Fuck tried to kill us," hissed Frances, menacing the man again with her gun.

"Don't," said Henry. "I want to talk with him."

"So, talk," she snarled, firing a single round into the man's kneecap. "You broke my scooter!"

"Owww!" said the man. "Owww! Owww! Owww! That really hurts. That really fuckin' hurts! Stop that!"

Henry reached under the man's arms and dragged him onto the road, the man grunting in pain. The light from the skewed headlight of the scooter, shining crazily out to sea, lit up his features. They were unfamiliar to Henry. He could see that the man had been hit bad. Apart from the knee, just now beginning to well up with blood, he was bleeding heavily from the thigh. It looked as if one of Frances's first shots had clipped the femoral artery. He'd been hit elsewhere too, Henry saw, earlobe shot off, upper chest, and foot. The man's face was already beginning to go white, and Henry supposed that soon he'd go into shock. He untied a helmet from the fallen scooter and propped the man's head on it, then applied a makeshift tourniquet above the thigh wound with the man's tie.

Feeling less generous, Frances kicked the man in the side of the head. "Look at that scooter."

"Chrissakes," the man cried, spitting out a hunk of bloody tooth, "willya get her *offa* me?"

"I'm mad," said Frances.

"I can see that," said the man. "Jeeesus." He squeezed a few tears out of the corners of his eyes, breathing heavily.

"You want to talk to me?" asked Henry.

"I ain't gonna tell you nothin'," said the man. "You gonna take me the hospital or what?"

"Gee . . . I don't know about that," said Henry.

"Then I ain't sayin' *nothin'*," said the man. "You gonna kill me anyways, right?"

"Probably," said Henry.

"At least keep *her* away from me. Awright?" he pleaded.

"What's your name?" Henry asked. "If you don't mind."

"Unnnn," said the man.

"I'll tell you mine. My name is Henry," he said.

"Petey," said the man. "My name is Petey."

"That's a nice name," said Henry. "New York?" It wasn't even a question really; the man's accent was unmistakable.

"Uh-uh," Little Petey grunted.

Frances was calming down a bit. She went to get the scooter, shutting off the motor and righting it on its kickstand. Henry sat down next to the man and crossed his legs. "You don't look too good," he said.

"I fucked up, I guess," said Little Petey.

"You tried," said Henry. "Really. You did the best you could."

"Henry," said Little Petey. "At least I got that right." He shook his head from side to side. "That . . . that must be Frances, right? The wife?"

"Yup," said Henry.

"The wife . . . they . . . they told me . . . somebody said something about that. I should . . . I shoulda listened. You went down, and I was lookin' at you. See what *you* was gonna do." He jerked a wet thumb toward Frances, now standing over him again, wild-eyed, the wind off the sea blowing hair across her face. With surprising robustness, Little Petey reached up and gave Henry a play-ful punch in the shoulder, leaving an imprint of bloody fist on his shirt. "I mean, Henry. What happens, youse two get in a argument? I mean, holy shit. That is one mean bitch."

Henry smiled and offered Little Petey a cigarette, lighting it for him and putting it in his mouth.

"Tell me somethin'," said Little Petey, lowering his voice a little. "Is . . . is she good inna sack? You don't mind me askin'? I'll bet she's un-fuckin'-believable."

"That she is," said Henry, grinning now. He gave a hopeful look back at Frances, relieved to see she was smiling now too.

"That's good," said Little Petey, closing his eyes, pleased with Henry's answer. "That's good. I thought so."

Henry put the muzzle of the H & K under Little Petey's chin and pulled the trigger.

27

It took all night, getting rid of the car, the body. Fortunately, nobody drove by until they got Little Petey down to the water's edge, the two of them carrying him, stumbling at one point on the steep, crumbling incline. Henry and Frances rolled and slid the last few yards, Little Petey's corpse with them.

"Leave him where he is," said Henry. "We'll come back for him in the dinghy after we dump the car." By this point, Little Petey was half in the water, head down, feet sticking out. Henry weighed him down with rocks, pushing the feet under, and marked the spot with a piece of driftwood.

They crawled back up to Little Petey's jeep. Henry collected shell casings and then got behind the wheel. Frances followed him on the scooter to the mangrove swamp behind Friar's Beach. They wiped down the car, put it in neutral, and rolled it into the dark, stagnant, algae-covered water, relieved when it sank completely from view.

They took the scooter back to the hotel and wearily rowed the dinghy out of the pond before starting the engine. The chop outside the protection of the reef was difficult to manage in the inflatable dinghy, but they made it to where they'd stashed the body without incident. Henry lashed Little Petey to a towline while Frances combed the water's edge for objects to weigh him down with.

Little Petey's final resting place was on the far side of Molly Beday, a barren, foam-flecked rock a half mile offshore. Henry cut Little Petey loose a few yards from its jagged face, a necklace of tire rims and broken cinder blocks pulling the corpse straight down through the black inhospitable surf, two hundred feet into a rocky trough.

When Henry and Frances finally limped up the steps to their rooms, the sun was coming up, the sky over the mountains glowing pink and purple with first light. Henry's hands were cut from the high-test monofilament he'd used to truss up the dead gangster. The two of them were covered in road dust, blood, and grease. Frances's jeans were soaked through at the knees, where she'd scraped herself falling from the scooter.

"We should do something about that," said Frances, pointing back down at the scooter. There was a single bullet hole in the front fender.

"Shit." Henry groaned, exhausted. He trudged painfully down the steps again with a roll of hurricane tape. He probed the hole with his finger until a 9-millimeter round popped through the other side. Then he stretched a piece of tape over the hole.

"I'll fix it tomorrow," he said, back in the room. "Right now, I'm just too beat." He helped himself to a long swig of tequila from a bottle by the refrigerator. Frances was already on the bed. She reached up and grabbed hold of his ponytail. When he looked down at her, she was already asleep.

At noon, Henry was wakened by an insistent tapping at the door. It was the housekeeper.

"I'm coming, I'm coming," he groaned through the fog of a miserable hangover and growing discomfort from having slept in his wet, dirty clothes, the H & K digging into the base of his spine.

He opened the door a crack and tried to smile into the blinding sunlight.

"You can let it go today," he said. "We were out late last night."

"You have an accident, Mr. Henry?" asked the housekeeper. "Your moto—"

"Yes," said Henry, accepting a pile of fresh bath towels through the narrow opening. "A little one. *C'est pas grave. Pas de tout.*"

"And madame?" the housekeeper inquired. *"Ça va aussi?"*

"She's fine, fine," said Henry. "Just a little spill. We sleep late today."

"It's very dangerous, Mr. Henry," said the housekeeper, casting a disapproving glance at the damaged scooter. "Very dangerous. You should have an auto."

"Estelle," said Henry. "You might be right. I'm going to give it some serious thought. Thank you."

"Have a nice day," she said, turning to go. "And be careful."

"Who was that?" groaned Frances from under her pillow. She propped herself up on her elbows, knocking the Colt and the Walther onto the floor.

"Estelle," said Henry. "I told her to come back tomorrow."

"Oh, God. Look at the bed," said Frances, peering through an unruly tangle of hair. The sheets were smeared with dried blood, dirt, and motor oil. Henry picked up the Colt and the Walther, removed his own gun from the small of his back, and put them all in a pile on the nightstand. He sat down next to Frances and pushed the hair out of her face.

"My head . . . my knees," said Frances. "I'm hung over. Are you hung over?"

"Yes," said Henry.

"Help me get my pants off."

Henry popped the buttons on her jeans, moved down near her feet, and gave a short tug on the ankles.

"Gently!" she protested. "Shit! They're stuck to my knees."

"We can soak them off."

"I'm not moving."

"What do you want me to do?"

"Fuck it," said Frances. "Just yank them off. Quick, okay? Try and get it over with quick."

"You sure? I'll carry you to the tub if you want."

"I'm not getting out of bed. Just do it, okay . . . I can take it."

Henry got a firm hold on her pants legs. "Count of three?"

"Okay," said Frances, gritting her teeth.

"One . . . two . . . *three!*" He pulled the dirty jeans down hard, as hard as he could, the knees tearing free. Frances did the rest, kicking the jeans off her feet and onto the floor, eyes filling for a brief second.

"At least that's over with," she said, brushing gravel out of a scrape on her elbow. She flopped back onto the bed and pulled the pillow over her face. "Wake me for happy hour," she murmured from under the pillow.

"You want the shirt off?" Henry asked her, but she was again unconscious.

So tired he could barely move himself, he got out of his own disgusting clothes and curled up on the bed, his head by Frances's feet. He was thinking—car, body, shell casings, fingerprints. The idea that Little Petey might have friends, that they might be asking around soon, almost kept him awake. He opened his eyes and thought about that for a few moments. There would be others, of course. He looked out the window, saw the masts of the moored sailboats in the pond, swaying gently back and forth, the motion somehow reassuring. Outside the French doors, the insistent cheeping of sugar thieves in the palms was the only sound. He listened for the hollow, chop of the waves against the reef but heard only Frances, breathing steadily under her pillow. He hugged her ankles and closed his eyes, freezing the moment.

28

Frances, in a pastel green sundress and yellow Bakelite sunglasses, stood outside the gate of the big stone house on the hill and pressed the buzzer. With her hair up and her scabby knees exposed to the air, she looked like a tomboy forced to dress for relatives.

"Frances Denard," she announced. "Here to see Rachel and Mickey."

Woody, on the other side of the gate, whispered into his radio. It took a long time for him to receive an answer through his earpiece. Finally, he swung the heavy iron gates open. The two weimaraners came bounding up and pounced playfully against her chest.

"Hey! Hey! Get down! Down!" Woody commanded in vain.

"That's okay," said Frances, bending over to pet the excited dogs. "Big babies," she cooed. "You're *nice* doggies . . . nice doggies."

Woody stood by impatiently as the guard dogs rolled onto their backs, Frances vigorously scratching their bellies, the dogs' legs pumping air in unison, tongues hanging out. When Frances started up the driveway, the dogs got to their feet and followed, pushing their heads into her hands.

"Nice dogs," said Frances.

.   .   .

Burke came out of the garage, looking worried. Frances showing up at the front gate had been a nasty surprise. He had just that moment sent off yet another fax to Washington, seeking any and all records of a Frances Denard. Now he stood there, unsure of what to do, what was going to happen next. How would she react when she turned her head and saw him standing there? Would she say anything?

He broke into a flopsweat, hating himself for his weakness. He should have just told Woody on the radio, "Forget it. No visitors." But then what would have happened? Would she have gotten pissed, filed a police report on the break-in? Complained to Woody about his boss? The damn woman was blackmailing him without doing a thing. Twisting his nuts. Walking right in here, pretty as you please, the supposedly vicious guard dogs greeting her like a long-lost friend.

Burke stood there waiting, his witness forgotten, more concerned now with what she would say when she saw him. Terrified that her first words would be "Hi, Don! Good to see you again!" That would be enough to incite real interest among the other marshals. The humiliating memory of lying on his belly, Frances holding him at bay with a Bic pen and his own gun, was making him queasy. There was something else, too. Mixed in with the fear and sweat was the tangible memory of that moment when he'd squeezed his hand down between her legs for his wallet and gun, and felt her pussy.

By the time Frances and Woody and the dogs reached him, Burke looked like he was suffering from heat stroke.

"It's okay?" asked Woody, concerned by Burke's appearance.

"It's okay," said Burke, his voice a little too high and strident. He held his breath as Frances's eyes met his. The green pupils drifted right by him, registering nothing. Woody led her out to the pool deck, the dogs yapping at her heels. At first, he felt relief, but almost instantly this was replaced by something else, anger and resentment that she'd said nothing, given him not the slightest sign that they had, after all, shared an intimate moment.

Burke stalked back to his room in the guesthouse, determined to send another fax.

"Frances!" cried Rachel from the diving board. She'd been demonstrating her double gainer for Donnie and Mickey, both sitting at the poolside breakfast table. "Watch this." She leapt feetfirst into the pool, grasping one knee and hitting the water with a big splash, showering Donnie and Mickey.

"Hi," said Mickey, pushing out a chair with his foot.

"Hi," said Frances. Turning to Donnie, she said, loudly enough for Woody and the marshal on the roof to hear, "You must be Mister Pastou. Pleased to meet you. I'm Frances."

"Yeah, right," said Donnie. He leaned forward and kissed Frances's hand, holding it for a long time. "Sit here," he said, patting the empty chair next to him, in preference to the one Mickey had offered.

Woody retreated to the gazebo, signaling Burt on the roof to keep an eye on the new arrival. The dogs lay down to sun themselves on the warm tile deck.

"What happened to your knees?" asked Mickey.

"Oh! They're *terrible!*" said Rachel, dripping from the pool, a towel around her shoulders. "What *happened?*"

"We fell down," said Frances, eyes not leaving Donnie's, a look of great amusement fixed on his face. "Nothing serious. Scooter was a little banged up. It still runs, though."

"You should put something on them. Won't they get infected?" said Rachel, sympathetically. "Bandages or something."

"They dry up quicker this way."

"But, the scars . . ."

"Forget it. I'm fine," said Frances. "Really." She moved her head one way, toward the building, saying, "What a nice house. And the gardens . . . beautiful," but her hand went another. She slid a driver's license with the name and photograph of a Peter Schiavone on it across the table and under the corner of Donnie's newspaper. He palmed it neatly, took a quick peek, and just as discreetly returned it under the table.

"Little Petey," said Donnie.

"Little?" said Frances.

"I know," said Donnie. "There's another one. Bigger. This person. You seen him lately? Round here?"

"He had to cut his vacation short," said Frances, breezily, her face becoming cold and expressionless in a way that made Mickey's blood chill.

Donnie was fighting a grin. Mickey started to say something, but he held up a hand, silencing him.

"We were wondering," said Frances, her expression growing cheerful again, "what firm he's with. He had to leave in a hurry, and we didn't have the time . . . we didn't exchange information. Henry might want to do business . . . with the, uh, parent company."

"I don't get it," said Rachel.

"Shut up," said Mickey. "Please. Sorry."

"Make like we're havin' a nice talk about sports or somethin', okay?" said Donnie. "I'm talkin' here.

"So," said Donnie.

"So," said Frances.

"We got a problem."

"We were kind of wondering how bad a problem it is," said Frances, lighting a cigarette.

"Petey wasn't such a bad guy," said Donnie, sighing. "He was with bad people. That was his problem. Youse already got an idea what people I'm talkin' about, right?"

"Pretty much. I mean, Henry's made an educated guess. Who he was with and all."

"Well," said Donnie. "He'd be right. Funny thing is . . . Petey's not the guy you would think to send. I mean, you wouldn't think a' him first, you hadda have somethin' done."

"He wasn't very good," agreed Frances. "Henry . . . Henry thinks it was kind of a rush order."

Donnie sighed. "Things must really be goin' to hell up there. . ."

"Well," said Frances, "we thought you should know."

"That's really nice a' you," said Donnie, looking genuinely touched. "An' I appreciate it."

"So," said Frances, taking a sniff of air. It smelled of frangipani, jasmine, and wet earth from Donnie's garden. "What are you going to do?" She looked over Donnie's shoulder at a cluster of younger marshals playing grab-ass in the gazebo, weapons unslung.

"Me? I ain't gonna do nothin'. I mean . . . what? I'm gonna tell the fuckin' Osmond brothers over there? Go cryin' to *them*? You think I wanna live in fuckin' San Diego, or Tucson . . . some fuckin' retirement village somewheres? No way, José. I ain't sittin' on some boardwalk in my fuckin' diapers feedin' no pigeons. This my house. They want me, they can come and fuckin' get me."

"That's my attitude," said Frances, smiling. She reached over and took Donnie's hand. "Henry's of two minds on this subject."

"Well," said Donnie, shrugging, "he's got a point. Face it; anything could happen . . . Look at those idiots over there," he said, referring to the marshals. "They gotta have a fuckin' meeting, decide they gonna take a leak . . . You coulda emptied a clip inta me,

they'd still be talkin' about it." He gave Frances's hand a squeeze before reluctantly putting it down. "You should prolly look like we
havin' some fun here, 'fore they get nervous. Take a swim, let
Rachel show you around. I want you to come again."

"You want a drink?" offered Rachel.

"No, thanks anyway," said Frances. She raised both arms above
her head and stretched, yawned, and removed her sunglasses. She
looked at the garden again, admiring the even flagstone paths, the
little Japanese-style carp pond, bocce court, the bamboo, neatly
laid out around a center hillock planted with bonsai trees.

"It's gorgeous here," she said.

"It is, ain't it?" said Donnie. "An' you . . . you look better than I
ever seen you. Marriage is good for you."

"I'm happy."

"Oh . . . one thing," said Donnie, leaning forward, an amused
look on his face. "Little Petey . . . was it Henry . . . or was it you?"

When Frances didn't answer, not even acknowledging the question, he just smiled contentedly and sank back in his chair. "That
musta been a bad surprise for him," he said. "You, I mean."

29

Did you see Burkie this morning?" asked Robbie, finishing a few stretching exercises against a telephone pole. "At the fax machine? He's talking to it now."

"I'm waiting for him to break it," said Woody. "He hits it, you know." They had reached the halfway point of their morning jog: two and a half miles from Donnie's house, on a hilltop in Orléans. Heavy black women in skirts and clean T-shirts trudged past them, crossed the street, and walked up the steps of the Baptist church. A sign in front of the church announced the day's sermon: HARD-SELF BUSINESSPERSON/GOOD CHRISTIAN. YOU CAN BE BOTH. WITH GOD'S HELP!

"I hope he takes early retirement," said Robbie, wiping his face with his terry-cloth sweatband. "The man is toast."

"He's what? Fifty-two, fifty-three?" asked Woody.

"Something like that. Old," said Robbie.

"What's he got going on with Justice is what I want to know," said Woody. "I mean, he asks for files, they send files. He gets all sulky and pissed off. He asks for more files. You ask me, he's losing it big time. Guy was crankin' out memos half the night last night."

"That chick set him off," said Robbie. "That guy Henry's wife. He wasn't getting anything about him; now he's on the wife's case."

"I saw some of the Henry stuff he was getting. Immigration, credit records, chamber of commerce filings. I don't know what he's got such a hard-on for the guy about. He's a fuckin' war hero. Bronze Star, did you know that?"

"Yeah. I knew that."

"Even the CI reports on this guy are good. Some douche bags the DEA got snitching for them down here . . . even they got nothing bad to say about the guy. And those guys have something bad to say about everybody. They didn't even bother to make anything up!"

"I know."

"Do you know about the Henry and Frances Denard Animal Rescue Center?"

"No."

"It's a little storefront over in French Quarter. They take care of cute little fuzzy animals. Mister Potential Organized Crime Associate put up all the money."

"The wife's good with animals. You see her with the dogs?"

"Yeah, I saw that."

"She oughta make dog food commercials. Like that guy—whatsisname—the one from *Bonanza*?"

"Lorne Greene. He died."

"Yeah?"

"Yeah."

"What about the other one—Little Joe?"

"He's dead too."

"Wow."

"The fat one, Hoss? He's dead too."

"Dude! That Ponderosa was some kind of dangerous place!"

"Yeah, the only one still alive is that Trapper John guy. He musta got out just in time."

"Maybe it was the MSG."

"What?"

"That Chinese cook they had. MSG."

"Stuff gives me a headache. Right here. You can feel it. I always tell them leave it out. But you know they still put it in."

Robbie peeled off his shirt. "Ready to head back?"

"Just a sec."

"Gettin' tan, man. I'm gonna look buff, time I get back home."

"See what Burkie's looking like these days?"

"The gut? Yeah . . . old school, man. You could get away with looking like that, the old days. He's eating the kid's food."

"Mickey's?"

"Shit'll kill you. I'd like to see what that kid's arteries are gonna look like a couple of years."

"Burkie doesn't like that they're friends. The kids and that Henry guy . . . his wife. The Denards."

"You know what I say? So what? I don't see what he's got such a bug up his ass for. I mean, she comes over. He doesn't want her on the premises, okay—so tell her to buzz off. No visitors. Mister Pastou and guests unavailable for medical reasons. Let the kids have fun on their own time."

"He's such a wuss. He wussed out, now he's like feeling bad about it."

"He got some old arrest records on the wife. That's what he was doing today. Old shit, her NYPD jacket from the seventies. The seventies! Misdemeanor shit. Soliciting, pandering, possession controlled substance . . . prosti shit."

"No lie!"

"No lie. I think the guy's fixated."

"He's fixated on his own dick, you ask me. I mean, who cares?"

"That's what I said. I mean, who cares? So she took dope in the seventies. You should see some of the pictures of my parents back then. And the other stuff . . . What? She was a ho'. What? Is she gonna storm the house? Fuck everybody to death? Get real. Get a life. That's what he should do."

Robbie took a few deep breaths and started back down the hill. "Come on," he called back. "I want to get back for a swim before Donnie wakes up. He's always needling me . . . It distracts me."

30

It was raining again when the man from Justice they called the Big Kahuna arrived. Burke watched his cab pull up from the gazebo, where he was drafting yet another request for information concerning the former Frances Brading of Amherst, Massachusetts.

The Big Kahuna, a Hawaiian with a mean disposition, saw Burke in the gazebo and came straight for him. He held only a briefcase. Burke was not looking forward to their meeting.

"What the fuck, *exactly,* did you mean with *this*?" he said, starting right in, Burke's cable already in his hand.

"It's a reasonable request for information," said Burke, trying not to show fear or anger. "I need some files. I need information."

"Reasonable request? Reasonable request!" shrieked the Big Kahuna, his voice higher than one would expect from such a large man. "Do you have any *idea* what happens, a rocket like this lands on a desk in Washington? A . . . A fucking ICBM makes less noise! I spent yesterday, the day before, the whole fucking *weekend* running my ass off doing damage control 'cause of this fucking cable, mister! I hadda call State, I had to call those stuck-up *pricks* across the river. I had to get down on my fucking knees and apologize to *them*!"

"But, all I did—"

" 'He's overworked,' I said. 'He's under a lot of pressure . . . very important case.' All fucking *weekend* I'm bowing and scraping to a bunch of pipe-smoking *fucks* who I wouldn't let look after my fucking houseplants much less a witness. I had to call the AG's office and sell my firstborn male fucking child, just to get a statement, for the most meager, pathetic amount of cover on this . . . this *abortion*." He paused to get a breath. "You out and out accused the CIA and Pentagon, on paper, in *clear* no less, of covering up! You think you're talking to an *idiot*? You suggested lack of cooperation, lack of *honesty* with the other branches. Do you have any idea how many people *saw* that memo? I'll be shocked if it's not in the fucking *Post* when I get back to town. You got a lot of people back there hopping fucking mad about this. People are scrambling around, pointing fingers with one hand and covering their assholes with the other. Well, it's over now."

The Big Kahuna sat his considerable bulk down on the thin bench in the tiny gazebo, looking like a sumo wrestler at a child's tea party. "You are off this detail as of now. Get your things together, 'cause you'll be coming back with me."

"They *are* covering something," said Burke. "This Denard. No way you're gonna tell me this guy's straight. He fucking reeks of spook! I know it and you know it! He's . . . he's dirty, goddamn it! He's dirty and his wife's dirty, and the two of them, they're all over my witness like a school of lampreys!"

"Of course they're covering something," said the Big Kahuna, using a singsong, condescending tone, "of course they're covering something, genius." He was hissing now. "They called. They laid out the facts for the AG. Some mogul out at Langley made the trip over to have a nice talk with him. The AG calls the USA. The USA calls me. You know what he says? Can you guess? He says, '*Shut this line of inquiry down now.*'

"This Denard . . . this Denard you're so hot and bothered about . . . did it ever *occur* to you that maybe you're right? That *maybe,* just *maybe* a person like this comes in contact with some interesting people, with other persons . . . persons of interest. Nobody said anything to me exactly. They didn't *have* to. But, speculating for a moment, is it *possible* that he belongs to somebody? For fuck's sake, you've seen the guy's service records. He makes GI Joe look like a fag! The guy has a rabbi over there at the Fool Factory. At the Pentagon . . . at the Pentagon they want to deny even hearing about him. They *don't* want some fucking sad-sack marshal sticking his nose in, then blabbing the guy's name across every desk in Washington. Can you see that?

"You got a lot of people worried. A lot of people pissed off. Your own career, well, that's in the shitter . . . and for *what?* The guy's on the board of People for the Ethical Treatment of Animals! He's a war hero! He's a goddamn Rotarian, for chrissakes! He could run for office. Shit! I'd vote for him!"

"He's dirty," pronounced Burke, sticking to his guns. "He knows our witness. He pretends he doesn't, but he does. The wife too."

"You've seen your last file on the Denards," said the Big Kahuna. "I can promise you. You're out. They're sending another guy down to replace you tomorrow. And you better change your attitude on the way back, because you are in serious jeopardy of becoming everybody's least favorite person of the fucking *year.* I'd forget about all of this shit or you'll be chasing bail jumpers in Dakota somewhere. You want that? Now hurry up and pack. The flight leaves in an hour and a half. The movie's *Harry and the Hendersons—* you'll love it."

31

It was the sound of Trung, snapping to attention, heels actually clicking together, that alerted Monsieur Ribiere to his old mentor's presence. The old man was suddenly, just, there—an apparition in the doorway of Le Jardin Indochine.

"*Mon Colonel,*" blurted Trung.

"*Dai Uy,*" murmured the old man, addressing Trung by his old ARVN rank of captain and returning the salute with the barest approximation of a bow. Trung beamed at the acknowledgment.

The old man was in his eighties now, Monsieur Ribiere guessed. Innumerable bouts of malaria, liver fluke, dengue fever, and God knew what other tropical afflictions had left his leathery, wrinkled skin a permanently jaundiced yellow. His skull seemed too large for his frail body, the discolored flesh stretched across the prominent forehead like an African drum.

He had retired, they said, from the service years ago, during one of the bad times at La Piscine, when the old Gaullists were being purged. Even the old man's long, and chillingly effective, service to a succession of presidents became, in the end, an embarrassment to

the incoming Socialists, a reminder of something nasty and un-
clean.

To his peers, of course, he remained a legend. Even now, in
every intelligence service in the world, people told stories of his
exploits. In the emerging nations of Africa and Asia, if a prime
minister choked to death on a fish bone, there were people who
would still talk, who would wink knowingly and mention the
old man's name. Long after he had ceased to operate, electoral
upsets, plane crashes, coups, assassinations, and every sort of political anomaly were attributed to the man's Mephistophelian in-
fluence.

He limped. He'd limped when he came out of the camps after
Dien Bien Phu, and his withered legs never improved. He wore a
shabby gray linen jacket that might once have been white, the
rosette of the Resistance pinned to his lapel. He smoked hand-
rolled cigarettes, was smoking one now; it dangled from the corner
of his mouth, the smoke curling around his eyes. Monsieur Ribiere
stood up to greet him, wondering what possible reason he could
have for being here.

As he extended his hand, Monsieur Ribiere knocked over a bottle of *nuoc mam*. Trung's young cousin, the busboy, made a move
to come pick it up, but a sharp gesture from Trung stopped him in
his tracks. He disappeared into the kitchen.

"I know what you're thinking," said the old man, sitting down
with difficulty. "And you're right."

"I thought you'd retired, Chef," said Monsieur Ribiere.

"I have. I have. Of course I have, old friend," said the old man.
"That is why they chose me to come. When you want to piss on
an ally, it is better to do it from a distance."

"This is official?"

"Don't be absurd," said the old man, primly laying a napkin

across the spilled fish sauce. "Oh . . . that smell . . . It still . . ." He paused to look around the empty dining room, doing so without moving his head. "I am here to pass along only a flavor, a sentiment, a new feeling in some quarters of which . . . of which I have become aware. A change in attitude, if you will."

"Can I order you some food?" asked Monsieur Ribiere, alarmed by how the old man looked, nearly mummified, how he'd shrunk.

"No, no. I don't have long. Listen. The Americans"—he sighed, crushing the ash of his cigarette between two fingers—"yesterday, we love them. Today . . . today we love them a little less." He paused to reach a bony hand across the table to Monsieur Ribiere's plate and snatch a rice ball with his nailless fingers. The Gestapo had taken those in '44, Ribiere remembered. The old man chewed slowly, swallowing before he continued. "This ridiculous affair with the American witness—"

"Yes?" blurted Monsieur Ribiere, without thinking.

"Certain . . . certain exalted personages," began the old man, with obvious distaste, "I am led to believe . . . that these guardians of the republic . . . would not be terribly unhappy, not unhappy at all, in fact, if the Americans were to suffer an embarrassing occurrence . . . on French soil."

He reached over again, snatching a spring roll from Monsieur Ribiere's plate this time.

"What am I . . . what is expected of me?" said Monsieur Ribiere, realizing that he was sitting bolt upright in his chair like an undergraduate. "Am I to do something?"

"Oh, no," said the old man, chewing. "Do nothing. Do nothing at all." He licked his fingers, wiped them on the tablecloth, and then handed Monsieur Ribiere a grainy surveillance photograph. Monsieur Ribiere recognized the photo as one of Trung's, taken at Juliana Airport. It depicted one Kevin Aloysius Coonan and a Peter Schiavone, walking across the parking lot. Ribiere was startled and impressed that they had gone so far as to give the old man access to such current intelligence. His mind reeled with the implications.

"These two gentlemen, for instance," said the old man. "It is felt back home that they look like fine, upstanding fellows . . . of no interest to anyone. Wouldn't you agree?"

Monsieur Ribiere felt a roiling in his stomach. He sat mute, waiting for the rest.

"You see how it is, yes?" said the old man. "You are to do nothing. Say nothing. Let the Americans make their own mess. If, as it appears, disaster is inevitable, they will need no help to cover themselves in the shit."

"And then?"

"Ah!" said the old man, smiling, the sight of his yellow, tobacco- and betel-nut-stained dentures distinctly unappetizing. "Well, as good friends and valued allies, we will be right there to help them wipe it off. What else are friends for?"

"You sure you won't have some lunch?" said Monsieur Ribiere as the old man plucked another rice ball off his plate. "The chef . . . I believe you know . . ."

"Yes . . . Trung's brother-in-law is it? Uncle? Another naughty boy . . . No. I must return immediately. I will continue my retirement. This . . . this was just a favor to a friend." He stood up and shook hands before limping to the door. "Go well, my friend," he said, his back to Ribiere. As he passed Trung at the door, already frozen in full parade-ground salute, he gave a limp wag of the wrist. Then he was gone.

.   .   .

Monsieur Ribiere sat silently at his table for a long time, turning things over in his mind. Trung kept looking at him expectantly, like a dog with a full bladder. For Trung, seeing the old man was like hearing the familiar jingle of keys, watching the leash come out, and he fully expected to be let out to play.

He would be disappointed. After reflecting long and hard, Monsieur Ribiere curtly dismissed him for the day. When Trung was long gone, Ribiere left through the back and walked slowly down the beach, looking occasionally over his shoulder, once stopping and kneeling, as if to tie his shoe. Near the end of the beach, he turned and hurried up an alley, doubled back toward the restaurant, turned onto a side street, and, joining a crowd of tourists, moved along with them until he came to the post office.

The third pay phone from the end was unoccupied, and Monsieur Ribiere stepped inside and dialed a number.

"Yes?" said the voice on the other end, in English.

"Pardon," said Monsieur Ribiere. *"Je suis en erreur."* Then he hung up, opened the phone book under the metal shelf, and on page 373, next to a name chosen seemingly at random, he drew a tiny clock face.

This time the man came dressed as an American tourist. They called it "natural cover."

When he found him on the beach out front of La Samanna, sweating over a John Grisham paperback in a beach chair, there was a zaftig, fortyish woman in a one-piece bathing suit on the blanket next to him and he wondered if she was the man's wife. Her hair was unnaturally blond, and like the man, she looked as if she drank too much. The man saw Monsieur Ribiere and strolled casually down to the water's edge, belly hanging over his cotton shorts, to meet him.

"Is that your wife?" Monsieur Ribiere asked.

"Good God, no," said the man. "You think my wife's going to hop on a plane, middle of the night, two hours' notice, and jet off to some island? Vick's a sport, but not *that* sporting. No . . . that's Heather, my secretary. To her, this sort of thing is appealing. Fake passport, meeting a source, palm trees, the whole bit. She's in heaven. She jumped at the chance, playing spy for a day. Reads too many spy novels, you ask me. They all do up there, if you want to know. Anyway"—the man glanced at his watch—"so what is it? You never used the emergency number before. I'm all atwitter."

"New orders," said Monsieur Ribiere, unhappily. He disliked betraying the old man's trust. "Through a very unusual, very unofficial channel."

"Yeah. I heard you had a distinguished visitor."

"You heard?" said Monsieur Ribiere, amazed.

"Oh, yeah," said the man, reaching down to skip a flat stone across the water. "You kidding me? That guy gets on a plane, there's people want to know. Back at the shop, they figured he came down 'cause one of your people is gonna get the chop. That's what he's known for, isn't it?"

"No, no . . . nothing like that. He's retired."

"Yeah, right," said the man. "There's sort of a betting pool going, you know, who's it gonna be? I'd hoped, frankly, meeting you, I might hear something, give me a little edge. They're so impressed, I can't tell you how impressed back home, if you know something like that's going to happen before it happens. Ah well . . . So what is it?"

Feeling silly in his bathing suit, Monsieur Ribiere waded a little farther into the water. "There appears to have been a change of heart, at the Palace. About the marshals . . . the witness . . . about helping."

"So?" said the man, irritably. "So what?"

"Well, we think something is going to happen. Soon. Already there are people here. There's a potential for violence . . . for exposure."

"For who?" said the man. "For us? Let me get this straight. You're saying somebody's gonna take a shot at that ginzo they got holed up here, right?"

"I thought it would create some problems."

"For Justice maybe. For the Marshals Service. Who gives a shit? That's what I say."

"My orders—" Monsieur Ribiere paused to rephrase. "The suggestion, you understand, is that I do nothing to prevent it."

The man laughed, surprising Monsieur Ribiere. "That's all? That's what this is all about?"

"We have current information that something . . . that an incident is imminent."

"You want to know what all this crap is about? I'll tell you. Paris is having a fit of pique over this Mustafa whatsisname they just let run back to his buddies in Lebanon. Our president, in his infinite wisdom, was rather blunt in his disapproval. What did he call it? . . . 'The cavalier attitude towards international terrorism.' . . . He must have offended . . . Personally, I thought his comments to the press unwise. *We* all assumed, of course, that your bunch had managed to turn the nice Mister Mustafa around during his stay with you. The president, God bless him, doesn't think the way we do. Immediate expression of righteous indignation was the course decided on. That always plays better on the six o'clocks."

"There are some hurt feelings, then."

"Apparently."

"So. Will you pass this on?"

"I don't think so," said the man, wiping his face with his hand, his nose already glowing pink from the sun. "No . . . I don't think so. One of those apes from the Marshals Service has been circulating some very unkind memos around town. Accusing us of all sorts of nefarious doings . . . No, they trip over their knuckles down here, nobody will be too unhappy about it where I work. We'll be able to say 'I told you so' in fact. Operating outside the country and all. We love it when we can say that. I can't see any exposure, can you?"

"My friend . . ."

"This Denard fellow? Don't bother about that at all. As a subject of official curiosity, he's done, permanently. Not to worry."

"How?"

The man chuckled, pleased with his own ingenuity. "Actually, I just implied that he was one of ours. Keeping an eye on the froggies for the greater good. Worked out great, too. Anytime we run somebody against an ally, it makes people very, very nervous. Everybody is suddenly in a hurry to not know about it. Course it helps that the NSC is pissed off at you guys. Best of everything. They're delighted about something they don't want to know anything about. Perfect."

Monsieur Ribiere squinted into the reflected glare. "So, I do as they ask. Nothing."

"Yep. I've got to agree with the old goat. I mean, what happens there's a big blowup? A few red faces at Justice? Just serves in the end to point up the value of good liaison. When nobody's talking to each other, a good, solid back channel, the value goes way up. Our respective employers will find new reasons to cherish us all the more."

Ribiere didn't respond.

"Marvelous hotel," said the man, referring to the elegant spread of white stucco bungalows and royal palms behind them. "I'd love to have you up for a drink by the pool, but . . ."

"No, no, that's alright. I've stayed too long already. I'm sorry, sorry if I got you down here for nothing."

"Not at all. It's lovely here," said the man. "And between you and me"—he winked lewdly, indicating the somewhat dumpy woman on his blanket—"that old girl there can suck a casaba melon through a garden hose."

32

The four of them had gone drinking the night before—a prolonged bar crawl from one side of the island to the other, winding up at Henry and Frances's hotel, where they did tequila shots in the empty bar and went skinny-dipping in the rain in the teardrop-shaped pool. Mickey's last memory was of throwing up into a hibiscus bush before Henry, Frances, and Rachel loaded him into the rear end of his pickup and drove him back to Donnie's house.

"I want to die," he muttered now, sweating alcohol in the early afternoon sun. "I can't believe you do this all the time."

"Have a beer," said Frances from the chaise lounge next to him, stubbing out a cigarette in a half-eaten croissant. "You'll feel better."

They'd gone for what Henry and Frances called the hangover cure at the Grand Case Beach Club: rented chaises, Bloody Marys, and fat joints of Henry's hydroponic weed on a beach crowded with young Frenchmen. French waitresses brought them food and drinks and adjusted their beach umbrellas to keep their heads in the shade. Frances even arranged for massages, administered under a tamarind tree near the bar by a breasty Afrikaner who hummed along with French pop songs from a portable radio while she worked.

Henry tucked into a plate of stuffed crab backs with both hands, looking completely unbothered by the vast amounts of liquor Mickey had seen him consume the night before. It was twelve-fifteen in the afternoon, and he was already, by Mickey's count, into his fourth beer—this *after* a Bloody Mary and two joints. Frances, too, looked no worse for wear. She was on her third beer after a hearty breakfast, and unlike Rachel, who was collapsed into her chaise, a wet towel over her forehead, she was fairly animated, petting a scraggly-looking dog with a limp who'd wandered down the beach and had seemed to recognize her and speculating on the private lives of the swimmers.

"Who's the fat guy with the girl from La Ronda?" she wondered out loud, noticing a balding, barrel-chested American embracing a thick, dark-skinned woman in the shallow water.

"The john?" asked Henry, sitting up in his chair. "I haven't seen him around. Doesn't look like a tourist—he's too tan."

"She's a prostitute?" asked Rachel, lifting a corner of wet towel so she could see. When she saw Violetta's slightly hunched laborer's body, held tenderly afloat in Kevin's longshoreman arms, she looked disappointed, having expected, no doubt, a more exotic figure.

"You know that big clapboard place by the dirt road on the way to Philipsburg?" said Frances.

"Yeah."

"That's La Ronda," said Frances. "It's a whorehouse. Not a bad place, actually. They've got a pool table, and they play good merengue. We used to go there a lot. The yachties used to go slumming there until the pool table warped. We'll take you sometime."

"That's okay," muttered Mickey.

"The guy with the big arms is a customer?" asked Rachel, becoming interested.

"That would be my guess," offered Henry.

"Ewwww," said Rachel, making a face. "I don't care *how* much you paid me . . ."

"He's not that bad," interjected Frances. "At least he's nice. He took her to the beach. Look. He really seems to like her."

Violetta was out of the water now, Kevin running ahead for her towel. When she sat down on the blanket, he dried her back and kissed her shoulders, and when she turned and dried his hair like a child at bathtime, he closed his eyes and grinned with pleasure.

"See the marks on her calves and ankles?" said Henry.

"Yeah?" said Rachel.

"Cane cutter. You get those marks cutting sugarcane in the fields. From a machete. That's a woman who's done some hard, hard work in her life."

"I guess next to that what she's doing now isn't so bad," said Rachel hopefully.

"Look at the big galoot with her," said Frances. "He's in love."

Kevin lay down next to Violetta, wrapped his Popeye arms around her waist, and went to sleep.

"Men are such babies," said Rachel. "They all want their mommies."

"You got that right," said Frances, expressionless behind her dark glasses. "And regular blow jobs."

33

There must be a million a' these fuckin' things in here!" complained Richie Tic. He tore another fragrance strip out of the new *Vanity Fair* and placed it neatly on the growing stack in front of Jimmy.

Jimmy took a cautious sniff, wrinkled his nose, and crumpled the cardboard strip into a little ball before tossing it into a trash can in the corner of the small, wood-paneled trailer office.

"Try this one," suggested Richie, yanking loose another one.

"This is nice," said Jimmy, taking an appreciative whiff. He licked the strip and wiped the cardboard surface on both sides of his jowly neck. "I like it. What's that one called?"

"Compulsion," answered Richie, already examining the photo layout next to another strip. "What about this? What's 'is cowboy shit? Smells like my fuckin' car? What's 'at, leather?"

"Yeah, yeah," said Jimmy, dismissively. "You wanna smell like you a cowboy from fuckin' Queens you wear that. Lookit the pitcher there—that little prick with the suntan. He don't look like nothin' you wanna smell like. Nice fuckin' hat." He laughed. "Can you see that guy walkin' around, that hat on his head in this neighborhood? Guys would be pissin' all over themselves laughin'."

"I'm a Rhinestone Jewboy," sang Richie, snorting with laughter.

The phone rang, three times. Jimmy looked over at Paulie Brown, who was deeply engrossed in a *Cosmo* sex quotient test on the leatherette couch.

"Hey, fuckwad. Get the phone," Jimmy commanded.

Paulie heaved himself up and got the phone. After a few impassive grunts, he put the receiver down and gave Jimmy the bad news.

"That was the fellow from the casino down there. You know, Jerry's guy?" he said.

"So? Whadduz he say?"

"He says he ain't seen Little Petey for three days. He says he ain't been in his room and his car's gone. He says he's worried and he wants to know what he should do."

Jimmy's thick eyebrows knitted together, and he began tapping his hairy fingers on the desk. The dark, double-breasted suit he was wearing started to shake, and out of his mouth came a sound that began as a low growl and quickly developed into a piercing, high-pitched wail, continuing without break as he first tore the heart out of *Vanity Fair,* then cleared his desk of everything on it with a sweep of his arm. He punched his desk lamp, sending it bouncing off the wall into Paulie's head. Then Jimmy, his head snapping this way and that, like a hyperactive tortoise, settled on a small end table covered with magazines as his next target. He kicked it across the room, knocking over a floor lamp and showering both Richie and Paulie with broken glass from a framed picture of Ava Gardner on the wall. Paulie brushed the bits of glass off his shoulders like he was ridding himself of some dandruff, a thin trickle of blood com-

ing down from a tiny cut on his forehead. He stood there, frozen
and expressionless, waiting for Jimmy's tantrum to end.

"SonofaBITCH!" screamed Jimmy, getting his second wind.
"MotherFUCKING SONofaBITCH!" He slammed his fists into
the desktop, put his foot into a metal filing cabinet, denting it
badly, then looked around the room for something else to hit.
There was nothing. The trailer rocked on its cinder-block supports
as Jimmy paced back and forth, the sounds coming from between
his clenched teeth resembling nothing human. Richie had managed to work himself down in his chair, a copy of Italian *Vogue*
held tentlike over his head.

When Jimmy finally sat down, Richie tried to mollify him with
a hopeful scenario.

"Maybe . . . maybe the guy's just gone native a few days," he
suggested. "You know, shacked up with some hooer . . . or maybe
he done it and he hadda like lay low for a while. That could happen."

"He's gone," said Jimmy, eyes wet and black. "He's fuckin' gone.
You can't see that? You can't see that, you can't see nothin'." He
pondered things for a minute, Paulie and Richie waiting expectantly.

"You. You're goin' down there," he said, looking at Paulie.

"But, you said—" Paulie started.

"Fuck what I said. You goin' down there. Tomorrow."

"My wife—"

"FUCK your wife!" screamed Jimmy, his face turning the color
of rare liver. "Get down there and straighten out that fuckin' Irishman. Find out what HIS fuckin' problem is . . . I can't . . . I can't
get nothin' done . . . It's un-fuckin' believable." He reflected for
another moment. "See that he gets that other thing done first. And
fast. *Then.* Then see that that hippie fuck who stiffed me for my
money gets done too. If he can't get it done, then you do it! I'm

sick a' the whole fuckin' lotta youse. I had enough a' this shit. This fuckin' mick down there takin' a fuckin' vacation or somethin'. I want some fuckin' action. Soon as that rat gets done . . . you see that the other one goes. I had enough."

"I bringin' somebody along or what?" asked Paulie.

"What? Who you gonna bring? You gonna bring Benny, Teddy, D.P.? Who? They all been called up the gran' jury. They gonna go buyin' airplane tickets NOW? What's the matter with you? You fuckin' retarded? I think you fuckin' retarded . . . 'My wife, my wife.' You better get yer fuckin' head screwed on straight, Paulie, or I gonna take it off an' shit in it."

"I got a subpoena too," said Paulie. "I got the same problem."

"That's right. You got the same problem. Same problem as me. Benny, Teddy, they don't fuckin' work for me. You do. It's your ass hangin' out there too, scumbag. So fuckin' do somethin' about it an' stop bawlin' about your fuckin' wife for a fuckin' change. Pussy-whipped . . ."

"I could go. I don't mind," said Richie.

Jimmy gave him a fierce look and raised a hand as if to slap him. Richie cowered almost imperceptibly. "You listening to me? D'you hear what I just said? I said HE'S going. Him. You, I need around here." To Paulie, he said, "Get goin'. I'm sick a' fuckin' lookin' at you."

When Paulie had gone, Richie began picking up the mess, crawling on hands and knees under the desk to get the magazines and fragrance strips scattered by Jimmy's outburst.

Jimmy, beginning to relax behind the desk, loosened his tie and said, "Hey, cupcakes—while you down there . . ."

34

The sound of deep water chopping against the hull, the squeaking of the lines as Henry let out the mainsheet a bit more, the snapping of sails as they filled with wind, winch cranking; these would have been happy sounds under other circumstances, but this was business. Henry scrutinized the waters around Isle Forchue from the mizzen deck of the seventy-three-foot Irwin, looking for other boats. Directly off the bowline, the island stood, barren looking and curiously uninviting, the choppy seas white around its rocky shoreline.

There were, mercifully, no other boats in Isle Forchue's one protected harbor. Henry dropped anchor and took the Irwin's powerful dinghy ashore, beaching her under some sea grape trees.

The hike to the heavy-weapons cache took around twenty minutes. Henry had no difficulty finding the spot. He took a shovel to the loose sand and soil and quickly unearthed the crate. Getting the plastic waterproofing off was a bit harder, but a while later the whole parcel had been undone. Henry unzipped his dive bag and began loading.

The Ithaca 12-gauge shotgun went in the bag first, along with eight boxes of number-four combat loads. A Car-15 and silencer went in next, for Frances. Fourteen clips of 5.56 ammunition. Seemed like a lot, but you never knew . . . Finally the Armalite. That was for Henry. He took out a darning needle and monofilament and, sitting cross-legged on the ground, carefully sewed up the waterproof wrapping before returning the remaining cache of weapons to the crate. He shoveled dirt back into the hole and raked some brush and scrub over the freshly turned soil.

Satisfied that the ground looked once more undisturbed, Henry hoisted the dive bag over his shoulder and headed back to the sailboat. People were going to die, and he hoped, he intended, that he and Frances would not be among them. If something bad was going to happen, it would not be for lack of firepower. Prior preparation prevents—he kept repeating it over and over, like a mantra, under his breath—piss-poor performance.

He changed over to Country Joe and the Fish, God only knew why; he'd hated that song then, hated it now—"One two three . . . what are we fighting for?" and found himself laughing out loud. There was a sudden noise from behind, and Henry fell onto his belly, his free hand reaching for the H & K at his waist.

It was a goat, hooves kicking at the rocky surface of the hill as it scrambled for distance from the horrible sound of Henry's singing voice. He was frightening the goats.

He lit a joint to calm down, his heart still racing from his close encounter with the goat. He sang all the way back to the dinghy, the sound of his own voice comforting on the lonely island.

With Henry gone for the day to get the guns, and not due back till eight or nine, Frances had invited Mickey and Rachel to dinner at La Case d'Or in Marigot. Even the perpetually misanthropic Mickey was excited at the prospect, for it was considered the best

restaurant on the island. The chef, formerly of a three-star place in
New York, was said to have had a nervous breakdown and so
moved to the less stressful environment of Saint Martin.

Frances picked them up in a hired car with driver, Rachel
squeezing excitedly between her and Mickey in the backseat, the
smell of French perfume and new clothing filling her nose and
making her nearly delirious with pleasure. They smoked a joint on
the way over to Marigot, the driver playing zouk on his cassette,
and watched the setting sun through tinted glass windows.

"Madame Denard!" crowed the proprietor of La Case d'Or. She
was an elegantly dressed matron of sixty or so, expertly made up,
her hair in a shimmering twist, a single strand of pearls around her
ample neck. She proffered both cheeks to Frances in pantomime,
then gave in and administered a warm, full-body embrace, and
kisses that left bright red lipstick. She dabbed the lipstick off herself, fussing busily over Frances and her guests, apologizing for the
damage, and signaling waiters and busboys all at the same time.

". . . *Et Monsieur Henri. Où est-il ce soir?*" she inquired.

Frances smiled warmly, and for Mickey and Rachel's benefit, responded in English. "Business, Madame Bigard . . . He regrets . . .
perhaps he'll join us later."

Madame Bigard led them past a gurgling, Florentine-style fountain, through an ivy-filled courtyard into the outer room of a re-
stored plantation house. The floors were wide, teakwood beams
stretched overhead, and in between huge floral arrangements, the
naked brick walls boasted impressionistic studies of local flora and
fauna. From the next room, Mickey could hear the clatter and
clink of diners, the intimidating murmur of people speaking
French, and, from somewhere, chamber music. As Madame Bigard
charged forward with her phalanx of hostess, front waiter, wine
steward, busboys, appearing from all sides, Mickey hesitated for a

moment, nervously reaching up once more to touch his hair. Rachel, next to him, dug her fingernails into his arm, holding on for dear life.

Frances, without even looking, slid her arm around Mickey's and placed her other hand on his, scarlet fingernails patting the back of his hand reassuringly as she whispered into his ear. "Relax. You're with the two best-looking women in this place." She gave him a nudge, and they stepped into the dining room.

It was true, Mickey realized in a moment of complete happiness. Madame Bigard led them across the peach-hued dining room, in between tables filled with envious-looking little Frenchmen and their wives and mistresses. He was having dinner with two smashingly beautiful women. Compared with Rachel, in her tiny black minidress, and Frances, her backless, dark green Chanel exposing a long expanse of tanned flesh, her hair up, two sizable emerald stud earrings flashing as she moved her head, green eyes looking greener than ever, the other women in the room looked like over-dressed crones.

Their table was right on the water. Underwater lights illuminated the coral below, and dark shapes of fish scooted about, breaking the surface with sudden splashes.

"Martinis okay?" inquired Frances. "No use pretending. Let's show the flag straight off."

Helpless to resist, Mickey and Rachel just grinned and nodded. Mickey, not a martini drinker, was swept along by the mental picture of himself and these two good-looking women, sipping martinis from chilled stem glasses. Who cared if he hated gin; James Bond drank martinis, and that was just who he felt like now. Time slipped by as if in a dream, and soon they were all having seconds, then thirds, Mickey growing more and more relaxed, now smelling food and thoroughly enjoying himself. He found his eyes returning repeatedly to the low cut of Frances's dress, fascinated by the way her chest rose and fell with her breathing. He gazed longingly at the junction where her neck met the emerald earrings, studied her lips as she ordered wine. He was watching the lips move, not listening, fascinated by the way Frances's expression changed from moment to moment; one second coquettish, another, deadly serious, moving from laughter to mimicry to seduction in the blink of an eye.

Rachel, though just as delighted with the surroundings, was not oblivious to Mickey's sudden interest in Frances. When she spoke to him for the third time and received no reply, Rachel reached under the table and tightened her hand around Mickey's nuts. Just short of causing him to yelp, she released him.

He looked at her, expecting a reproach. But something strange and marvelous happened: To his astonishment, she laughed, Frances joining in, the two of them watching Mickey's ears redden with increasing delight.

"What am I going to do with him?" Rachel was saying. "He has such a crush on you. It's disgusting." Her speech affected by the martinis, she said to Frances, "Look at him."

Completely unflustered, Frances extended a hand, leaning across Rachel, and ran those fingernails gently, gently down the side of Mickey's face, the two of them watching his reaction, clearly enjoying his torment.

"It's sooooo obvious," said Rachel.

"I'm flattered, if it's true," said Frances, somewhat charitably, Mickey thought.

"It's true," said Rachel, sighing.

Really feeling the martinis now, Mickey just shook his head and smiled weakly. He was having too good a time to say anything. What could he say, anyway? Rachel didn't seem pissed off, everybody was having fun, the whole dreamlike quality of the evening made even the embarrassment pleasurable. He wanted it never to end.

The smell of French cigarettes, the perfume, caramelized shallots from the next table, the barest hint of fennel and saffron wafting out of the distant kitchen, the gigantic tulips everywhere, and these two fantastic-looking women—he felt narcotized with joy.

By entrée time, well into a second—or was it a third—bottle of wine, Mickey was afraid that any second he would throw caution to the winds and make a blunt and probably unrealistic sexual overture to both women. The thought of the three of them, a sweaty tangle of limbs, in his big, round bed was lurking dangerously close to vocalization. He shook his head, trying to banish the thought.

"Talking to yourself?" said Rachel.

"Just thinking," he answered.

"He's been so quiet," said Frances, her mouth full. "Do you think we damaged him?"

"He's not broken," said Rachel, kicking him playfully under the table with her high heel. "Yet . . ."

"At least he's eating. That's always a good sign," said Frances, mopping up sauce with a hunk of bread.

"This is great," pronounced Mickey. "This is really great." It was all he could think of to say. In his mind, he was making love to both of them, imagining an orgasm so enormous that the top of his skull would lift off like a Sputnik and bounce off the ceiling.

"He looks happy," said Rachel.

"He's smiling," said Frances.

For dessert they all had harlequin soufflés. Mickey was drizzling Grand Marnier sauce onto his plate from a silver sauceboat when he heard Madame Bigard laughing flirtatiously at the dining room entrance.

There was Henry, striding across the dining room, his arm around Madame Bigard's thick waist, lasciviously nuzzling her neck the whole way. She was shrieking with obvious delight, to the annoyance of the remaining diners. He looked like he owned the place, a possibility that occurred to Mickey as Henry grabbed an empty chair from the next table and pulled Madame Bigard roughly onto his lap.

"God!" said Rachel. "Everybody's horny today."

Henry's suit looked like sharkskin, sharp edges at the shoulders, thin lapels, a slim metallic-blue tie. Instead of the usual chunky steel Rolex, he wore a paper-thin platinum Piaget on a narrow alligator-skin band, and the shoes, though ancient, looked expensive and well cared for. In full view of the appalled diners, Henry ran his hands over Madame Bigard's chunky thighs and into her armpits. Flushed with excitement, she held up a hand for a waiter and called for *digestifs* for the table.

"The kitchen is still open, Henri, you bad boy . . . *cochon*," she said. *"Mange, j'insiste."*

"Non, Mimi," said Henry, leaning around to peck first Rachel, then Frances on the cheek. "Just cognac."

When Henry's lips approached Frances, she turned her face to him and fastened her teeth on his lower lip, holding it for a full two seconds.

"Gawd!" said Rachel, fanning herself with her napkin. "You look great!"

"Merci bien, mademoiselle," said Henry, charmingly. "And may I say you look pretty damned ravishing yourself." He looked perfectly at ease, leaning back in his chair, one arm slung across the back of Rachel's chair, the other continuing to massage Madame Bigard's neck.

Mickey, unhappy with the indisputable fact that he was no longer the center of attention, ordered a double espresso, determined to sober up.

Rachel accepted a crème de menthe from an insistent Madame Bigard, following Frances's example.

Madame Bigard was brought a snifter of cognac with Henry's, the two of them clicking glasses and exchanging chin-chins.

"How was your trip?" inquired Rachel, still gaping at Henry's suit.

"Fine, fine," said Henry, exchanging a conspiratorial glance with Frances that no one at the table could miss. "Had the wind the whole way back."

A waiter arrived with a plate of petits fours, and Madame Bigard forced Henry to eat one, feeding him by hand, Mickey getting the idea now that this was a relationship that went back a few years— probably a lot of years. Henry looked so goddamn at ease in his sharkskin suit, the imposing-looking Frenchwoman wriggling on his lap, the whole floor staff of La Case d'Or hovering attentively while other customers paid their checks and slunk away in a huff.

"Henri knew my hoosband," said Madame Bigard, reading Mickey's mind. It seemed everybody was doing that tonight. "My hoosband . . . a very bad man." She laughed. "Like Henri . . .

"Are you a bad man too, Mickey?" she asked. "I think you must be."

"Mickey's a very nice man," said Frances, cutting him to the bone, then adding, "but he's a little bit bad, I think." She gave Mickey a piercing, flirtatious look that made his heart race. Across the table, Rachel looked almost sorry for him.

"Do you know each other from here?" she asked, eyes on Henry.

"*Non.* Marseille," said Madame Bigard. "Henri, my hoosband, they are friends . . . from business. Restaurant business. You see?" She gestured around the room. "When my hoosband die . . . Henri helped me."

"What happened?" asked Mickey, feeling mischievous, sensing

an uncomfortable subject, wanting Henry to sweat a little for a change.

"He was shot," said Madame Bigard, without skipping a beat. "Corsican," she pronounced, as if that explained everything. "They are all either gangsters or policemen. *N'est-ce pas?*"

Mickey was pleased to see Henry blushing.

35

Kevin was happy. Little Petey's mysterious disappearance had allowed him an undisturbed week of lolling around in the sun. Whether Little Petey was at this moment back in the City, burning pictures of saints in his hand and swearing *omertà,* or festering in a car trunk somewhere, or simply oiling up poolside at the casino, it made no difference to him. He was happy for the extra time with Violetta, who, to his delight, had actually begun to return his affection.

The Dominicans didn't mind the time off either. Kevin had advanced them some money to run off and amuse themselves, and though they hadn't run very far (he could hear them now, downstairs at Ruben's bar, arguing over who among them was the bigger *maricón*), they had been content to spend their days drinking and whoring with only a minimal discharge of firearms.

Kevin unwrapped the stuffed panda he'd bought for Violetta at the Dawn Beach gift shop and propped it up on the pillow for her to find when she returned from the shower. He slipped on a new white, short-sleeved, button-down shirt, pleased with how tan it made him look in the mirror. He fussed with his hair for a while, trying to comb it over the bald parts, then giving up, thinking it was possible, just possible, she could love him anyway.

He certainly hoped so. Though lulled into occasional forgetfulness by the week off, his mind kept returning to the money he'd get when he finished the job. Enough to stay on this island forever. The day before he'd seen a lot for sale, a ways down the dirt road, and Kevin, experienced in construction, imagined himself building a small cottage, with maybe a garden, having a whole slew of multihued, barefooted children, the rest of his life spent dreaming in the sun, drinking milk stout (similar enough to Guinness), and making love to Violetta. Fifteen thousand could go a long way down here. If he needed more, later, he could work construction—they were always putting up hotels and condominiums.

Kevin put on cotton slacks and huarachis and waited for Violetta to come out of the bathroom.

She wore the Indonesian wrap he'd bought her that afternoon, and though she still looked shyly down at the floor, he was sure she must have liked it—it looked so damn good on her; she looked like the woman in those Bob Hope, Bing Crosby films—what was her name? Her long black hair shone under the single naked bulb, and he was pleased to see that she wore the necklace. When she saw the stuffed panda, the corners of her mouth rising, her eyes widening with pleasure, Kevin wanted to shout with joy. He looked forward to dinner like a kid on his first date. Maybe tonight she'd talk to him.

The Wednesday meetings of Alcoholics Absolutely Always were held at the Surf Club in Grand Case. All the Dinghy Dock regulars, Henry and Frances included, were charter members, and most proudly sported their AAA T-shirts, given out at the first meeting a year ago. Each member, at the beginning of meetings, would fork over twenty bucks to the club's secretary-treasurer; he, in turn, would pay the cooperating bar owners at the Surf Club, Cha Cha Cha, and Jimbo's. Members were then allowed one hour of unrestricted drinking at each establishment.

On this Wednesday, the Surf Club had laid on music, a trio of French kids playing Bob Marley covers. They had set up a tent next to the rear beach deck for the musicians, and the place was packed with dancing people. The harder core AAA members, identifiable by their shirts, or in some cases by reputation, were staked out at the bar, three deep, gulping down shakers of margaritas and tall frosted glasses of Long Island iced teas. The more sensible members and most nonmembers (paying customers) stuck with beer, distributed at high speed by two hardworking part-time bartenders who labored over an ice chest, popping bottle caps and handing out Foster's and Red Stripes and Heinekens to the heaving mob.

Though it was early in the evening, things were already degenerating into the usual spectacle of public lewdness, bad behavior, and profligate urination. A gnarled tamarind tree that grew from the center of the Surf Club's deck was already filling up with brassieres. According to accepted custom, women would tear their bras off in full view of the chanting crowd and try to hurl them as high into the branches as possible. The brassieres would then stay in the tree until they blew away or fell apart.

Aussie windsurfers smoked spliffs with ex–ski bums from Colorado under the sea grape tree. Irish carpenters and machinists went shot for shot with South African army deserters, retired firemen from New Jersey, tax evaders from New York, off-duty French paratroopers from the barracks in Marigot; all arm-wrestled, sang along, argued, groped, boasted, bitched, and generally raised hell around crowded wooden tables, saying things that no one would remember in the morning.

Henry and Frances were listening to Day Tripper's theory that

repressed farts were the direct cause of cellulite. Day Tripper's girlfriend, Janet the Planet, whose own crenulated thighs had no
doubt inspired his theory, lay facedown in a plate of chicken wings
nearby, draped in a French tricolor after having thrown not only
her brassiere but every other one of her garments into the
tamarind tree.

"It's the mee-thane," insisted Day Tripper, barely understandable
after countless drinks. "Great bloody enormous fucking air pockets . . . 's why she's such a cow . . . 's it . . . Mee-thane."

"You're a pig," said Frances, not bothering to show the AAA's
president for life and chief operating officer the respect a person of
his high office would ordinarily expect.

"I'm off," he said, slobbering beer into his beard. "I'm going to
Cha Cha Cha." Most nights, this pronouncement would cause the
whole AAA mob to surge onto the street, forming a loud and unruly procession to the next bar. But people were enjoying themselves too much, the music was loud. In a few minutes, when the
Surf Club reverted to cash bar, most people would be too whacked
to care. Day Tripper left alone; Henry and Frances were relieved by
his exit.

In the tapas garden, Kevin struggled to make sense of the menu
while Violetta smiled at him from across the table and a French
waiter hovered at his elbow. The bartenders, bracing for the on-
slaught from the AAA, hurried to load ice buckets with beers,
shove rented Portosans into place, and close off the main dining
rooms.

"I'll have one a' these . . . *accras,* then," said Kevin. "Howzat, Vi?
Accras. Bueno? And gimme one a' these *satays* and a quesadilla,
whatever that is." The waiter jotted all this down and skipped off
to the kitchen without comment.

"Superior fuck," muttered Kevin. "Thinks he's too pretty for the home team." He sipped his whiskey and calmed himself by admiring Violetta in her new Indonesian wrap. Brazilian samba issued from hidden speakers somewhere, and tall, bronzed French girls in cutoffs so short you'd need forceps to remove them chatted amiably with shorter, paler men in pleated slacks and neatly pressed button-down shirts. It was a young crowd, mostly French, but quiet compared with the place down the block, where Kevin could hear screams and shouts, breaking glass and live music.

"Merde!" said their waiter, as he put the plates down at their table. He'd just caught sight of Day Tripper at the front entrance, weaving through a group of tourists on a beeline for the bar. The waiter turned and called out a warning to the bartender, *"Ils sont arrivés!"*

Day Tripper staggered into the garden, shouting hellos to friends real and imagined. "Margarita," he was calling, reaching for his fly at the same time. "Gotta have a piss first." He looked around for the Portosans; then, like a bad dream, Kevin saw his lunatic gaze fasten on Violetta, and Day Tripper changed trajectory and came toward their table, an out-of-control cruise missile with a leering, idiotic grin on his face.

" 'S my girlie," he said, resting a tattooed arm on Violetta's shoulder and sending a shock wave through Kevin's brain. Violetta looked up at Kevin like a trapped deer. "My favorite little girlie," slobbered Day Tripper. "Give us a kiss."

Noticing that Kevin was standing up, and, even in his drunken condition, seeing that those thick, muscular arms could cause him serious pain, Day Tripper sounded a belated retreat. "Sorry . . . sorry, Dad. Didn't see she was on duty. I got it, got it . . . got it. Good for you. Cheers." He offered a conciliatory handshake to Kevin, who was still considering whether he was going to plunge his fork into Day Tripper's thorax or simply grind his glass into the

man's face. Kevin slapped his hand away as Day Tripper dug his
grave deeper. "She's bloody good, mate . . . Cheers, really . . .
Good bang for the buck, right? Right!"

The waiter, seeing how Kevin's face was lighting up, the veins in
his neck throbbing like hungry boa constrictors, stepped between
them and pushed Day Tripper toward the exit. *"Non, non, non,"* he
said. *"Pas ce soir.* You bozzer ze customers." A bartender joined him,
making sure that Day Tripper was pointed toward Jimbo's down
the street and gave him a gentle shove.

Day Tripper, torn between his desperate need to piss and his
natural instinct for belligerence, chose to follow nature's call and
tottered on a serpentine path to the beach.

Kevin, his evening ruined, felt a gesture was called for. He had
been humiliated by this rotten Brit; he could barely bring himself
to look Violetta in the eyes. Leaving her at the table with a casual
smile, he strolled back to the rear beer garden, where the Portosans
were. But he didn't use one. Instead, he kept walking, disappearing
into the dark backyards of Grand Case. He ducked under clotheslines, kicked a few chickens out of his way as he doubled around,
circumventing the restaurant. He almost tripped over a barbecue
grill, avoided a stray dog, and finally made it back to the street,
darting unseen across the narrow lit space between shadows to
catch up to Day Tripper. His rage building, he opened and closed
his hands, eager to wrap them around his tormentor.

When he found him, Day Tripper was standing, facing the bay,
still pissing over the seawall. He was singing, "I'm a little teapot,
short and stout. Here is my bollocks, and here is my spout."

Kevin walked up behind him and, without even bothering to
look around, clamped one hand on top of Day Tripper's head with
near concussive force. He grabbed a handful of Day Tripper's hair
between his fingers, clapped his other hand across his chin and
mouth, and, with a single, swift, and terrible jerk, snapped the

man's neck. A thin stream of urine continued down Day Tripper's pants leg as Kevin picked him up by the belt and hurled him headlong over the seawall.

There was a wet slap below as the body hit the beach, and Kevin felt immediately better. As he walked back to the tapas garden, he realized that that teapot song was still with him. Maybe later he'd sing it to Violetta. After he cleaned up the lyrics a bit.

Henry and Frances, along with a few of the more well-behaved AAA members, eventually made it to the tapas garden. They had no reason to notice Kevin, nor he them. They had a quick drink at the bar, wolfed down a couple of quesadillas, and soon left for Jimbo's. After nachos and a few shots of tequila, they had a taxi drive them back to the Oyster Pond, taking along Janet the Planet, who seemed to have lost her ride.

The official investigation into the death of Reginald Joseph Stang, aka Day Tripper, of Manchester, England, was pretty much concluded moments after the discovery of the body.

That this notorious drunk, brawler, braggart, and professional urinator had been found dead at the foot of the seawall was hardly an unforeseeable consequence of a less than laudable life. No one, not even his friends, was surprised. Some said it was a long time coming. While taking a leak, the inebriated Day Tripper had simply toppled off the wall and broken his stupid neck. He was bundled onto a gurney and covered with a sheet without anyone for a second considering the possibility of foul play. And, even had the French police suspected as much, it would have mattered little. Most were damned glad to be rid of the loathsome foreigner. They were all too accustomed to answering calls complaining of the late

Mr. Stang's destructive antics. Day Tripper was gone. That was all that mattered.

Henry and Frances read about it the next day in the *Chronicle*.

"You know," Frances said, "I'm trying to think of one good thing to remember him by . . . and I can't. Is that bad?"

"Fuck him," said Henry. "Didn't like him then. Don't miss him now. Rest in piss."

"Still . . . I feel kind of bad. Janet . . . you know."

"Janet is way better off without that turd. And Saint Martin's drinking establishments and adjoining properties, they smell better already. What do they call it? A communal sigh of relief. Are we going to the wake? It's inevitable."

"Ask me after I get over this hangover . . . before I start planning on another."

36

"Things to Do Today," wrote Kevin on his yellow notepad. Next to the number one, he wrote, "Pay More Attention to Personal Hygeene."

When he'd rolled into bed the night before, he'd caught Violetta in the mirror wrinkling her nose at him. This morning, with her asleep in the ratty, upstairs room at La Ronda, Kevin sniffed his own armpits and could tell she'd had reason for offense. It was all so new, what was happening to him. Giving a shit about somebody else. That was new. Suntan. New. He was thinner. All the swimming and the work on the vans—that was something too. Black. Violetta, after all, was black. That was definitely new. By the time he'd got it settled in his mind that, yes, no question about it, she was black, he was already in love with her, and it was too late to worry about how improbable such a thing was. Kevin, after all, had spent most of his life referring to anybody who wasn't as white as he'd been as a nigger. Indians, Puerto Ricans, even Italians, the darker ones—they'd *all* been "niggers."

Maybe he wasn't going to go out and join the NAACP, but something was happening to him. His head was changing. Things were looking different now. He would need this list to keep track of the changes. The things he was going to do. His plan for this newer, better life.

He couldn't think of item number two yet, so he decided to take care of the first thing on the list. After his shower, maybe something would occur to him. He grabbed a towel and walked down the hall to the communal bathroom.

When he opened the door, Paulie Brown was sitting on the toilet, reading a year-old copy of *Time*.

"There you are," said Paulie. "I din't wanna wake you."

"Jaysuss," said Kevin, not expecting this. "What happened the other fella?"

"Little Petey?" said Paulie, unembarrassed to be caught on the bowl. "You . . . you go ahead there, you gotta shower. I'll be done in a minute . . . Yeah. Little Petey? Well, we gotta talk about that . . . Lemme get through here on the crapper, and I'll see you downstairs there at the bar. I can't believe this shithole. A real fuckin' tropical paradise he puts you in. I don't blame you it was you that greased him." He looked around. "Fuck! No paper."

A squeaky-clean Kevin joined Paulie at the empty bar. In the rear kitchen area, some of the whores were feeding their children breakfast, watching the Spanish soap operas on TV, and gossiping.

"Jimmy wants to know what's goin' on down here," said Paulie. "He's pissed off, big time. He says you should know you only got a couple a' days to do the job. The guy . . . the guy's only gonna be here a few more days, then he goes up to New York, where nobody can get to him . . . It'll be too late."

Kevin's heart sank. He'd gotten used to not thinking about the job. He'd half-believed that the whole thing would go away, that he'd be able to keep the half they'd fronted, that, somehow, no-body would come, they'd forget him. Now this.

"I din't hear nothin'," said Kevin. "One day, Petey was here . . . the next . . . gone. I waited. Nobody came. I was waitin' for some-body to tell me somethin'."

"Yeah. Well. I'm here," said Paulie, not too thrilled either. His wife was going to give him a whole ration of shit when he got back, for leaving her alone for a week, and he'd taken a big risk coming down here, what with a grand jury subpoena hanging around his neck. Richie had tried to scare him, spouting legalistic mumbo jumbo about the difference between "subject" and "wit-ness" of a grand jury inquiry, and he'd made "subject" sound like a real bad thing. He wanted this big Irishman to hurry up and get things over with so he could go home.

"Yeah . . . well . . . ," said Kevin, his thoughts wandering up to Violetta, still asleep in his bed. "I'm ready, I guess . . . anytime. The vans are all set. The guns . . . those fuckin' kids . . . they'll be around somewhere. No problem."

"No problem. Good," said Paulie. "There's somethin' else we got for you. After. After you pop the old man . . . there's another guy, if yer innerested. We'll pay, a' course . . . Somebody else down here that's gotta go."

"Yeah. Sure," said Kevin, sadly. "Whatever."

37

enry and Frances were taking a bath.

Leaning back in the tub, water up to his chin, eyes half closed and Frances's ankles up over his ears, Henry picked up an oversize loofah and began to soap her calves. There was, blissfully, nothing on his mind other than how white the soapy lather looked against her brown skin, and the notion, growing more powerful by the moment, that any second now he'd raise himself a few inches out of the water so he could run his tongue along the undersides of her toes.

The chattering of automatic weapons fire, coming from somewhere across the pond, made Henry sit bolt upright, suddenly chilled.

"Is it from Donnie's?" said Frances, alarmed.

"Gotta be," said Henry, pulling himself out of the tub, unsure what to do first. "Clothes, clothes, clothes . . . FUCK! Where're my CLOTHES!"

The gunfire grew more constant. Henry could hear a shotgun working now. BOOM, BOOM, BOOM, a louder, more authoritative roar. Still unable to locate his pants, Henry wrapped a salt-stiffened kaffiyeh around his waist, tied it in front like a sarong, and stuck the H & K next to his kidney before charging barefoot and still dripping out the door.

"Wait!" yelled Frances, only throwing on her full-length silk kimono, no time to find the belt, and running after him across the parking lot to where they'd tied the dinghy. When she leaped into the boat, Henry had already pulled up the watertight container from the bottom of the pond. Now he was struggling to unwrap the heavier guns.

"Let's GO!" yelled Henry. "Go! Go!"

Frances cast off the line and yanked desperately at the starter cord. It took three tries, both of them feeling more helpless and exasperated with each pull, before the engine kicked in. When they were halfway across the pond, the shooting seemed to lessen. The red and green tracer fire became less frantic. Now Henry could see the windows of Donnie Wicks's house lighting up from the inside with the muffled reports of shotgun fire.

"What do you want?" yelled Henry over the engine noise.

"Give me the shotgun!" Frances responded.

He jacked a few last rounds into the Ithaca and tossed it astern. She caught the weapon one-handed, rocking back and forth as if she could make the dinghy move faster.

"You want this too?" he asked, showing her the Car-15. She just shook her head, her eyes set on the house, growing closer and closer in the dark. He tossed a box of extra number 4 combat loads at her feet, and she opened it and emptied the shells into the pouched sleeve of her kimono.

Henry taped two clips of ammo together end to end and slapped one into the magazine of his Armalite. He thumbed the selector into position for full auto, a painful lump in his throat as the shotgun blasts grew louder. There was a new exchange from outside the house, a hellacious sequence of explosions.

Shit! Shit! thought Henry. An automatic shotgun. He listened for the sounds of Kulspruta fire from any surviving marshals and heard only a short burst, followed immediately by the familiar staccato of an M-16, and what sounded like a machine pistol, an Uzi or a TEC-9, he couldn't tell. More shots. More return fire. Then silence. It didn't sound good.

When the bow of their rubber dinghy bounced noiselessly against Donnie's wooden dock, all was quiet at the house.

The lead van, just as planned, smashed headlong through the front gate, the heavy hunk of backhoe projecting from the grille slamming the thick iron bars backward so they rebounded off the stone wall, knocking Woody onto his stomach. The van was already past him, screaming up the drive in first gear, automatic weapons fire pouring out in all directions from its crude, X-shaped gunports.

Woody, on all fours and bleeding from the ankle and head, had turned and was raking the rear of the first van with his Swedish K when the second van came hurtling round the bend and hit him, the front left wheel passing neatly over his neck.

The strap of his weapon got caught up in the metal plates that Kevin had welded over the tires, and Woody's body was dragged into the rear left wheel well. His legs flailing as he was pulled up the steep drive, he came to rest only when the second van banged into the first, in a dead stop at the head of the drive.

Kevin was in the passenger seat of the second van. Determined to survive this night, he quickly opened the door and rolled unseen into the bushes, the Dominicans in the vans firing wildly, ejected cartridges flying everywhere in the confined space, ricocheting off the metal plates, filling the vehicles with smoke as a marshal on the roof of the house directed fire down on them.

One of the marshals emptied a full clip into the driver's seat of the first van. The driver—Kevin remembered him as one of the cousins, Hector, he thought—caught the full force. Kevin saw him bouncing up and down in the seat, glass shattering all around him as bullets tore through the windshield, his head vaporizing into a scattered mess. The side doors of both vans opened, and the Dominicans came tumbling out, anxious to escape what had clearly become the target of choice for the still unseen marshals.

Alfredo, with an Uzi, took a round in the face, the bullet passing in one cheek and out the other with a soggy, slapping sound. He sat down hard, looking surprised, the Uzi between his legs.

Kevin, his eyes growing accustomed to the dark, tried to pick out the marshals' positions from their muzzle flashes as Flaco, God bless him, waded straight at the enemy, doing it John Wayne style, the automatic shotgun roaring at his hip, blowing great holes through the foliage with each detonation. The light from the pool showed through, illuminating dark, firing figures in the garden.

Kevin, his Remington pump still silent, watched from hiding as a marshal was sent spinning away with a grunt into the hibiscus by the edge of the patio. Each time the automatic shotgun went off, it lit up Flaco's face, revealing an eerily ecstatic expression. With his one drifting, milky eye, his mouth half open, a tiny bead of saliva hanging from his lower lip, Flaco looked as if he might, at any moment, begin speaking in tongues. He looked happy, really, really happy, moving ahead to the pool area now, the automatic shotgun scattering patio furniture, sending chairs and tables skittling across the tile. Kevin got up and moved forward in a crouch, his Remington held out in front. Through the trees and bushes, he could see a woman's legs sticking up from the jumble of patio furniture, a sad, keening noise coming from beneath the wreckage. It sounded like a dying rabbit.

The marshal on the roof was still a problem. Kevin heard something move behind him and turned just in time to see Papo take a bullet in his spine. He went down without making a sound as Kevin hurried to get clear of him. He ducked by the trunk of a royal palm, drew a bead on the rooftop marshal, popped up, and let go with three blasts from the Remington. A body came tumbling off the overhang, trailing loose shingles, and slapped onto the concrete near the shallow end of the pool, the dead marshal's torso hanging into the water.

There was Flaco, reloading the drum canister. A dark figure fired from inside the house, hitting him broadside, clipping the bridge of Flaco's nose. It disappeared in a spray of blood and cartilage, but Flaco didn't even turn. He calmly finished reloading, raised the ugly gun, and began working the house, methodically blowing out the windows and shooting through the walls.

Kevin saw Flaco react to another hit, this one in his calf. Identifying the source of the shot as the gazebo, Kevin opened up with his Remington until another marshal, bristling with splinters like a bleeding porcupine, stood up to take a shot at him. Kevin put him down with his last shotgun shell, taking him full in the chest, then he sat down to reload and take stock of the situation.

Somebody was still moaning near the pool. Kevin thought the sound was coming from the woman. Her legs were moving slightly as the moaning trailed off into a persistent whimper. He got up and moved closer to the house, Orlando joining him from wherever he'd been lurking in the dark. Kevin wondered where the dogs were. There were supposed to have been dogs. He pointed at a spot where he wanted Orlando to stand guard while he entered the house.

Just then somebody opened up from inside the kitchen, sending Orlando to the ground, bleeding from the head. Kevin reached for a fragmentation grenade, pulled the pin, and hurled it through an opening in the glass. He waited, but it refused to detonate. The marshal inside the kitchen, however, was not so certain the thing wouldn't explode. He came running out the door firing hard, but Flaco, half blind yet still game, knocked his legs out from under him with a lucky blast, bits of glass and buckshot making pinging sounds as they bounced off the copper pots and pans.

Then there was no more firing.

Kevin waited. Flaco saw him and smiled, his teeth smeared with watery blood, before wandering off to hunt the wounded. Kevin stepped over the broken glass, loose shingles, and broken patio furniture and entered the house, the screen door to the kitchen coming off in his hand. It was time to find Donnie Wicks. An hour from now, resolved Kevin, he'd be counting his money. He'd make love to Violetta in a pile of fifties, in a good hotel, not a whorehouse, and drink cocktails with paper umbrellas sticking out of them.

The iron gates were wide open, one nearly torn off its hinges, and there were no dogs. Henry knew that that was what Frances would be thinking first: What happened to the dogs? The smell of cordite was everywhere, and smoke still drifted through the beam from a lone security light at the head of the drive.

Somebody was muttering something in Spanish, and Henry held a finger to his lips as they followed Woody's blood trail in the drive, coming up carefully behind the rear van, where the dead marshal's legs stuck out, at impossible angles, from the wheel. There was an atrocious amount of blood. Henry and Frances had to walk through it, their bare feet becoming sticky with the rusty-smelling liquid.

Peering around the corner of the van, Henry saw a delirious-looking man with a face wound sitting with his legs splayed against the side of the vehicle, his gun resting between them. Henry moved right past him, concentrating on the light from the pool as Frances moved in on the injured man and butt-stroked him with the shotgun. He slumped over on his side and stopped talking.

There was somebody lying, half in, half out of the pool—a marshal. Henry recognized the nylon sweatpants. There was another marshal, facedown and bleeding from legs that looked as if they'd been hit by lightning.

"Rachel!" whispered Frances, seeing the legs protruding from the pile of furniture. She ran to her and began to dig through the chairs, heedless of the noise she was making. "I'm comin' baby," she said. Henry nervously covered her from poolside, uncomfortable with their exposed position.

Disentangled from the chairs, her legs finally down, Rachel lay, still alive but gravely injured, on the cold patio, a throaty whistling sound coming from the chest wound below her shoulder.

"Henry!" barked Frances. "What do I do? Do something, for fuck's sake! You're supposed to be good at this." Henry saw she was crying with exasperation, a startling enough occurrence even with Rachel lying there nearly dead from shock and loss of blood. He had to plug the hole first. So she could breathe. He found an oil-cloth table cover nearby and folded it into a compress. Frances put the Ithaca down and wiped bloody foam from Rachel's lips as Henry pushed the oilcloth square onto her wound.

"Keep the pressure on," he said to Frances. "That's all you can do. And get her knees up, she's going into shock."

There was a sudden exchange from inside the house, and Henry leaped forward with his Armalite.

"Oh, God," said Frances, looking up at him for a brief, terrified second. "Mickey and Donnie." She felt around for the Ithaca, her other hand still pressing down on Rachel's wound. Henry hesitated, but another glance from Frances sent him on his way. She looked angry. "Go!" she said. He cut his feet on the broken glass slipping, as quietly as he could, into the house.

Mickey and Donnie were playing pool in the downstairs rec room when the shooting started. A second later Burt was with them, shouting for them to take cover behind the bar while he took up a position at the foot of the spiral stairs behind a green leather easy chair.

There was more firing and more, sounding like a war through the narrow doorway to the upstairs. Mickey, hyperventilating, nauseated with worry about Rachel, found himself trying to see up through the pool, craning his neck at the bottom of the Plexiglas window. It was no good.

"Get your head down, you idiot!" yelled Burt, and then Donnie had him by the belt and dragged him to the floor. Mickey could feel the old man's body trembling as they huddled together on the carpet, the greenish light from the pool playing over them.

Mickey heard breaking glass, and the sounds of metal on metal, bullets hitting his pots in the kitchen upstairs. Silence. More shooting. Silence again. Then Burt opened up with his Swedish K, firing at a dark shape at the head of the stairs.

The wood paneling over Burt's head exploded into chips. Burt ducked, then came up and fired again, but it was tough, shooting through the curving iron banister of the spiral staircase. His bullets veered dangerously in all directions, tearing up the pool table as they spun off the metal railing, breaking the fish tank, and sending the PARK YOUR BUTT HERE ashtray skittering across the bar like a hockey puck.

The man at the head of the stairs had no such trouble with the shotgun. His next round went right through the easy chair, sending stuffing everywhere. Burt never got up. He just sagged to the carpet, a long, pink spume staining Donnie's sand-colored carpet.

"We're fucked," said Donnie, no longer trembling. He held Mickey's hand tightly in his and kissed him on the cheek, tenderly. "I just hope it's nobody I know," he said. "I always hated that part."

Mickey, still thinking of Rachel up on the patio, couldn't speak. His tongue felt frozen in his mouth. He could only blink.

Henry recognized the big man at the head of the stairs instantly, felt a sickening sense of disappointment with himself for having missed him when he'd seen him on the beach. Hadn't he been at Cha Cha Cha that night too? He should have recognized the man for what he was immediately, when he first saw him frolicking with his whore at the Beach Club.

In his anger, he made another mistake.

Having come up on him without being detected, he jammed the muzzle of the Armalite into Kevin's kidney, blowing his advantage completely. Reacting instinctively to the sharp impact, Kevin, as anyone would feeling a blow to the sensitive organ, flinched. The shot from the Armalite only bit a harmless trail through Kevin's love handle, setting his T-shirt momentarily on fire.

Kevin whirled around with the Remington but banged the barrel into the doorframe. Henry fired a second time, panicked by the completely untroubled look on Kevin's face. The barrel of the shotgun exploded where he held it, his fingers bursting open like microwaved sausages. Without pausing for a second, Kevin simply dropped the shotgun and punched Henry full in the face with his bloody stub.

The punch sent Henry reeling onto his ass, ears ringing, as Kevin stepped forward and attempted a field goal with his heavy work boot. It sent the Armalite bouncing off Henry's brow and into the kitchen. Then Kevin was stomping with both feet, doing a murderous hokeypokey on Henry's abdomen as he tried vainly to crawl away. He managed to sink a bare foot deep into the half-mad Irishman's nuts, but he kept coming. Henry bit him in the thigh as he clubbed the side of his head with both hands, allowing him time only to stand up, gasping for air against the wall, as he tried to find somewhere, anywhere on the big man's body that might hurt if hit.

Kevin charged him with his whole body, flattening Henry against the wall with his bulk and knocking the wind out of him. Henry remembered the H & K, reached for it, and realized his kaffiyeh had come loose. It lay on the floor, the pistol under it.

Henry took a punch in the face, then another, the flesh over his left eye tearing and filling it with blood. He let Kevin hit him in the mouth so he could bite him again, this time sinking his teeth into the injured hand, then attempting a head butt. Kevin just brought his knee up and knocked Henry's head back into the wall. He heard shots from outside.

There was an explosion. From downstairs. It shook the whole house, and then there was a sound like waves breaking. Kevin turned just long enough for Henry, already sagging, to reach the H & K under his kaffiyeh. He got his fingers around it and let go with the full clip, shooting up from the floor. He was not going to let this man get his hands on him again. Round after round went up and into the big man's abdomen, puncturing liver, spleen, pancreas, Kevin's white T-shirt blossoming like a rosebush in a time-lapse nature study. When Henry's last round tore a nice-size hunk out of Kevin's backbone, the big man jerked. His head moved suddenly to the side as the light in his eyes turned off, and he fell over like a building coming down.

Through the blood in his eyes, and the pain, Henry lay on the floor, hearing the ocean. He could swear he heard water rushing somewhere.

"Rachel . . . Rache . . . sweetheart . . . you're gonna be okay," Frances was saying. The whistling sound had stopped, and she still leaned her full weight on her friend's chest, looking around for something better to fasten it with.

She noticed the man with no nose too late. He stood across the pool, clicking the empty chamber of an automatic shotgun. Cursing herself for putting down the Ithaca, Frances felt for it as the skinny Dominican dropped the shotgun and came around with an M-16 from a strap on his back, unslinging it with one hand.

A bullet snipped a piece of bone off the ridge of Frances's brow before she could get her gun up. A second shot, in the chest, punched her backward into the tangle of deck furniture. When she raised her head, she saw the man was reaching for something.

Getting onto her knees, Frances realized the man was nearly blinded by the wound to his face; she couldn't see his eyes, the upper part of his face was so disfigured. She snarled like a mad dog and brought up the Ithaca to fire. The first shot took him in the throat. It was enough. He touched his chin, something falling from his hand into the pool, then fell after it, leaking from the neck like a garden sprinkler.

This fragmentation grenade went off as advertised. Frances had just flopped her full weight onto Rachel's chest as the blast sent a geyser of chlorinated plasma fifty feet into the air. It rained down on the two women. Frances slipped into unconsciousness, the whistling from Rachel's chest starting again in her ear, drops of water falling around her.

.   .   .

Donnie was drowning. He was drowning in his own house. They were crouched down behind the bar, he and Mickey, watching the dead Dominican float past the picture window, a red halo emanating from his ruined head, when suddenly everything went white and Donnie was alone in the dark.

Then he was trying to dog-paddle, something heavy and soft between his legs. Donnie reached down, choking on water, praying it wasn't Mickey he felt. He saw matchbooks from the Havana Hilton float past, pool cues, novelty coasters, playing cards with big-titted women on them. As the water level rose (his tropical fish slithering past him), it reached the Tiffany chandelier over the pool table and shorted out the light. He tried to reach whatever, whoever it was between his legs. It seemed to be following him. He hooked a thumb into something unpleasant and got a quick, horrifying look at a dead Dominican, face only inches away, wounds washed momentarily clean by the water. Floundering, Donnie managed only a final full turn in the water, seeking Mickey, before he went under. He saw stars, felt an otherworldly calmness come over him that he assumed to be death.

Then someone was pulling his hair.

Donnie sat weeping at the edge of his emptied pool. Mickey's body lay next to him, a long shard of broken Plexiglas jutting from just below the Adam's apple. He wasn't sure about Rachel. Henry had said something hopeful, but he was busy now, working over Frances in a chaise lounge a few yards away. Frances's blood-soaked kimono was spread out around her and Henry tried to bind her wounds with strips from his kaffiyeh. Donnie saw that there was a sharp piece of rib protruding from Henry's back, but he was too shattered to mention it. He looked down at Mickey again, then turned away.

Soft cries for help were coming from somewhere in the garden, but neither Donnie nor Henry was in any position to do anything about them, and Frances, awake now, didn't care.

"How is she?" she asked, worried about Rachel.

"I don't know," said Henry. "It's all a mess."

"She still alive?"

Henry glanced over at the fallen girl, her chest rising and falling unsteadily. "Yes," said Henry, his eyes, too, filling with tears.

"Mickey?"

Henry shook his head.

"Oh," said Frances, closing her eyes. "It's . . . really bad, isn't it?"

"Yeah," said Henry. "It's bad . . . Donnie made it . . . He's just over there."

"Whooop-de-fucking-doooo." Frances sighed. "Is . . . is somebody coming?" she asked. "Did you call somebody?"

"Yeah," said Henry, his voice filled with sadness. "We gotta get you to a hospital, baby . . . You're shot up pretty good."

"The cops . . . ," said Frances. "This doesn't look . . . good."

"We're a little past that point," said Henry, with a bitter laugh. "Love me?" he asked, looking to save something.

"Yes," said Frances, closing her eyes.

He knew they'd arrived when he heard their silenced MP-5s. They were moving through the grounds, shooting the wounded. Marshals and Dominicans alike, dead or alive; each got a single round to the head. Trung appeared first, looking like he'd come from a lawn party, in a casual shirt and checked pants and huarachis. The others wore hoods and the black fatigue uniforms of Ribiere's shock troops. One dark figure stepped over to Henry, pushed him gently aside, and looked down at Frances. He whispered into a throat mike, and more hooded figures appeared out of the dark, bearing stretchers.

Henry heard the thrashing sound of muffled rotors overhead. A searchlight reached down from the sky and fixed him in its beam as the black helicopter moved over the house and set down in the rear bocce court.

"She needs immediate medical attention," said Monsieur Ribiere, lifting Frances's wrist to take a pulse. He barked out an order, and two hooded medics loaded her onto a stretcher.

A dark figure threw a hood over Donnie's head and marched him off into the darkness. He didn't resist. Henry held Frances's hand until Monsieur Ribiere patted him on the back and reassured him. "They will take her to hospital," he said. "You may go with her, if you like." He cast a dispassionate eye on Henry's face, on the length of bone that had torn through his back, sticking out like an aerial. "Yes," he said. "Someone will have to attend to you as well."

Monsieur Ribiere walked over to where Rachel lay. "This one," he said ominously, "will need . . . special attention. We'll take her on the helicopter . . . to Curaçao. They have better facilities there. Trung!"

Two hooded figures put Rachel on a litter and loaded her into the chopper. The rotors started up again, and, to Henry's dismay, Trung hopped aboard. As it lifted off, he took a place in the open hatch of the helicopter, his feet resting on the skids. When he smiled at Henry, it made his blood run cold.

The searchlight went out, and the black chopper disappeared into the night sky. Henry followed alongside Frances's stretcher as they carried her down to the blue van.

"Are we okay?" she asked, opening her eyes for a second and seeing him there.

"We're fine," said Henry, not sure at all.

38

The *New York Times*'s headline the next day read, MASSACRE: U.S. WITNESS, U.S. MARSHALS, OTHERS KILLED IN SHOOTOUT. Few details were offered, and it took several days for the follow-up story to appear:

D'Andrea "Donnie Wicks" Balistieri, whose burned and bullet-riddled corpse was found in the early morning hours Tuesday here, was apparently cooperating in a grand jury investigation aimed at other organized crime figures when he was killed.

Six U.S. marshals, guarding his residence, were also slain in what is reported to have been a furious firefight with as yet unidentified, armed intruders. Six Dominican nationals and a Caucasian male were also found dead at the scene, and two other persons, Michael Pistone of New York City, reputedly a friend of Mr. Balistieri, and Rachel Solomon of Lynbrook, are reported missing.

Sources say that Mr. Balistieri was scheduled to be a witness at the expected trial of James "Jimmy Pazz" Calabrese on murder and conspiracy charges. With Mr. Balistieri gone, the government case against Mr. Calabrese is said to be in doubt.

Alerted by reports of gunfire and explosions in the exclusive Oyster Pond section of Saint Martin, local French police rushed to the scene to find Mr. Balistieri's residence in flames. In all, thirteen persons were found to have been killed, and photographs and records recovered from the burned home led authorities to conclude that Mr. Pistone and Ms. Solomon were missing. It is not known how many assailants escaped.

In Marigot, the capital of this tiny West Indian island, local officials and officers of the military and intelligence branches, speaking on background, expressed dismay at the carnage at what had been a quiet vacation retreat for the affluent, most of whom are French citizens.

Lt. Governor Vance Richards, interviewed on a local television news show, said, "It is unconscionable that a person whose criminal activities and apparently imminent testimony against other violent criminals made him a likely target for such an attack should be staying in Saint Martin without our knowledge or consent. We would like, at the very least, to have been informed."

Mr. Richards pointed out that Mr. Balistieri had been the victim of an earlier attack a year previous and produced what appeared to be a French passport with a photo of the dead man, portraying him as an M. Pastou, resident of Marseille.

"There is the safety of our citizens to consider," said Mr. Richards. "And of course, the business of Saint Martin is tourism. A disaster like this can only hurt. I am very disappointed that the United States government, in connivance with Mr. Balistieri, allowed such a thing to happen—that this felon was provided with a false passport and encouraged to live here under false pretenses. My government and the government of France are both extremely unhappy with these developments, and an official demarche will be presented by end of day to the American ambassador."

Calls for comment to the U.S. Attorney's Office in Manhattan were not returned by press time, and the Justice Department issued a terse "No comment."

Unnamed sources in the U.S. Marshals Service, however, quoted elsewhere, complained bitterly of Justice Department mismanagement and lack of investigative zeal on the part of French and Saint Martin authorities. One man said the service is "in a state of shock" over the loss of so many U.S. marshals. "We blame Justice for this," said one source close to the team who guarded Mr. Balistieri. "We never would have allowed the man to stay in his own home if they hadn't pushed us."

He went on to say he had little faith in a satisfactory resolution to the many unanswered questions in the case, saying, "It's a French show now. Justice has egg on its face and doesn't want to press. And the French have already dropped the ball." He claimed that a purported offer of an FBI forensics team had been pointedly refused. "They have zero interest in finding out who did this. They hate this Al Capone stuff. It embarrasses them, and they just want it to go away."

A local French observer agrees. "There is little cooperation. People here are angry. There are a lot of hurt feelings."

The impact on the expected trial of Mr. Calabrese is yet to be seen, but as Mr. Balistieri was said to be the key witness in a complicated RICO case involving many jurisdictions, it is an open question when, or even if, the proceedings will continue.

As Fred Mishkin, the veteran crime reporter for UPI, said, speaking on C-SPAN this morning, "Unless they have Jimmy Pazz's fingerprints on the gun that got Donnie, the show's over for the government. It's back to the drawing board."

39

B e happy!" said Richie Tic, struggling to pull the brand-new strawberry blond Dynel wig over Jimmy Pazz's basketball-size head. "You read the paper. He's dead! Whaddayou bustin' the guy's balls for?"

"No pitchers," complained Jimmy. "There should be pitchers." He finally managed to pull the wig halfway down his forehead. Paulie Brown sat across the desk from him, looking sheepish.

"You din't see nothin'?" asked Jimmy again.

"Jimmy, it was like World War Three in there," said Paulie. "I'm layin' up inna weeds all fuckin' night. I'm gettin' bit like crazy—you should see my legs—there's things crawlin' around. But I stayed. I stayed there all fuckin' night. They were still haulin' bodies outta there when two dogs start lickin' my face. I hadda get outta there. There was cops all over the place, army guys, guys with fuckin' *hoods* on." He scratched his ankles and groaned. "I musta been bit a million times. I'm surprised I still got any blood left."

"Henry . . . he looked like he was gonna make it? I mean, there's nothin', *nothin'* inna papers about him, they don't say anything," said Jimmy, not letting go of the subject.

"The cops took him out. He got pinched. They put him inna back of a van and took him off. What can I say? What was I gonna do? The wife too. She didn't look too good. She looked pretty messed up. There was a lot of blood." Paulie looked up warily. "They was haulin' stiffs outta there left an' right . . . it was hard to keep track. Then the house went up. He musta been still inside."

"I just don't get it," said Jimmy. "It don't make no sense."

"The Irishman's definitely dead, though, right?" said Richie. "That's a good thing. That's good. Right, Jimmy? Now you don't gotta pay the guy the other half. You like accrued a considerable savings, know what I mean?"

"I still woulda liked to see a pitcher. And that fuck . . . that hippie, Henry . . . him. I'da liked it if he'da died."

"It went good," insisted Richie. "I talked to the lawyers. They all miserable 'cause now we ain't goin' to trial an' they ain't gonna be gettin' no fuckin' money like they thought . . . What shoes?"

"The black wedgies," said Jimmy.

"I couldn't . . . I couldn't find those before."

"So *he* can look," said Jimmy, pointing at Paulie. "Look in 'at fuckin' closet there. Pair a' black shoes, toeless."

"I ain't lookin' for no shoes," said Paulie. "Fuck that. I got calamine from the top a' my neck to the crack a' my ass, I ain't crawlin' aroun' no floor lookin' for shoes. I mean, jeez, have a fuckin' heart."

"Have a fuckin' heart?" screeched Jimmy. "Have a fuckin' HEART? I just paid for you to go down the fuckin' islands, tropical fuckin' paradise . . . an' . . . an' you don't even get the job fuckin' done right! You lucky I don't eat the fuckin' eyeballs outta yer fuckin' head, you prick! Now get down there an' find my fuckin' wedgies. You believe this?"

"I got it," said Richie, looking warily at Paulie. " 'S okay. I'll get 'em. I know what they look like. He don't know from shoes."

Jimmy stood in front of the full-length mirror next to his desk. He was in a black leather Versace, the wide buckled belt disappearing under rolls of flab. "I think I look fat. Do I look fat to you?"

"No, Jimmy, you look good," said Richie, emerging triumphant from the closet with a pair of black, open-toed shoes. "You look like Ivana Trump."

"I still don't like it, that Henry guy's alive," said Jimmy, sucking in his gut with some effort. "I don't like it they don't say nothin' inna paper."

"What? You worried the guy's gonna say somethin'? What's he gonna say?" said Richie, bending over like a prince to slip the size fourteen shoes onto Jimmy's hairy feet. "He can't say anything. He's capable. Culpable. He tried to whack the guy himself once. He's prolly a suspect. I mean, what's he doin' there inna first place? He's makin' another try. He finds out Donnie's down there, livin' next door like fuckin' Millie Helper there, an' he figures he better finish the fuckin' job."

"Maybe," said Jimmy, trying to make his cheeks look hollow by biting the insides and holding them between his teeth. "Still . . ." He looked over at Paulie, sitting morosely in his chair, saying nothing. "What's the matter with you all of a sudden? He turned to face Richie, arching his back, hand on his hip. "I *still* think I look fat."

40

Saint Rose Hospital in Philipsburg, on the Dutch side of the island, had been closed for over two years. A more modern, much larger facility had been built to replace it over in Cole Bay, so the ancient but picturesque sandstone structure had lain shuttered and vacant until the night of the mayhem at Donnie Wicks's house, when it reopened its doors for two very private patients.

They let Henry see her on the second day. Trung drove him over from the hotel. His fractured ribs had been repaired and bound, and the tears and abrasions in his skin had been sutured and dressed. His arms, back, chest, and feet, cut by broken glass, had been bandaged with adhesive and gauze, the worst of the cuts requiring only a few stitches. Henry's face, however, was horrifyingly swollen and discolored from the pounding he'd received. One side was puffed out twice the size of the other and splotched with reds and blues and various shades of green, one eye nearly closed still.

The whole way to the hospital not a word was exchanged. Trung, thoughtfully Henry felt, refrained from playing his usual country yodelers on the radio, and in return Henry avoided the subject of Rachel and what had happened to her.

At the hospital gate, a French para in civilian clothes, blue eyes too wide apart and a Beretta casually tucked into a rear pants pocket, let them into the courtyard. The central fountain had been drained, and like the cobblestone drive that surrounded it, it was littered with dead leaves from the overhanging flamboyants. Geckos darted about under the leaves, making a dry, crinkly sound as they searched for overripe berries fallen from the nearby guavas.

Another unsmiling Frenchman, with the unmistakable bearing of a lifetime military man, met them at the door to what had once been a fully equipped emergency room. Bandage wrappers and bloody gauze were still strewn about the floor. Frances's blood-soaked kimono lay in a sad pile next to a rubbish pail where the doctors had discarded their rubber gloves and syringes. Two pale and bleary-eyed French doctors, no doubt dragooned into this affair by Monsieur Ribiere, sat unshaven and sweating by a broken gurney, smoking unfiltered cigarettes and playing cards. A portable television silently flickered images of soccer players from a counter clogged with leftover take-out food. They looked put out by it all, not even raising their eyes when Henry entered the room, as if the work they had done in the late hours a few nights ago had somehow diminished them.

The second Frenchman led Henry down a long, mustard-colored hallway, open on one side to the Great Bay. Wisteria had worked its way up one side of the columns, and there were more lizards, roaming freely across the walls and floors. They passed what had once been the patients' dayroom, now populated only by rusting wheelchairs and some empty cases of Ting. Henry limped after the Frenchman, hurrying to keep up, his sandals making a flip-flop sound that counterpointed the martial sounds of the Frenchman's paratrooper's boots on the mildewed floor.

An Asian Henry recognized as a Nung, a Thai-speaking ethnic Chinese, guarded Frances's room. The Frenchman put a finger to his forehead, and he jumped back from the door to attention, boots thumping.

Inside, at least, it was cleaner. Frances was propped up against new white pillowcases, her eyes closed. The color had gone from her lips, had leeched out from her suntanned skin. A mustachioed nurse with a mole on her cheek acknowledged Henry's presence by standing up and leaving the room, her eyes on the floor the whole way.

An IV rig on a wheeled stand was next to the bed, dripping clear liquid into Frances's arm. There was a thick square of gauze over her right eye, the skin around it yellow and blue. The closed eye under it was golfball-size, but Henry had been assured that the eye itself was essentially undamaged. The dressing on her chest went completely around her back and across one shoulder. The first spots of watery blood and bright orange antiseptic had begun to ooze through.

"Sweetheart?" said Henry, unsure if she was asleep. "Baby?"

"Hey," she answered, one eye opening.

"You okay?"

Frances nodded her head and closed the eye again, keeping it closed for a moment as if gathering strength. Henry's eyes wandered over to the drip, drip of the hanging IV bottle. When he looked back at her, she was crying, tears running from the corner of her open eye and onto the pillow.

"Fucked up," said Frances. After a few more seconds, she said, "Rachel?"

"No," said Henry, shaking his head. He took her hand in his, gently. "She died on the chopper on the way to Curaçao." He didn't tell her his real thoughts on the matter. In Henry's mind, the only question was whether Trung had first pinched Rachel's nostrils closed and stuffed a rag in her mouth, or had simply kicked her out the open hatch into the ocean. He was practiced, Henry knew well, at both. Either way she was dead, of that he had no doubt at all. She was dead, and there wasn't a damn thing to do about it.

"We did the best we could," he said instead.

"Fucked up," said Frances. "So . . . fucked up . . . I feel . . . so . . . guilty."

Henry just nodded, unable to speak. He sat down on the edge of the bed and ran a finger across an undamaged section of Frances's brow. An air conditioner, recently jerry-rigged into the window with wood planking and hurricane tape, droned monotonously, struggling with the thick, humid air.

"So," said Frances. "How bad do I look? Bad as you?"

"Better," said Henry. "Your face isn't nearly as messed up. One of the doctors, he's a plastic surgeon. He says you were lucky. He doesn't usually work on fresh wounds. Usually they call him in later. He says you'll look fine."

"Maybe I should get my tits lifted while I'm in here," joked Frances, cutting short a laugh because of the pain.

"Trung said something like that," said Henry. "He was asking about his wife. Wants the guy to make her look like Dolly Parton."

"How 'bout you?" she asked. "You ever gonna look better than this? You look like Quasimodo."

"I'm fine," said Henry. "Couple a' new dings and scratches. Once the swelling goes down, I should look pretty normal."

"Henry . . . you *never* looked normal."

"Well . . . you know what I mean."

"How about the rest of you?" she said, reaching down and cupping his balls. "Everything in working order?"

"Still intact," said Henry, smiling.

"Well," said Frances. "That's something at least. I thought I saw you limping."

"Just some cuts on my feet."

"Good . . . How's Donnie?"

"We'll talk about that later," said Henry. "Don't sweat it. He'll be fine."

"Oh, Henry," she said, starting to cry again. Stopping suddenly, she squeezed his arm and pulled him closer. "Kiss me, alright? I want to make sure you're still there."

When he leaned forward to put his mouth on hers, intending a careful kiss, she tugged him violently closer, kissing him so hard his lip split. Breathing fiercely through her nose, she fumbled frantically with his belt buckle.

"Are you *out* of your *mind*?" he said, in a loud whisper.

"I think," she said, ignoring his protest and throwing back the sheets, "I think we can just manage." She pulled up her hospital gown. Henry started to draw back, but she already had his pants open and was kneading him, guiding him toward her by his penis.

"How?" he spluttered. "I mean . . . look." He gestured to the IV rig, her chest wound. He could have cited the Nung, just outside the door, the nurse, who could reappear at any moment, not to mention his own wounds, already beginning to spot through his ill-chosen white sailcloth shirt.

"Just shut up and give me a hand here, okay?" she hissed, un-clenching her teeth from his lower lip with a brief lick. "I'm fine below the waist. But this is gonna take some cooperation." She put her knees up, legs apart. "Just watch where you put your hands . . . and try not to pull my plug. Okay?"

Too far gone by now, excited by the familiar sights and scents of his wife, Henry moved his head down between her thighs and laid the relatively undamaged side of his face against her pubic bone. She was already wet, beginning to move rhythmically against him. "Sorry. You're going to have to do most of the work." She took hold of his hair and pressed his mouth onto herself.

Henry could feel his sutures straining as he twisted on the nar-row hospital bed, trying to get his tongue into her. She spread her legs wider, moaning quietly now, her heels grazing his back, the shirt starting to feel sticky against his skin.

"Good," she said. "Now . . . get up here."

He crawled up the middle of the bed, the unchocked wheels beneath them beginning to protest. The whole bed began to move away from the wall with his first thrust, the IV rig rolling after it. But he was inside her now. There was no stopping. "Good," she was saying. "Good. Gently . . . gently . . ."

She was squeezing him so hard around the neck, he thought for a moment he'd black out. They forgot about any pretense of discretion, the bed bouncing loudly on its squeaking wheels. He saw the clear contents of the IV bottle go suddenly pink, a red flower erupting into its base. Frances's blood, running back through the tube from her hand, which was now wrapped in a choke hold around his neck. He had to keep slapping her arm down to reverse the flow as they hurried to finish.

"Keep your fucking arm down, you idiot!" he said, wanting to cry.

"Shut up and fuck!" she yelled back. "I know what I'm doing."

"Christ," he muttered, seeing the red stain expanding on her chest bandage. More blood, his, hers, he didn't know, made a raindrop pattern on her gown and bedsheets.

But he was lost now. Oblivious to the pain, the blood, the approaching footsteps.

When it was over, the IV had popped completely out of Frances's wrist, the contents of the bottle spewing across the floor. The mustachioed nurse was slapping Henry on the injured side of his face, screaming, *"Salaud!"* Then she was running about the room, reconnecting a new bottle, taking in the blood, the mess. *"Quels affreux!"* she barked. "You want she is to die? *Animaux!"*

Frances was laughing. Henry's shirt was a connect-the-dots game of red, rapidly becoming a solid color. His facial wounds flowing freely, blood droplets falling from his chin. As he put a hand up to touch his cheek, he realized his pants were still open, his wet prick hanging at half-mast. Frances, still giggling as the nurse fussed with her dressings, wiped some errant spermatozoa off her belly with her fingers, then pulled the sheets up around her chin, a glazed, satisfied expression on her face. This infuriated the nurse, who tore the sheets off of her with one motion and threw them on the floor so the doctors could get more easily to her dressings.

Henry stood, duncelike, in the corner, buttoning up his jeans while the nurse took inventory of the damage.

"He was just taking my temperature," explained Frances through tears of pain and laughter. "Really. We . . . we just couldn't find the thermometer. Feel better now." The nurse, unamused, produced a corpsman's Syrette and jammed it rudely into Frances's arm before tossing it into the corner. Frances's open eye fluttered back into her head, and she fell asleep. The nurse, like a vicious border collie, herded Henry out of the room. The Nung guard, smiling with embarrassment, covered his mouth with his hand and turned away as the two card-playing doctors pushed past Henry without a glance.

They redressed Frances's wounds and then got to Henry, waiting for them under guard in the former emergency room. He thought they restitched his wounds less gently than they had the first time, pissed off no doubt at how cavalierly he had treated their earlier work.

When, finally, they let him see Frances again, it was out of the room, under the watchful glare of an even more imposing nurse, this one with the shoulders of a linebacker. They met in the over-grown garden that looked out on the Great Bay, Frances in hospi-tal slippers, pulling the wheeled IV rig with her as they strolled down the flagstone path. In the distance, pelicans groomed them-selves atop the pilings and terns flew overhead, racing to meet the incoming cruise ships. Two of the floating cities were already out in the bay, the ever-present chum of Cheez Doodles, soggy pret-zels, Fig Newtons, and Pringle's chips attracting birds from all over. Henry could see the big boats disgorging water taxis full of chubby, bargain-hungry tourists who'd soon choke the streets of Philipsburg.

"So, what happens now?" said Frances, letting out a deep breath.

"We go on," answered Henry. Not so sure.

41

Without Frances, Henry felt disconnected, lost. He wandered, aimless and useless, unable to take pleasure in anything, seeing no light anywhere. What had seemed charming about his island yesterday looked squalid and somehow menacing today. He drove the scooter around for most of the day, unable to stay in one place, unable to relax, stopping at each beach, each bar, only long enough for one drink.

Leaving the Mariner's Club, he took the mountain route back to the pond, the scooter handling differently without Frances holding on in the rear. On top of the mountain, he cut the engine and just stood there awhile, listening to the crickets and geckos chattering in the dark. A few hundred yards ahead, the road took a steep drop down the other side of the mountain to the sea. The road was ungraded and unbanked; one could easily fly right off the side of the mountain, and Henry considered that option, toyed with the idea as if playing with himself, not serious, just to see how bad things were.

But Frances would be out in a couple of days. He had the hotel bill to pay. Dinner reservations at Frogs. Bad manners to kill your-self. Realizing how drunk he really was, Henry started up the scooter and drove cautiously home.

The pitiably empty bed at his hotel put him right back into the hole. He cracked a bottle of tequila and sat out on the balcony, his feet up on the rail. He tried, for an hour, to drink himself to sleep, his head filled with faces: Frances. Jimmy Pazz. Mickey. Rachel. He considered going over to Cole Bay, scoring some gummy, gasoline-scented, jungle-brewed cocaine, thinking for an ill-considered few seconds that that might make him feel better. But even the memory of that taste in the back of his throat made him gag. No way out. No way to fuck up with honor. No way to forget. Just go forward. He lay back in his chair and drank some more.

Henry didn't know how long he'd been out when he became aware he was no longer alone on the balcony. A few feet away a dark shape sat studying him, the glow from a cigarette illuminating a patch of pale, unshaven skin. Henry struggled to sit upright, one hand reaching behind his back for the gun that wasn't there.

"You look like shit," said the voice.

"I know you," slurred Henry, paralyzed with drink. "You're the marshal dude. From the dock that day. You must like it here. You came back."

"I know who you are," said Burke. "And I know what you are."

Burke moved forward in his chair so Henry could see his face in the moonlight. He looked almost as bad as Henry did. Dark circles ringed his eyes, he hadn't shaved in days, and Henry realized that he too had been drinking. In Burke's hand a few ice cubes melted in a water glass of Henry's tequila.

"War hero. Two fucking tours . . . and you end up selling out to the French. I know what you are. What you do."

"You don't know shit," said Henry, too drunk to care. "Have another drink. And fuck you."

"Froggies not have enough work for you? Was that the problem? Havin' a hard time keepin' Dragon Lady in beach towels?" Burke paused and took a long swig of watery tequila. "Don't worry. This isn't official. I'm on my own time."

Henry said nothing, focusing on a narrow corridor of moonlight on the wave tops and wishing he was sober.

"I met the wife," said Burke, bitterly. "Made me look like a jerk. Got me all fucked up in the head. They sent me home . . . and look what happened."

Henry looked over at Burke, wondering where the gun was, expecting one. Burke didn't move, one hand on his drink, the other rubbing his face now.

"My witness . . . my whole team . . . gone. I . . . I . . . told them . . . I said I told you so. They don't like that. You don't get points for being right when everybody else is wrong, do you? No. I'm an embarrassment. I'll be lucky to be a fucking guard at a convenience store." Burke sat up a bit, making a show of putting aside his drink. "I saw you at the hospital. Visiting the little woman?"

"Yes," said Henry.

"I thought it was you, you know. When I came down. But it wasn't you, was it?"

Henry just shook his head sadly.

"I had it all figured out. You're the one got Junior . . . gave Donnie a new asshole. I'm right about that part. I should have got that right away. Tall, dark, Spanish speaker. *Habla Español?* Yesss. And a king-hell sharpshooter from what I can tell. Oh. I can't touch you. Officially. Oh no. Too sensitive . . . James fucking Bond over here . . . our man Flint . . . The French pimping you out like a two-dollar whore."

"So what do you want?"

"I want Donnie fucking Wicks. He's alive, isn't he?"

Henry said nothing.

"He's gotta be. French are saying sweet fuck all on the subject. Say he went up with the house. But that's not what happened, is it?"

"He's dead. Leave it alone."

"The fuck I'll leave it alone. Five marshals dead. I trained some a' those kids . . . The case ruined. And they blame me. Of course. They blame *me*."

"I tried" was all Henry could say. He felt sympathy for the wreck of a man across from him. He was a danger to no one in his present condition.

"Have another drink." He poured a large splash of tequila into Burke's water glass.

"I want him back. I want Fat Jimmy Calabrese frying like a big juicy steak in the electric chair. You know they got the death penalty back now."

"Yes. I read that."

"I want my fucking witness back. I want my fucking witness back or things are gonna get real fucking hot for you down here— your little vacation paradise you got for yourself. Maybe . . . maybe I can't take you back. Maybe Washington don't want to know about you, and maybe the French love you like they love pussy . . . but I can still make things complicated. I been talking to the press. What do you think? You think they'd be innerested in a guy like you?"

"You're not getting Donnie," said Henry, his voice an affectless monotone. "Ever."

"What? Are you pals? You shoot him in the ass. You clip his boy Junior . . . now you're blowin' each other? I don't fuckin' get it.

What I can tell, Jimmy's pals fucked you real good. And the lovely wife . . . I don't know how bad she is, but I take it she's worse than you."

"She is."

"So whassa fucking problem? I mean . . . who are you fucking loyal to anyway?"

"I'll give you Jimmy," said Henry. "How about that?"

42

He wore a hat. Always taking care to stay out of the sun. He let his beard go in the last days of summer, cutting it down to a neat Vandyke. He watched his skin go from a dark brown to a golden brown to an ashy palomino, then, finally, white.

The day before he left, he plucked his eyebrows, changing their natural shape entirely. The effect of such a simple adjustment was remarkable, and he had to hide in their rooms so that no one would see him. He made Frances cut his hair.

"I can't believe you're making me do this," she said, holding his ponytail and hesitating with the scissors.

"Cut it," said Henry.

"You look geeky enough. Believe me. No one will recognize you. I hardly recognize you."

"Cut it."

She chopped, and Henry's ponytail fell to the tile and lay there, sad looking, like a dead pet.

. . .

It was already getting light when Paulie turned the Olds into the driveway of his Howard Beach home, a modest, two-story, aluminum-sided structure with a birdbath in the front yard and an American flag hanging limply from a pole next to the front door.

He parked the car, got out, and reached into the backseat for the two bags of groceries he'd picked up at the 7-Eleven on the way home from Brooklyn. Two economy-size bottles of diet cola, four rolls of toilet paper, assorted cold cuts, hermetically sealed in plastic, a box of Count Chocula breakfast cereal, five cans of crab and tuna catfood, a loaf of Wonder bread, a six of lite beer, coffee filters, and a pint of Ben & Jerry's Cherry Garcia. He hoped he hadn't forgotten anything—he'd lost the shopping list somewhere between Jimmy's office and Eddie's Clam Casino in Sheepshead Bay, where he'd closed the bar, playing rummy with Chickie Scalice.

He walked slowly to the front door, keys at the ready in one hand, the two bags in the other, opening the screen with his foot. Leaning on the edge of the stoop, half into the hydrangea, was a copy of the Sunday *New York Times,* a paper Paulie did not subscribe to. Assuming it was a fortunate mistake and looking forward to reading the sports section over a bowl of Count Chocula, he leaned down to pick up the thick stack of banded paper, got his hand around it without spilling any groceries or dropping his keys, and was standing up again when he felt the cold barrel of a gun pressed hard against the back of his skull.

"Hello, Paulie," said the voice.

"Hey, hey . . . take it easy," said Paulie, freezing.

"Let's go inside, Paulie," said the voice. "Don't turn around. Just open the door like a good boy, nice and quiet, and step inside."

Breathing heavily, Paulie put his key carefully in the lock and opened the door. The pressure of the gun in the back of his head did not abate until he was standing inside his darkened foyer, the door closed behind him.

"Can I turn around?" he asked. "I ain't carryin' nothin' but groceries."

A hand slipped up and down his sides, patted the small of his
back, traveled briskly around his waistband. "Sure," said the voice.
"Turn around."

At first he didn't recognize the man in front of him. He was tall
and thin, with a sickly complexion, hair cropped close to the skull,
receding on top. He had a neat beard, and he wore gray sweats and
athletic shoes like he'd been jogging. The headset to a Walkman
hung around his neck. Paulie thought that was a nice touch.

Things were bad. That much he knew. Paulie knew the kinds of
people in his business who were likely to come visit you with a gun
at five-thirty in the morning, and he was running down in his
mind who he might have pissed off lately.

"You can put the bags down, and the paper," said the man.

Paulie obediently put the groceries on the floor, leaning them
against an umbrella stand. A sneakered foot came up and kicked
him in the belly.

"Whatchoo do that for?" he asked, keeping his voice down in
spite of considerable discomfort.

"Sorry," said the man. "Just trying to impress upon you the gravity of the situation."

"Awwww, jeez . . . it's you, ain't it, Henry?" said Paulie, finally
recognizing the voice, the way the man spoke. He looked into the
cold, unblinking eyes, glanced down and saw the silenced gun, and
realized he was never going to eat that bowl of cereal. "You look
like half a fag."

"Really? You think so?"

"I don't mean that in a bad way," said Paulie. "I mean . . . I know
you ain't one."

"It's my fiendishly clever disguise, Paulie," said Henry, turning
his head a fraction of an inch to listen to a passing car. "You know,"

he said, returning his full attention to Paulie, "I'm awful pissed with you . . . I'm seriously, killing mad at you, in fact."

"Yeah . . . I can see that."

"My wife . . . she got shot up pretty bad down there. My friends . . . they're dead, Paulie. My home . . . well, I just don't feel safe there anymore. You can see that, can't you?"

"Yeah, sure. I unnerstand." Paulie was thinking about his wife in the upstairs bedroom. Would she wake up when Henry pulled the trigger? Would the sound of the shots, or of his body falling to the floor, wake her up, bring her downstairs? "Believe me, I unnerstand," he said. I'm dead already, he was thinking. He wasn't going to plead for his life or anything. He wouldn't crawl or make excuses. This was how it ended. He found himself hoping the cold cuts wouldn't go bad, hoping maybe, at least, Henry would take him somewhere else to shoot him, the backyard, or the garage. He shook his head sadly, thinking about his wife's reaction when she found his body.

"Let's go sit down somewhere," said Henry, wagging the gun. "Have a nice talk. You got a kitchen? Down there?"

Paulie sighed and led Henry down the unlit hallway to his small kitchen. The sun was coming up over the airport now; light streamed through the yellow and orange daisy print curtains, illuminating the worn linoleum floor he'd promised her he'd replace but never had, the faded wallpaper, the brand-new refrigerator, swag from some hijacking Jimmy'd got a piece of. The refrigerator door was festooned with colorful magnets of fruit and vegetables, each holding down a child's crayon drawing.

"Very talented," commented Henry. "Whose?"

"My niece."

"She doesn't live here, though?"

Paulie shook his head and sat down where Henry was waving him with the gun. Henry sat across from him, resting the weapon on a stack of *Self* magazines and mail-order catalogs, the barrel level with Paulie's throat. He identified the gun as a .22-caliber Hi-Standard, with silencer, and noticed, too, that Henry was wearing gloves. He looked around his kitchen, missing it already.

"Where's Jimmy?" asked Henry. "Right now, I mean. Will you tell me that, please?"

"You gonna kill me anyways, Henry, right?" said Paulie, shrugging rather heroically, he thought. "So why I gonna tell you somethin' like that?"

"I don't care *why* you do it, Paulie," said Henry, in a flat, uninflected monotone. "As long as you *do* tell me. And understand me, please . . . you *are* going to tell me . . . If I have to lift your eyeballs outta their sockets with a fucking butter knife, one at a fucking time, you *are* going to tell me. So don't be silly. I'm a *very* determined man right now."

Paulie shuddered slightly, sweat running down his back into the crack of his ass, making him itch. He squirmed in his chair, but still he shook his head, his lips pursed.

"You know I did two tours in Vietnam. Did you know that?" said Henry.

"No . . . I din't know that."

"You?"

"Me? No . . . bad back. I woulda, but . . ."

"I served for a while with a bunch of fellows, Vietnamese, Cambodians, called PRU's. Nice enough boys once you got to know them, but hell on the enemy. We did some ugly things over there, Paulie. Real, real ugly. Things hadn't been going well for us. Sometimes we had to know things. *Had* to know, if you see what I'm saying. I didn't much like that kind of thing . . . Still don't. But . . . lives were at stake, and I did them. Like now, Paulie. Way I see it, lives are at stake here too. So don't just sit there like a dumb lump and think you aren't gonna tell me what

I want. Because that's bullshit. You will. Everybody does. Everybody."

"Fuck you, Henry. Sorry," said Paulie, keeping his voice down.

"Hell, just looking around this kitchen . . . why, I see four or five common household objects which properly applied'll have you bucking up and down and shitting yourself. They tend to do that, I'm afraid, shit themselves. You won't even *know* what you're telling me, okay? But you *will* tell me. I'm a serious man."

"Fuck you. You ain't gonna do nothin'."

"Fuck *me*?" said Henry, getting loud. "Fuck *me*? Fuck *you*! You think I'm some sort of nice guy, I don't go in for some a' your Sicilian hijinks before? Is that what you're thinking? That was then. This is now. I'm talking about protecting my *wife,* asshole. My home! You think for a second what you'd be willing to do, right now, keep me from walking up those stairs and feeding your wife's tits into the toaster. I've got to think about Jimmy fucking Pazz for the rest of my life? No way. I will cheerfully, *cheerfully* eat my fucking breakfast outta your wife's empty fucking skull, I have to, Paulie!"

He tightened his hand on the gun, and the muzzle wandered around over Paulie's body for a while, looking for someplace painful.

"Can't you just take me out the fuckin' garage an' get this over with, Henry? I don't wanna wake her."

"*My* wife . . . *My* wife," said Henry, his face tightening.

"I'm sorry about that," said Paulie. "Really. You . . . you got a legitimate beef wit' me. I see that. You wanna take me outside, inna garage, put a few inta my head . . . I can't complain. I unnerstand that. But, c'mon . . . You wouldn't do nothin' to my wife, would you, Henry? She didn't do nothin'. That wouldn't be right."

"I'm sorry too, Paulie. But I just *have* to know."

Paulie did not like the look on Henry's face at all. He was getting ready to do something, he could see that. He considered diving for the gun, pictured himself dead, stretched out on the kitchen table. He thought about what Henry had said, about shitting yourself, how undignified that would look.

"Paulie?" came a thin voice from the stairs. "That you, honey?"

Paulie went pale. Across the table, Henry's face showed uncertainty for the first time as the padding of slippered feet drew closer. Neither man moved.

"Oh! You've got company," said the tiny woman in the canary yellow housecoat. She might have been pretty once, without the curlers, the slippers with the bunny faces on them—a pleasant, child's face, gone to fat under the frosted curls. "You get everything on the list? Remember the food for kitty?"

"Yeah, yeah. I got it," said Paulie, his voice cracking.

"Crab and tuna flavor? She don't like the other kinds."

"Yeah. I got it."

Henry had just slipped the gun onto his lap, mind racing. He was stunned by what happened next.

Mrs. Caifano leaned over and, without a moment's hesitation, picked up the silenced pistol, holding it between her fingers like a schoolmarm impounding a slingshot. She headed off to the foyer.

"What I tell you, Paulie, about bringing guns inta the house? You tell your friend. House rules . . . He can pick up his thingy when he leaves. It'll be right in the drawer there."

Henry sat dumbstruck, listening as the middle-aged woman in the housecoat shuffled sleepily down the hall, dropped his gun into a bureau, closed the drawer, and returned carrying the two bags of groceries.

She immediately set about putting away the perishables.

"You're being very rude, Paulie, not introducing me."

"Sorry, Marie. This is Henry . . . Henry; my wife, Marie," said Paulie, looking sheepish.

"A friend from work? You boys work together with that terrible man?"

"Yes," said Henry, finding his voice. "Work." He felt utterly foolish, wondering whether Paulie was going, at any second, to come lunging across the kitchen table at him.

"He calls here all the time . . . always . . . Tell Paulie do this, tell Paulie do that. I don't see how you boys work with a person like that. He's got no respect for privacy, that man."

She put the half-empty shopping bags on the table between Henry and Paulie, who played peekaboo while she put the remaining items in the cupboards, maintaining a steady, friendly patter the whole time.

"Have you had any breakfast? How 'bout I make some nice scrambled eggs with some sausages?" To Henry, she confided, "Paulie was so good to remember the groceries. He always forgets." And Henry saw, beneath the familiarities, fear in Mrs. Caifano's face, hidden by the talk of breakfast and groceries, but there. It made him feel ashamed of himself, and he tried to smile sympathetically.

"And so late," she babbled on, "always so late . . . the drinking, the smoking. Henry . . . you should hear this man, he gets up inna morning, the coughing and wheezing. I swear." She shook her head.

"I could use a cig right now," said Paulie, searching his pockets for a pack. "Shit. I knew I forgot something . . ."

Eager for a smoke himself, Henry pulled out his own, a crumpled pack of Gitanes. He lit one for himself, then, seeing the look on Paulie's face, trying to suck smoke into his lungs from across the table, passed him the pack.

"Thanks," said Paulie.

"Oooh, are those French?" asked Mrs. Caifano. "I never seen those. You from France, Henry?"

"No, ma'am," said Henry. "I just like them."

"So can I get you somethin' to eat, Paulie? Henry looks so skinny. Let me make you something—"

"We ate," said Paulie, his stomach growling. "At the diner, we had somethin' before."

"Well, you'll have some coffee. I'm just gonna make a little toast for myself, you don't mind. If you boys wanna talk business, I'll be out of your way inna min. Will you have some coffee, Henry? I grind my own beans."

A roar settled on the house as a jet passed low overhead. Henry could hear the tires squeal as the plane settled down onto the nearby runway. When the noise was gone, Henry looked across the table and saw an amused look on Paulie's face, much less worried now.

"Sure," he said. "Thanks, Mrs. Caifano, I'll have a cup."

"You wanta show Henry the yard, Paulie. I'll call yez when it's ready," said Mrs. Caifano. "We're putting in a pool, you know, Henry. Paulie, show him what you done so far. I'll give a yell. Youse can have it onna patio, it's ready."

Paulie stood up, turned his back on Henry, and walked out the screen door into his backyard, holding the screen until Henry followed.

"Thank you," said Henry to Mrs. Caifano.

"Nice lady," said Henry.

"Twenny-two years married," said Paulie, not looking at Henry but gazing distractedly into the empty pit in the center of the small, fenced-in yard.

"Really? That's a long time," said Henry.

"You know . . . all 'at time, I never fucked around on her. Not once. The whole time."

"That's . . . extraordinary," said Henry, taken slightly aback. "I mean . . . you know . . . people in your outfit—"

"Twenny-two years. Not once."

"That's . . . admirable, Paulie. Really. I imagine most of your colleagues don't share your views on the sanctity of marriage."

Paulie laughed. "No . . . no they don't." He hoisted up his pants and stepped down into the half-empty pit, kicking at a rock on his way to the deepest point. "You know, I saw youse that night down there. I saw your wife there inna stretcher. She gonna be okay now?"

"Yeah . . . she'll be okay."

"I felt bad about that."

"I get the sense . . . that . . . Well, let's just say you're an unusual man, Paulie."

"Yeah." Paulie chuckled. "I guess so."

"So. What do we do now?" asked Henry. "We going to wrestle around the backyard for a while? The wife gonna come out with my piece, take a few shots at me? What's next?"

"Nah . . . she ain't gonna do nothin' like that."

"She calling somebody on the phone?"

"Who she supposedta call?"

"I don't know."

Paulie stepped in front of Henry, hands at his sides. "You ain't gonna hurt my wife, Henry. Even you had yer gun now, you wouldn't do nothin' like that. You ain't gonna shoot no old lady in her bunny slippers."

"No," admitted Henry. "I guess not."

Paulie nodded and looked up at the sky for a long time. If Henry wanted to, he could have killed him right then. A hand across the windpipe, maybe. He let the moment pass. "I guess I could beat you to death. Kick in the nuts, chop in the neck . . ."

"Yeah, right. We'd look pretty fuckin' stupid, rollin' aroun' inna dirt."

Another plane came in low, the noise building to a deafening whine as it dropped out of the steel gray sky over Paulie's house. The neighbors were waking up now. Henry could smell cooking bacon and burning English muffins. Somebody was yelling at kids in the next house over.

"I don't know, Paulie," said Henry, sighing. "You got any ideas?"

Paulie smiled, his eyes turning to slits as he took Henry's arm. "Actually," he said, "I'm thinkin' a' somethin'."

43

Paulie Brown was a film star. "Popping up everywhere at a theater near you," joked one of the bleary-eyed FBI men, watching a grainy surveillance tape of Paulie having a midday walk-talk with Jerry "Dogs" Camino.

Paulie's sudden emergence as social butterfly over the last few days was causing a lot of speculation in the Foley Square offices of the Organized Crime Strike Force. From Jimmy Pazz's rarely seen factotum to roving diplomat in the blink of an eye, Paulie had been observed having espresso in Brooklyn with Benny "Red" Merlino, lunch in the Village with Jackie Essa, midafternoon walk-talks with Jerry Dogs, as well as his usual schedule of errands and meetings with his "known associates," Jimmy Pazz and Richie Gianelli.

"Jimmy's gotta be makin' a move," said one of the experts assigned from OCCB to the strike force after viewing Paulie's third appearance on videotape that day. "What are we hearing from snitches?"

"Dick," answered the exasperated FBI guy. "We're getting dick. Nobody knows nothing."

"Then *what* the fuck is going on?" railed the OCCB guy. "*What* is he doing?"

Informant reports continued to hint at nothing. Nobody got shot. Nobody disappeared—all the usual faces were observed showing up at their usual haunts. There were no unusual outbreaks of cheek kissing or backslapping to indicate a shifting of power or loyalty. Life went on. The only thing different was that Paulie Brown had suddenly gone from knuckle dragger to Kissinger, and nobody could figure it out.

Surveillance was stepped up, of course. Jimmy Pazz's trailer was watched more closely than before. Paulie was followed from pay phone to pay phone; but as he never used the same one twice, it was impossible to listen in. An effort was even made to run a wire into Paulie's house; an agent dressed as a cable TV repairman tried to get past Mrs. Caifano one afternoon. The old lady had a lawyer pulling into the driveway before the agent was halfway through his pitch. What little Jimmy said on his office phone was indecipherable and useless, and, since his offices were swept for listening devices twice a week, a room mike was out of the question.

Then, just as suddenly as it started, it stopped. Traveling Paulie Brown became good old Predictable Paulie Brown again, and things went back to normal. Eleven A.M., Subject Paul Caifano woke up, had breakfast with his wife, and went to the racetrack. One-thirty P.M., Paul Caifano had lunch with his usual associates, Edward "Boy" De Cecco (known gambler), Robert "Ruby" Marx (suspected loan shark), and Charles "Chickie" Lowenstein (known bookmaker). They ate, as always, at the Turf and Surf Lounge at the track. Paulie was known to favor the pastrami. At four P.M., Paul Caifano visited the West Side Poultry Barn, a business in which he was known to have a controlling interest; from there he went to the Best of Friends Social Club on Arthur Avenue, where Jimmy's crew were known to assemble. At nine P.M., Paul Caifano had dinner with Richie "Tic" Gianelli (alleged soldier in the Calabrese crime family), finishing up at eleven-thirty. He had drinks, alone, at Mary's Bar near his Howard Beach home, after which he retired.

In short, exactly the same routine.

Henry fed pigeons on the boardwalk in Brighton Beach. He ate smoked fish and black bread, pierogies and hot borscht, and drank a little but not a lot of vodka. When not sitting on the boardwalk in an old man's coat with a fake cane, he lay around his rented room, watching television and sleeping. His next-door neighbor, a taxi driver from Azerbaijan, knew him as an out-of-work machinist who spoke a few words of Russian and had an interest in coins. He'd seen him go into Sammy's, the coin shop a few buildings down. It was good, thought the taxi driver, to have a hobby.

44

Henry stepped back and admired his work: two hexagonal warning signs, bright yellow with black lettering, one admonishing the reader to WEAR HARD HAT AT ALL TIMES, the other warning, EXPLOSIVES! USE OF TRANSISTOR RADIOS, WALKMANS, AND CELLULAR PHONES IS FORBIDDEN!

The signs were about four feet high, sunk in two cone-shaped concrete stands, and unusually thick, about six inches. Henry didn't think anybody would notice. He sat down in Sammy Avakian's cluttered storage lockup and smoked a cigarette, thinking.

Jimmy Pazz, watching *House of Style* in his trailer office, heard the whooshing sound first. He thought for a second it might be coming from the television and was irritably reaching for the remote when there was a loud *thud,* a jarring impact that rocked the whole trailer on its cinder-block foundation. Richie Tic looked up from his magazine in time to see the wall beginning to glow, something white hot coming through the paneling right next to the photograph of Connie Francis, spitting flame and sparks. He was opening his mouth to say something when whatever it was erupted into the room in a concussive fireball. Jimmy was on his feet in time to see Richie's upper torso bounce off the acoustic tile ceiling, his lower body, clothes smoking, crumpling to the floor.

Everything was on fire. Jimmy knew that. He could smell his own flesh singeing, and the blond Dynel wig—it was melting over his head, long, gooey strands of blond plastic running down his face like hot lava. Screaming like an impaled wolverine, Jimmy used his 320-pound bulk to smash through the office door and out of the burning trailer.

In the last few seconds of his life, Jimmy saw things with an unusual clarity. Through burning eyelashes and melting Dynel, he actually noticed the Calabrese Construction panel truck double-parked across the street, realized he'd never owned or even seen it before. The signs were new also, he noticed, one on each side of the entrance to the site, and he ran at them like goalposts, hoping to flop into the puddle of rainwater between them and put out the flames.

When the backs of the two signs erupted in unison, spraying hunks of irregularly shaped shrapnel through Jimmy from his knees to his collarbone and throwing him back onto the steps of the trailer, he had a half second of consciousness left—time to realize what had happened.

By the time the cops arrived, running from their observation post a block away, the van was gone and Jimmy looked like the smoldering remains of a shaved buffalo. The charred heap of flesh and smoking Dynel smelled unbelievably acrid.

When the fire department finished hosing down the trailer and went looking for Richie, they found his head and one shoulder wedged in an open desk drawer, strangely unburned; the rest of him was ashes.

The guys at ATF were called, and after sifting through the

wreckage and arguing with the crime scene officers, the Fire Department Arson Team, and the medical examiner over who got what and what exactly constituted a body part, one agent in a blue nylon parka briefed some curious Fibbies from the strike force on his initial findings.

"Looks to me like somebody fired a fuckin' LAWS right up Jimmy's Hershey Highway," he said, grinning at the novelty. He walked over to the trailer steps, where two young men from the ME's office were trying to figure out how to get Jimmy Pazz's corpse onto a gurney and retraced the hapless capo's last steps.

"Jimmy comes runnin' outside, feelin' pretty uncomfortable already, I guess, and he gets a bellyful a' Claymores right about . . . here. That's an antipersonnel mine, in case you didn't know," he added.

"That's . . . like . . . military hardware," ventured one of the Fibbies. "What are you telling us? Jimmy piss off Abu Nidal? I mean, maybe you see this shit in Beirut . . ."

"Don't ask me." The ATF agent shrugged. "All I can tell you is this was real creative work. Whoever done this, I'd like to meet. I haven't seen anything like this since . . . since nineteen sixty-nine, and that was in fuckin' Vietnam. I *like* this guy. This guy is a pisser."

45

So the parrot . . . he comes outta the freezer," said Donnie Wicks, his whole body shaking with suppressed laughter. "And he says, '*Brrrrrr, brrrrr* . . . I'll be *good,* I'll be good! I promise! Just tell me one thing, though. What did the turkey do? Ask for a blow job?' "

Henry laughed politely. Frances was not amused. "I don't like what she did to the parrot," she said, turning to pet the weimaraners. She'd heard the joke before anyway, from Captain Toby, who told it better. Toby got the parrot's voice just right. Donnie, struggling for breath between hits on a joint and long, noisy inhalations on his portable respirator, made the parrot's struggles too painful, too tragic.

Henry sipped his rum and gazed out over the water at the lights from Saint Martin, looking forward to going home. Donnie lived right on the beach now, and Henry could even see the headlights from cars over there, moving up and down the mountain roads. The weekly trips to Anguilla to see the increasingly dependent Donnie were becoming a burden, like visiting a tiresome grandmother, and Henry yearned to be back in their rooms at the Oyster Pond—holding Frances between clean hotel sheets, listening to the familiar chop-chop of the waves below their balcony, the New York City weather playing silently on the cable TV.

"Ya got any more a' this marahoochie you can leave with me?" asked Donnie, enjoying the last of the torpedo-size spliff. "Sidney Poitier back there—whatsisname? Agnes? Angus?—he won't get me none for love or money. Fuckin' creepin' Jeesus."

"Yeah, don't worry. We'll leave you a couple ounces. Enough to last you till next time," said Henry, keeping an eye on Frances, who had gone down the beach a few yards. "When are you gonna learn how to roll your own, though? I'm not gonna keep rolling 'em all up for you. If you want a pipe I'll get you a pipe. How about a nice big bong, Donnie? Would you like that?"

"Fuck that," said Donnie. "I can fuckin' roll. I been practicin'." He reached inside his robe and pulled out a perfectly ballistic one-paper joint, evenly packed and rolled like a nonfiltered Camel. "See?"

They sat on Donnie's porch for a while without saying anything, watching Frances play tug-of-war with the dogs. Donnie lit another joint and started complaining again about Angus, the owner of the small Anguillan guesthouse where he'd lived for the last months.

"He's a religious fanatic, the guy," he said. "Him an' the missus, and everybody else on this miserable fuckin' island. You should try listenin' to the radio down here, watchin' TV. Especially Sundays . . . Forget it. You got yer Jerry Fuckin' Falwell on one channel, Oral Roberts on the other. Change stations you got Jimmy Swaggart askin' for some more money so's he can go and get another hand job. They even got that fuck with the hair—Benny, Benny somethin'. This prick—he *blows* on people. Blows that curry breath on people an' it's suppose' to be magic, 'cause their eyes roll up an' they fall onna ground, and the next thing, when

they stand up, they ain't got that brain tumor no more. I'm tellin'
you, every fuckin' station there's people cryin' or about to cry,
askin' you to send money."

"What about the VCR?" asked Henry, growing annoyed.
"Watch a fucking tape."

"I *seen* 'em all," complained Donnie. "I send Angus or Mrs.
Angus down the video store. I say, 'Get me somethin' good. Somethin' with a little excitement in it, some good car chases, some
broads.' Whaddya think they bring back? *Free Willy!* I thought it
was a fuck film . . . it's about some kid and his fish! I go fuckin'
nuts!"

"Okay, okay. We'll bring you some tapes next time."

"Get me some good gangster movies. Ones I ain't seen. Jesus,
Henry, you know what I like."

Henry took another sip of rum and swept his hand reflexively
over his head. The hair was growing back; it was already over his
ears, tangled, sun bleached, and sticking up in spots like a Rastafarian's. It was grayer, though, and Henry, when he caught sight
of himself in a mirror, thought he looked old. He was tan
again—it had taken only a couple of weeks once he'd returned
from New York, and it was nice, of course, to live without shoes
or socks.

Frances's wounds had healed. Yes, there was a large, star-shaped
scar over one breast, but her face looked fine, only a slight crescent
of dead tissue over her right eye to remind of that night. They almost never talked about it.

"You gonna hog that whole joint?" she asked, back from the
water's edge, the weimaraners trailing sleepily behind her. She
snatched the joint out of Donnie's hand and took a hit. "Still pissing and moaning about Anguilla?"

"What do you think?" said Henry.

"You're becoming a real whiner," she said, sitting down in the sand and cracking a beer. "Read the paper today? I figured that would cheer you up."

"What? About Jerry Dogs? Yeah, ain't that a bitch! They say he's been in 'at trunk for two weeks. Can you imagine the stink? I guess . . . I guess he had a fallin' out with Paulie." Donnie sat up in his rattan armchair a little, warming to the subject. "Jerry was always a pain. And him and Jimmy was close. That was probably his problem. Paulie was smart havin' that guy clipped, believe me. I woulda done the same thing. You can't have people walkin' around harborin' bad feelings. It's bad for everybody."

"Good luck and God bless, that's what I say," said Henry. "Maybe we should send him a card. 'Congratulations on your new job.' "

"Paulie the Boss," said Donnie, shaking his head. "Well . . . see how *he* likes it."

One of the weimaraners came over and licked Donnie's hand. "Hello, Useless," said Donnie, leaning over to nuzzle the dog's face, kissing his nose. "Government dog. Half the fuckin' Dominican army lands on my house an' they run away—don't even bark." He scratched the dog's head while it looked up at him adoringly. The other weimaraner came over and plopped down under his chair. "Maybe they wasn't so dumb after all."

Frances, seeing Donnie getting sad again, came around behind him and began massaging the old man's neck. It didn't help. Donnie's shoulders started to shake, and tears came, running silently down his cheeks. He didn't bother to wipe them. No one said anything for a while. Donnie coughed and snuffled and took a sip of wine before settling back in his chair and closing his eyes. Frances took Henry's hand and led him to the water. They stood ankle deep in the gentle surf and wiggled their toes.

"You think he's sleeping?" asked Henry.

"Yeah. He does that a lot lately, drop off like that. He's old. Old people do that."

Henry put his arm around Frances's waist, and they stood there for a while, looking up at the sky, the bewildering array of stars, the horizon purple and orange around a fat, yellow moon, the silhouette of Saint Martin in the distance. A light breeze rustled the palm trees behind them, and Henry turned to look back at Donnie, sleeping in his chair, the dogs at his feet.

 46

*A*fter a long day at the beach, they ate dinner at Talk of the Town, on the bay in Grand Case. It started to rain. The tin roof of the clapboard lolo was soon drumming with heavy raindrops, water leaking through in spots, so they had to move their chairs to a dark corner near the tiny kitchen.

The wind picked up, and on the street people ran for cover, huddling in doorways, suddenly crowding the Talk of the Town's makeshift bar, jabbering in loud patois, the rain louder now, making sounds on the roof like a machine gun.

An American couple hurried from their open jeep to take refuge in the smoky shack. The man, a rosy-cheeked retiree in white, and the wife, a pained-looking creature in a blue jacket and scarf, appeared lost. They stood frozen in the dark shelter, eyes adjusting, clearly looking for a friendly face to direct them back to their hotel.

"Ask *them,* honey," said the woman, seeing Henry and Frances in the corner. "They probably know," she whispered loudly.

The man gave Henry and Frances a careful look, measuring them against the sea of black faces pouring into the lolo's bar area.

He took in the faded jump vests, the kaffiyehs worn around their waists like South Sea natives'. He saw how Frances was feeding chicken bones to a flea-ridden dog under the table, the animal's jaws making crunching sounds as he wolfed them down. He waited for one of them to talk, to look up at him, acknowledge a white man's presence in the room, but they didn't. They just sat there, drinking beer and eating chicken, saying nothing.

These were clearly not people you asked for directions back to the Great Bay Hotel and Casino. With their too-dark skin, bare, dirty feet, and ragged clothes, the way their teeth flashed eerily white when they opened their mouths to take a bite of chicken, their wild, tangled hair and somehow debauched expressions, he was not comfortable approaching them.

He turned to his wife, confident that the feral-looking couple in the corner would be of no help, and said, "No, honey . . . They aren't American. They don't speak English in here. C'mon. We'll ask at a gas station." He hurried his wife out the door as if the place was alive with anthrax spores, preferring the downpour to this cramped, frightening place at the end of the world.

When they were gone, Henry and Frances burst out laughing. Hearing them, the proprietor came out of the kitchen and asked if they wanted anything. Henry called for more beer.

"*They* aren't *American,*" he said, mimicking the middle-aged tourist. "They don't speak English in *here.*"

Frances, still smiling, leaned back against the stained plywood wall and put her head on Henry's shoulder. "I feel kind of good about that," she said. "I guess we've really gone bamboo."

"Yes," said Henry. "And we're never going back."

ANTHONY BOURDAIN is a writer and chef who has run the kitchens at New York City's Supper Club, One Fifth Avenue, Coco Pazzo Teatro, and Sullivan's. His first novel, *Bone in the Throat*, was a *New York Times* Notable Book of the Year and has been optioned for film by New Line Cinema. He lives in Manhattan with his wife, Nancy.